TRANSFORMATION
SUMMER

TRANSFORMATION
SUMMER

To Jack —
A great boss,
an even greater friend
Sean

SEAN SMITH

atmosphere press

To my parents, Thomas H. Smith (1930-1994)
and Nancy H. Smith (1932-2021)

To my wife, Shawn Stamm (1959-2021)

To my daughters, Kirsten and Shalyn, and
my thoroughly remarkable grandkid Hosea

To my friends and beta readers, Francesca Forrest,
Michael Keith and Daniel Accardi

Special thanks to the Atmosphere staff –
especially my editor Justin Bigos, for his support,
encouragement, and darn good ideas.

PART ONE

GETTING THERE

Arriving

Even now, after all this time, I can still do it. All I need is a half-decent road map of California.

I unfold the map, spread it out, and my eye immediately travels north, until I find San Jose. Then I look a little to the southwest until I find Route 1, put my finger on it, and trace the route as it hugs the coast, rounding past Monterey Bay.

And I can remember being in our car when we reached that point in the journey. More than that, when I close my eyes I can *feel* myself in the car. I can hear the drone of the engine, I can feel the forward motion, the rise and fall of the road underneath, and the warmth of the afternoon sun through the windshield. I can see the landscape pass by, the occasional road signs that remind me of how far we're getting from home. I am there.

Yes, I step back from the memory, analyze, second-guess, put it in perspective relative to subsequent events.

But I prefer letting myself fully inhabit the memory instead.

I am there. The memory plays on.

"Seth, honey? Better wake up," my mother said. "We'll be turning off the highway pretty soon, I think."

I opened my eyes and made a pretense of yawning.

3

"You've been missing out on some pretty amazing scenery," she added, trying not to sound reproachful.

"Hmm-mmm," I mumbled, looking out the window at the rugged-looking coastline on the right-hand side, and the bare hills rising up on the left.

I hadn't been asleep. I'd only been pretending, because I had no desire to have any conversation with my mother. So somewhere north of San Jose, I'd settled back in my seat, turned my head to the window and closed my eyes. I figured that my thoughts could provide me with sufficient entertainment.

Except that all I thought about was how mad I was at my mother – both my parents, actually. About eight months before – barely after we'd finished Thanksgiving leftovers – Mom and Dad suddenly decided they couldn't be married anymore. Try as I might, I couldn't get any kind of reasonable explanation from either of them as to why this had happened: There was no other person involved, they said; they simply couldn't be a couple. Dad moved into an apartment shortly after that, and although they hadn't gotten divorced yet it was practically a foregone conclusion.

It had been a rough time since then, for all of us. Mom and Dad could barely talk to one another, and didn't do a particularly good job of talking to me, either. Then again, I was pretty pissed off at them, not to mention generally embarrassed and humiliated: not so much because my parents were practically divorced but because I thought it was something I should've seen coming, somehow, since I was a high school sophomore convinced I knew all about relationships. What signals had I missed? I felt now as if there was some vast space between my friends and me, and instead of looking to them for comfort and reassurance I had kept them at arm's length.

My anger had cooled somewhat in the interim, but it boiled anew when my mother told me that the two of us were going to a two-week summer camp near Big Sur called Toward Transformation, or simply "Transformation" for short –

a place she'd heard about from a friend of a friend, and which she was certain was what the two of us needed.

For me, there were three immediate associations with the phrase "summer camp," and none of them were particularly pleasant. First was making handcrafts – a wallet or a pouch or something that you convinced yourself would be practical and aesthetically pleasing, when in fact it went straight into your junk drawer and stayed there. Second was horseback riding: Now, like a lot of kids I knew, I'd watched "Bonanza" and "Gunsmoke" and other TV westerns, and yet the prospect of riding a horse never interested me in the least. Finally, there was archery. I was convinced that any self-respecting summer camp had to include archery, and I was no more thrilled about trying my hand at it than horseback riding.

"So what goes on in this camp?" I'd asked her, with all the sullenness I could muster. "Do we make leather handcrafts and ride horses? Learn archery?"

"Well, I don't think there's archery," she'd said. "I guess there's arts and crafts, but it's not like you have to make anything special. I don't think they have horses there, but see, you don't have to stay in the camp all the time. You've got lakes, and mountains and hiking trails to explore, if you want, and nearby you can probably find a place where there's horseback riding—"

"Then what do you do in this camp?" I interjected impatiently.

She looked at me and continued quietly.

"You attend seminars – discussions, you know? See, many of the people who go to Transformation have some kind of special expertise or knowledge about a topic, and they share it with others at the camp. It might be something to do with business, or education, or the arts. Even personal counseling. Apparently, they call them 'Transeminars' – you know, a combination of 'Transformation' and 'seminar.'"

Mom seemed to expect me to say something, but I didn't.

"The point is, everything is very informal and there's lots of leeway," she finally said. "You see what's being offered and you go to what interests you. C'mon, Seth. It's two days there and back, and in between we'll be in this wonderful place for two weeks – Christine said the camp has running water and the cabins have electricity, so even though you're in the wilderness you practically have the comforts of home. We can get away from the familiar. It's a way to find some new experiences, new insights, new possibilities."

I thought it was an incredibly stupid idea, from the core of my 16-year-old being.

But no amount of negotiating, cajoling or pouting could get me out of going, so here I was.

The drive was a long one, about 14 hours we'd split over two days, so I had collected a whole batch of cassettes to listen to on the way. I made sure to include some that would be agreeable to both my mother and me: The Beatles; Crosby, Stills, Nash & Young; Simon & Garfunkel. Most of the rest I figured she could at least tolerate: Kansas, Boston, Meatloaf. If she wanted silence, I had some collections of short stories to read – *Nine Tomorrows*, *Welcome to the Monkey House*.

What conversation there was between us that first day was fairly brief and perfunctory. Mom pointed out some feature of the landscape she deemed interesting – a funny billboard, a souvenir shop, horses in a field – or asked if I was feeling hungry or needed a bathroom. My replies were along the lines of "I see it," "Pretty neat," "Nope."

We had stopped at a motel somewhere near the California state line, gotten some fast food, and Mom was fast asleep by 9. I watched the TV at low volume, but the only thing on that was even barely half-decent was a movie about truckers and bikers. I turned it off after about 20 minutes.

Who were you then?

Many years later, that question was asked of me by a woman I'd been hoping to get to know better, as we broached the subject of defining experiences in our youth. She had a habit of stating fairly standard conversational inquiries in ways that seemed unnecessarily portentous or profound: Instead of *What do you do for a living?* she would ask *Do you find fulfillment in what you do?*; or, instead of, *How have you been?* she would ask *Was this week challenging for you?* And rather than *What were you like as a kid?* it was *Who were you then?* For all that, I found her other traits endearing enough to want to spend time with her. In fact, I actually caught myself occasionally using her phraseology, and sometimes I still do (my current sort-of-girlfriend finds this tolerable, within reason).

So, who was I that summer?

Saying I was a "typical" teenage kid didn't pass muster with the aforementioned lady of interest. And yet in many respects I do think I was typical. A good, not great student. Charming enough to attract girls, clumsy enough to not retain them for any significant stretch of time. Somewhat musically inclined, but not to the extent that I felt it in my soul (more on that later). Grateful for my friends, of which I had plenty, and fond of my smallish hometown in Oregon, but convinced that I had a more sophisticated inner essence that nobody could understand – therefore, my destiny lay in far distant vistas.

Like a lot of kids, I also had what you might call a tendency to shoot my mouth off, except putting it that way suggests I was aggressive, even obnoxious about it. If I was in a discussion, I tended to offer over-simplified solutions to problems that were complex or of an unfamiliar nature to me. But people often seemed to appreciate this – maybe because I didn't sound judgmental or arrogant, but empathetic and engaging in a low-key, non-threatening way.

Once, hearing a guy on the school basketball team complain about what a bastard his coach was, I told him that his

7

coach must've had an unhappy childhood and was taking out his past trauma on the team. Another time, my friend Jen spent a good 20 minutes lamenting how she and her childhood pal had grown apart, couldn't figure out what to do with each other.

"So go bowling," I said, matter-of-factly.

Look, it's not as if I kept case files or anything, but it sure seemed like my advice got some results. The basketball player caught up with me a few weeks later and said that he got a kick out of imagining his coach as a sad little boy, and it made practice easier to bear. Jen had initially bristled at my bowling suggestion, but later decided, what the heck, worth a try – and she and her friend wound up having a great time. ("It didn't solve everything," Jen added, "but it was fun. I'll take that.")

So for whatever reason, I developed a modest reputation as that guy you could talk to – sometimes a problem-solver, always a sounding board. This wasn't a role I sought or relished, but I guess at some point my ego got wrapped up in it. So now here I was, the listening ear for friends and acquaintances, unable or unwilling to seek out someone who'd be the same for me.

Not that I was mulling such ironies that summer day en route to Transformation. All I thought about was how miserable I was going to be.

Our car crested a small hill, and Mom began looking carefully to the left-hand side of the coast highway. After about ten yards or so she saw a sign, "Hilltop Campground," and turned onto a smaller road. And I felt my stomach, which had been dropping for about the last hour, slowly drop some more.

It was that special feeling of helplessness where you don't want to arrive at your destination, and there's really nothing you can do about it – except open the car door and try to escape, like some action hero you've seen on TV or in the movies. But even if you manage to hit the ground without hurting yourself, where do you go, and how do you get there? So you sit and settle for the compromise: The arrival is a dreadful certainty, and although anxiety builds as you get closer, at the same time you're grateful for every second you're still not there.

We drove along on the camp road, from where we could see open fields as well as forests, and glimpses of mountains farther away.

"I guess the first night is supposed to be pretty casual," my mother said. "You know, check in, unpack, get a bite to eat in the dining room."

"Uh huh," I replied.

"They'll probably have more information on activities and things like that when we get there, so we can figure out what you might like to do."

"Great."

Mom was silent as we went over a rough piece of road.

"So," she said, "you think you might actually say more than two words to me sometime?"

I could've stayed silent, I suppose, but I'd found it wearying to keep up this foul mood. I guess a part of me was even curious as to what I might find at the camp.

So I turned toward her, smirked a little and said, "Whatever you want."

We pulled into a Little League field-sized parking lot. A small grove of trees stood at its edge, and beyond it I could see a large wooden building, facing three rows of cabins arranged in a semicircle. Off to the right, in the distance, was a good-sized lake.

The parking lot was about half full, and several people were unpacking their cars. I had kind of expected to see beat-up VWs and garishly decorated old school buses, but it was mostly station wagons and mid-size cars – one even sported a

"President Ford '76" bumper sticker – much the same as those in the neighborhoods of our town.

I lugged my gear across the parking lot toward the cabins, with Mom ahead of me, holding a piece of paper that showed where we were staying. We passed various people along the way, either hauling their luggage or chatting with one another. Then, off to the right about 20 yards away, I spied a small cluster of kids who looked roughly in my age range, hanging around the steps of one cabin. Two of them were facing me: a rather dusky guy with big, bushy hair and equally lush mustache and beard, and a Black girl who looked like some Neal Adams-drawn space goddess, beautiful to an almost intimidating degree.

As I passed by, the guy gave me an upward nod and a more-or-less friendly smile, and the girl gave me a brief wave. Another girl, her back to me, looked over her shoulder in my direction, caught my eye and then quickly looked away.

Mom and I went along the second row of cabins until we came to one marked "211." It looked solid, wooden, a small concrete stoop in front of the door, all pretty nondescript, since it was much the same as all the other cabins in sight. Mom opened the screen door and the wooden secondary door, and we stepped inside. There were two single metal-frame beds, one against each wall; at the back of the cabin was a large wardrobe next to a chest of drawers.

"Well," said Mom, turning toward me, trying not to sound as if she was making conversation, "guess this is home for the next couple of weeks."

"Terrific," I answered, mustering as much lack of enthusiasm as I could.

Mom frowned briefly, then threw her sleeping bag on top of the bed on the left-hand side.

I felt an impulse to needle her.

"Hey," I said. "Why do *you* get to choose who gets which bed?"

She paused in the midst of opening the sleeping bag and turned her head toward me.

"Because I'm the nicest person in this room."

Grace and Marcus

We unpacked our stuff. Well, Mom did – I took each item out of my suitcase at an excruciatingly slow pace and placed it on my bed, as if that was going to be my only task for the foreseeable future. She watched me, shook her head, and went out the door, saying she wanted to see what was happening with dinner.

I stopped my unpacking (such as it was), and sat on the bed, convinced that I was somewhere between martyrdom and political prisoner status. After a few minutes, I became aware of someone on the front stoop.

"Hey," said a young female voice, instantly bringing me back to reality at blinding speed.

The screen door opened, and in stepped a girl I recognized as the one who had given me that quick smile. I hadn't gotten a good look at her before, and I still remember the inviting first impression she made on me: very straight brown hair that hung around her shoulders, azure eyes, a slight, charmingly upturned nose, and a jaw line that, for some reason, captured my fancy in a way that no jaw line ever had before – firm, but also pleasingly feminine. She was wearing an ankle-length denim skirt, and a knock-off of an Army jacket over a white T-shirt. She also wore a smile that, nervous as it was, I instantly realized I could enjoy seeing.

"I'm Grace," she said, sticking her hands inside the Army

jacket-like pockets as she slowly moved toward me.

"Uh, I'm Seth," I said, and reflexively stuck out my hand. It was just the way I was taught.

Grace took my hand and shook it ineptly, smiling as if she thought this was all hilarious but determined not to offend.

"So," I said, "you're the welcoming committee?"

"Yep, that's me," and she seemed to relax a little. "A committee of one."

God, how I tried to think of something witty to say.

At that moment, Mom came back through the door.

"OK, I guess we can go over to the dining hall any time now and – oh," she paused, as she spotted Grace. "Hello."

"Hi," said Grace. "I'm Grace, the welcoming committee. Of one." She looked over at me as if it was a private joke.

"Oh," said Mom, and it dawned on her that this was a good thing. "Well, isn't that nice?"

Then Grace seemed to shake off any lingering uneasiness or awkwardness, and addressing me – but also looking in Mom's direction out of a sort of benevolent inclusiveness – said, "Anyway, you should definitely feel free to come sit with me and the other 'kids' at dinner tonight." Her phrasing of "kids" was a sop to Mom, but also a sincerely delivered invitation to me.

"Thanks," I said. "I will."

Grace gave a little wave and went out the door, and Mom smiled in a way that said, "See, it's not going to be so terrible after all." I smiled back in a way that said, "Maybe, but don't think I'm letting you off the hook yet."

A few minutes later, there was another knock on our door, and in came a guy who looked a youthful 40ish, tall, thin and vigorous, with stringy graying hair, and a brilliant smile.

"Joanne and...Seth, right?" he said, clasping his hands in front of him. His voice was soft and gushy, like a bad FM radio DJ. "I'm Marcus. I got a nice little note from Christine a couple of weeks ago; she said you'd be coming."

"Hi, Marcus," said Mom, shaking his hand. "Yes, I don't really know Christine all that well, but she had great things to say about this place."

Marcus extended his hand to me, and I shook it grudgingly.

"Are you the camp director?" I asked.

Marcus chuckled a little and shook his head.

"No, Seth. There's not really a 'camp director.' But I guess you could call me one of the co-founders of Toward Transformation, and I do help run things, along with other friends."

He stepped back a little so he could address Mom as well as me.

"The reason I stopped by, actually, was just to give you a better idea of what we're all about here. I don't know how much Christine might've told you, so maybe I can fill in any blanks."

He paused for a second, and when neither Mom nor I said anything, he went on.

"Well, Transformation has been going for a decade now, and if you go back 10 years, you know what was going on." Marcus stopped and looked at me indulgently. "Seth, you were a little boy then, of course, so I don't know what, if anything, you'd remember."

He looked reflective for a minute. "RFK. Martin Luther King. The Vietnam War – Khe Sanh, Tet, My Lai. The *Pueblo* and North Korea. Prague Spring. Student riots in Europe. The Democratic Convention."

"I remember some of those things," I mumbled, sulkily.

Marcus smiled again and raised his hands slightly, as if making a concession.

"The point is, it just seemed that there were so many troubling things going on, and a lot of people were very worried. And about a dozen of us living in Monterey County – some of us were old college buddies who'd stayed in touch, some were co-workers, some were friends or neighbors – decided we should get together over Labor Day Weekend, just shut out the rest of the world, talk and enjoy one another's company. So Jerry – you'll meet him later – invited us to his place, which was out in the country and had lots of room; most of us were married, and a few had kids.

"It was a great time. And one of the things that made it enjoyable was each one of us had a particular perspective or expertise to contribute to our conversations: Jerry, for example, is a history teacher, so he gave us some background on Southeast Asia; another person worked in urban planning, and she talked about what was happening in the cities; another had a background in media and shared some impressions on news coverage of various events. And so on.

"So that weekend we all broadened one another's understanding of the things we had read or heard about, or seen on TV. It felt like we were doing something for each other, on our own, instead of depending solely on institutions – schools, the media, the government. And so we thought, 'Why not do this again? And with more people?'

"In the months afterward, we all told a few of our closest friends about the idea, and they were tremendously interested; there were somewhere around 30 in all. Clearly, Jerry's house wasn't going to be big enough to hold another gathering. But we got a break: Someone in our circle was connected to a trust that had acquired this campground" – he waved his right arm behind him – "Hilltop, which was built in the 1930s. They'd snazzed it up pretty nicely, put in electricity, running water, full bathroom facilities, and so on, and made it available for use by scout troops and other youth organizations, church groups – anyone willing to pay the rent. Seemed perfect. So we raised enough between us for about a week during the summer, and we were off and running. Well, maybe not running, but at least walking pretty fast."

Marcus paused and flashed us another grin. I think that was about when I decided that if there was one person in this camp, other than Mom, who would be the target of my contempt, it would be him.

"As we expanded the circle, and brought in different kinds of knowledge and experience – everything from social work to graphic arts to personal investment – we changed the format from simply conversations to seminars, so there would be an expectation of coming away having learned something. And we set a goal, if you will: The idea wasn't to change your life, exactly, but to put you on the road toward change – toward transformation; that's why we call them 'Transeminars.' If nothing else, the camp would at least give you something to think about, and in the company of sympathetic peers."

Mom nodded and asked, "So, how many people come now?"

"This year, we have about —" Marcus closed his eyes and seemed to do a quick mental calculation – "40 or so adults, and maybe 20 children." Marcus looked in my direction. "Children meaning anyone 18 and under. More or less." He smiled at me as if he thought he was being clever.

"That's very impressive," said Mom. "But how do you do it? I mean, I know you charge a fee, but..."

"The fee covers the cost of us renting Hilltop, running utilities – electricity and water – and for food," said Marcus, who really seemed to be enjoying himself now. "The beauty part is, we're not paying for guest speakers or 'faculty,' if you want to call them that: That's all us. Everybody pitches in to do the day-to-day cleaning and picking up. Even the food is a do-it-yourself thing. One of the couples here, Bill and Tess, run a catering business, so they know where to get good stuff cheap and they prepare and cook everything. And if there are some people who maybe need a little help paying their way, well, we have a little scholarship fund.

"See, as we started to broaden the scope and purpose of Transformation, we looked among our growing network of friends and acquaintances for people who had skills that would be especially helpful. For example, there are three different adults here who have lifeguard certification, so that means we can go swimming at the lake. And there are other people who have basic medical training, or are good with their hands, can work with electricity, and so on. So we don't need to pay to hire staff because, again, they're already here."

He extended his arms toward us. "And we all learn from each other."

"What happens if you don't go to any of the classes or Transeminars, or whatever you call them?" I said, putting a hint of challenge in my voice.

Marcus and Mom looked at me as if I had unleashed a string of profanity.

"It's not a school, Seth," said Marcus patronizingly. "Nobody takes attendance. There aren't any grades. You could, theoretically, just do nothing but lounge around camp all day. And in fact, sometimes families take a 'day off' and go hiking, even head off to the ocean, which is perfectly fine – after all, for a lot of people, the two weeks at Transformation is their summer vacation. But that's not what we come here for: We want to expand our awareness, our knowledge, of the world and what's in it."

"You said there were something like 20 kids here – what do they do while their parents go to the seminars?" I asked.

"Well, it's true that the programs are usually not appropriate, or of interest, to smaller children. So we leave it to their parents to figure out how they handle the situation. Sometimes, a mom and dad will swap off – one goes to a seminar, the other looks after the kid – or if they both want to go, they'll make some sort of arrangement with other parents.

"Now, if we're talking about kids who are more your age, that's different. They know they are certainly more than welcome to sit in on any Transeminars that might interest them – and Seth, I really hope you will. But we realize they don't expect to be 'babysat,' and want to have time and space of their own. Again, we leave it to families to make sure everyone understands their responsibilities, to themselves and others.

"And you know, you'll find that most of the children and

young people here have been coming to Transformation for years, so they have a certain investment in themselves, in the camp – and with one another. Does that make sense?"

Marcus gave his sunniest smile.

"I guess," I said. "Thanks."

Mom moved over to me, touched my arm with a clear quit-being-such-a-shithead squeeze, and looked at Marcus.

"It all sounds wonderful and fascinating," she said, and then hesitated. "It's just that..."

Marcus inclined his head toward her. "What, Joanne?" he asked with such manufactured gentleness that my stomach turned.

Mom shrugged. "It's just that I don't really have any special kind of skills or knowledge to share. I mean, I did go to college and all that, but mostly I've been—"

I knew she was about to say "a wife and a mother." Mom looked in my direction, and a look of dismay briefly crossed her face, as if her saying that would seem like an insult to herself and to Dad and me.

Fortunately – in this case, anyway – Marcus' apparent need to dominate conversations came in handy.

"Joanne," he said, "don't devalue yourself like that. There are people who've been coming here for years and have never led a Transeminar, and it's perfectly fine; Transformation needs folks who do the listening as well as those who do the talking. Anyway, we all have things to share. Sometimes it may take a while before you discover what they are."

He stepped back a little, raised his arms above him and slowly lowered them, spreading them outward as he did.

"And, perhaps, being here will help you do that."

He smiled at Mom as if he were a game show host charming a female contestant.

If I had known how to drive, I think I would have picked up Mom, dragged her out to our car, and driven like hell, far away from this guy and this place I still didn't understand and wanted to get away from.

The Dining Hall

A parent's default answer to a kid's complaint about having to go somewhere unfamiliar? "I'm sure there'll be kids your age there."

It's blithe and hopeful and dismissive all at the same time, and doesn't really make the kid feel better. For one thing, "kids your age" can mean – to the parent's way of thinking – anyone within five years of how old you are, which for adults may seem like no big deal, but is hardly an insignificant span to the kid in question.

And even if the kids are, in fact, actually your age (or reasonably close), that doesn't automatically imbue them with any kind of virtue. There's a perfectly good chance that they'll turn out to be antisocial, territorial, exclusionary or just plain mean, for the simple reason that you're not them.

That was what went through my mind as Mom and I headed over to the dining hall.

Now, it's true that I'd had a promising overture from Grace, and the other two "kids" I'd spotted at least seemed welcoming. But how much did that really mean? For all I knew, they would all close ranks once I was with them, make me feel even more of an outsider than I already did. If "alienation" had been on my list of things to achieve while a teenager, as far as I was concerned, I had checked that box.

But there I was, pulling up a chair to a round table at

which sat Grace and the others I'd seen on my way from the parking lot. Grace, who sat next to me, introduced them: The very hairy guy was Rafe, and the goddess was Diana. There also was Funk, a tall, skinny guy with stringy hair kind of like Marcus had, and Mishy, who was petite and a little plump, and seemed thoroughly pleasant.

Basic information was exchanged. It seemed that we six were the oldest "children" in the camp, although Rafe's status as a "child" was a little uncertain in that regard, since he'd graduated high school the previous year. Diana, Funk and Mishy were all about to start their senior years, and Grace was a sophomore-in-waiting. Apropos of what Marcus had said, all of them were longtime veterans of Transformation: Rafe and Diana had been to every one since it had started at Hilltop, Funk and Mishy nearly so, and Grace was attending her seventh. None of them lived in the same place, but they were close enough to usually see one another at least once or twice between camps.

"Did you meet Marcus yet? He usually likes to visit with newcomers," asked Diana, who had a glorious, full afro and wore a low-cut peasant dress. I had expected her voice to be regal and imposing, but it was a classic mellow, friendly California drawl.

"Oh, yeah," I said. "We got the whole speech."

"We're all here to learn from one another," said Rafe, imitating Marcus' voice and hand gestures. "It's in this way that we move forward, and toward transformation, in a very real and fulfilling sense."

Everyone at the table laughed.

"OK then, since you got the official adult version, now let's give you the 'kids' version,'" said Rafe, reverting to his natural, raspier voice and making quotation marks with his fingers.

He looked around the room and leaned toward me.

"It's like this," he said, conspiratorially. "We – all of us at the table here, plus the kids who were older than us at the time

– realized a few years ago that you can really enjoy yourself here if – IF – you don't do any stupid shit. You wanna smoke weed? Or drink some booze? Fine. But don't get so wasted you're gonna do some damage to yourself or someone else. Just take a few tokes, instead of the whole joint. Don't walk around camp with an open bottle of Boone's Farm. Pop some gum in your mouth to hide the smell. And for God's sake, just make the hell sure you're with someone so they can hopefully keep you out of trouble."

Diana leaned over to chime in. I tried not to look at her cleavage.

"Marcus probably told you about being welcome to go to the Transeminars," she said. "Do it. Seriously. Just go to two, maybe three. I mean, there are actually a few you may like. It keeps all the adults happy because they feel like you're 'invested' in the program, if you know what I mean."

I remembered Marcus' comment about "investment" and nodded.

"Be nice to the littler kids," said Funk, "even if some of them are real shits."

"Don't slouch around the camp so much," said Mishy. "Stand up straight!"

We all laughed.

I turned to Grace.

"Any advice to add?" I asked.

"Smile and nod," she said, giving me a sweet, wry grin. "Smile and nod."

From the other side of the room, I heard somebody shout, "Hi! Can I just have your attention for a minute?" I looked over to see a stout man with glasses standing up and waving his arms over his head. When everyone quieted, he began to speak.

"That's Jerry," Grace whispered to me. "He helps run things."

"Welcome to you all," said Jerry, gazing around the room. "I'll keep it short."

There was a quick burst of applause from a few people, followed by laughter.

Jerry nodded and laughed himself, then continued.

"Anyway, here we are, together for another year of Toward Transformation. And it's a special year: our 10th one here at Hilltop. That's pretty amazing when you think about it. For a decade, we've gathered each summer to talk and think and learn, and most of all, relax and enjoy one another's company. Democrats, Republicans, liberals, conservatives, Catholics, Protestants, Jews, atheists, business executives, teachers, contractors, writers, moms, dads."

He paused. "No grandparents yet, right?"

There was light laughter.

"Hell, there are even Dodgers *and* Giants fans here!"

More laughter, and someone shouted, "Go, Angels!"

Jerry held up his hands to quell the noise, and continued. "We should feel good about what we've accomplished, and it should inspire us to keep it up for another decade – if not more! That's all I wanted to say. Enjoy your meal."

Everyone applauded, including the kids at my table.

Seth and Mom

Later that night, in our darkened cabin, I settled into my sleeping bag.

After a few minutes, I heard my mother ask softly, "You still upset about being here?"

"I'm not 'upset,'" I replied. "I'm pissed off."

Then I added, "But maybe not as much as I was."

"So, how are the other kids?" she asked after a short while.

"They seem fine," I said. "They were telling me about the camp and things like that."

"Uh-huh."

Mom seemed to be expecting more, but I didn't elaborate.

"Well, I sat with some nice people. One of them is the mother of a girl who was at your table – Misha? Mitchy?"

"Mishy."

"Oh. Anyway, Trina said they've been coming here for a long time, and she told me about all the ways Transformation has helped them over the years: They used to hate cooking big meals, like for Thanksgiving or dinner parties, but at one Transeminar they learned how to plan better so that it wouldn't seem like an overwhelming task, and also picked up some simple recipes. Now they love it. And then a few years ago, Trina's mother-in-law died, and that particular summer Transformation had something about dealing with deaths of loved ones; it was a big help to both Trina and her husband.

"Best of all, Trina said that for them it's like having a whole other family – even if they don't necessarily see each other except during Transformation. It's just very comforting."

I didn't say anything, but I knew intuitively that Mom – an only child whose father had passed away not long after I was born – had sometimes felt she was really on her own, even with a husband and son, especially when her mother had grown senile in recent years (Grandma hadn't recognized me when we had last visited her, and got so agitated that we left after only a couple of hours). I wondered if this might have contributed to her problems with Dad.

But at the moment, I just couldn't bring myself to respond. So, since it had worked once pretty well already today, I pretended to be asleep.

"Seth? Honey?"

I heard her sigh a little, then turn over.

The Dream

I woke up sometime just before dawn – I didn't know the exact time, but I could hear birds starting to sing. I just lay there for a while and eventually began to doze, waking up and falling back asleep.

"Seth?"

I snapped back to consciousness, though I kept my eyes closed.

"It's going to be time for breakfast soon. Maybe you want to take a shower or something?"

I mumbled something that approximated acknowledgement. I couldn't see her, but I could sense my mother lingering at the door.

"Seth? Don't fall back asleep and miss breakfast. You'll be starving for the rest of the morning."

I tried to say "Don't worry. I'm gonna get up in just a minute," but it came out, "Din worr. Ga geddp in mimmit."

Mom let out an exasperated sound, opened the door, and left.

I was in no hurry to join her. As far as I was concerned, I was just going to lie here as long as I could. I still didn't want to be in this place, still didn't understand what my mother thought I would accomplish by being here. Marcus had definitely rubbed me the wrong way, and if he was supposed to represent what Transformation was all about, that didn't bode well. The overtures from Grace and the other kids had been nice enough, but I was still convinced that it was all some kind of pretense, and they'd shut me off if I tried to befriend them.

I lapsed into sleep again, and had one of those dreams that begins with you imagining yourself doing whatever it was you were thinking about just as you dozed off.

In the dream, I get out of bed slowly, resignedly, and put on my clothes with an equal lack of enthusiasm. As I go out the door, I realize something: The birds have all stopped singing.

I stand in front of the cabin and look around. There is no sound at all, no sign of activity – I would've expected to see at least a few people walking around, going to the bathroom or showers, but nobody is in sight.

By this age, I'd seen enough science fiction/supernatural TV or film fare to know the protocol for when you suddenly find yourself apparently, inexplicably all alone: You dutifully set out to search the area.

I walk toward the dining hall, and there is no scent of food in the air, no sound of pots and pans banging about in the kitchen, no conversation. Tables and chairs are set up, but nobody is there.

I continue my exploration of the camp, making the rounds of all the rows of cabins. I peek into some of the cabin windows and see no evidence of inhabitants: no suitcases or knapsacks, no clothes or other belongings, no blankets or sleeping bags, just bed frames and mattresses.

I'm aware of some anxiety building within me, but I don't feel compelled to run around the camp wildly, as if I was George Bailey in Pottersville, shouting "Mom! Mom! Where are you?" It dawns on me that not only are there no people, but there's no food, either, unless I want to try my hand at hunting or fishing, neither of which I've ever done. Besides, if the birds are gone, maybe all the other animals – my potential meals – are, too?

And then I notice something else: I feel cold, as if it were

January or February. This doesn't make sense, because I know it's still summer – I can see the flowers and other vegetation. Yet even standing in the direct sunlight doesn't make me feel any warmer.

So I realize that I have a decision to make: Do I stay here in hopes of figuring something out, or do I go someplace, anyplace other than this – eventually home, I guess?

And then, I'm at the parking lot – I don't dream myself walking to it, I'm just there – and, of course, there are no cars.

I take a long look at the road beyond the parking lot, stretching into the distance. If I start walking down it, maybe at some point I'll magically appear on my street, in front of my house. That's how dreams work, don't they? Well, sometimes they do, anyway.

I begin to walk toward the road, but I don't make any progress; it's as if I am walking in place. It's unclear to me how long I keep walking, but at some point I begin to feel exhausted, as if I've been at it for hours. Finally, I stop and catch my breath. I pivot 180 degrees, facing the camp, and take a step.

And then I wake up.

I've never been much for interpreting dreams. For me, dreams are usually chaotic and surreal, and seldom, if ever, contain any meaningful nuggets of wisdom. Not that there aren't any insights to be gained, I suppose: If you dream about being naked in public, that's supposed to indicate a fear of vulnerability, or that there's an aspect of yourself you feel you want to keep private – but I can't help but think an overwhelming majority of the human race has that same anxiety. Big deal.

However, this dream, so vivid and realistic, *did* make an impression on me. It told me that, for better or worse, I was stuck in this camp, and that the way things were going these two weeks would be just like what I had seen in the dream. I would be cut off (or, rather, I would cut myself off) from any human contact, from warmth and nourishment – of the spiritual rather than literal kind.

And what would all this accomplish? I would leave at least as miserable – and probably more – than when I'd arrived. Not to mention that I would antagonize and likely alienate my mother. This wouldn't help me any and, if I was being honest about it, would be a pretty crappy thing to do to her, given that her marriage was all but over. I guess, in retrospect, this is when I reached that point where you realize that there are actually limits to how much you think you hate your parents.

I don't know how long I lay there processing all this, and I'm not sure how much crystallized in my mind at the time. But I finally got out of bed, put on my clothes and walked out of the cabin toward the dining hall.

I wasn't choosing between life or death, exactly, but between a life that could only get worse or a life that maybe, just maybe, would at least be tolerable.

Initiation

I got to the dining hall just after they'd stopped serving hot food, but there was still a choice of cereals – including some I'd never even heard of and a few of which looked like they might have been homemade – and various fruits, plus make-your-own toast.

Just as I had filled my tray, Jerry stood up to get everyone's attention. I quickly found an open spot at a nearby table and sat down. I looked around for a few seconds and spotted my mother sitting several tables away; she had been chatting with someone next to her, and when she caught sight of me she gave a quick wave. Then I tried to find the other kids, and finally caught sight of them clear on the other side of the hall. They were busy eating and talking with each other so they didn't see me.

When all the conversation had petered out, Jerry walked into the approximate center of the room. "Hi again, folks. As you know, we like to kick off the first morning of camp with our traditional 'Transtestimonial.' So as always, we invite you to share some thoughts about what Transformation has meant for you – you know, to remind us of why we come, what we hope to gain, and so on. And, of course, being that this is a special year, it seems particularly appropriate to, uh, reflect on our experiences. So, anyone have anything to say?"

I was a little surprised to see quite a few hands quickly

raised; I suppose I'd been conditioned by school to believe that volunteering one's viewpoint was something to avoid. The people Jerry called on at first, however, said pretty general, vague things: "I've made so many dear friends here"; "It's the thing I look forward to the most every year now"; "Such a beautiful, peaceful place where you can feel at ease."

Then Kevin, a portly, balding guy in a Hawaiian shirt, got up to speak.

"To me, Transformation – the place and the word – means being able to be both changer and changed," he said, solemnly. "I'll always remember taking that Transeminar on community organizing from Millie, and the impact it had on me: to think that I could make a difference in ways that might seem small but were significant, nonetheless. So that became my new vocation, part-time at first, but three years ago I accepted a full-time administrative position, and it's been wonderful."

He briefly described some of what he'd been doing, which included phrases that, to me, were unenlightening: "voter empowerment," "economic opportunity," "public-private collaboration."

Summing up, Kevin said, "So, because I was changed, now I can help make change."

He paused, and a small smile appeared.

"The changer and the changed," he said. "Or vice-versa."

Several people applauded lightly as he sat down.

A prim-looking, tentative-voiced woman, Alena, came next.

"I learned how to read here," she said, raising some chuckles, which she joined in on. "Did anyone else take Ruth's Transeminar – oh, what did she call it? Ah yes, 'Trashy Books You Should Read for the Hell of It.'"

There were a few murmurs of assent in the room.

"Well, I think many of you know me, or me as I used to be: When I read something – a book, a magazine, a newspaper article – it was a serious business. There had to be a *purpose* to reading, as far as I was concerned. The idea of it being for fun, pure, unadulterated whimsy, was alien to me.

"I don't know why I went to Ruth's seminar: I guess it must've been one of those occasions where you think that hearing a talk on something that is so opposite of what you believe will reinforce that belief – do you know what I mean? But then Ruth described how she too had always been a 'serious' reader, in every sense of the word, but had once wound up at a friend's lakeside cabin with nothing to read but *The Love Machine* and *The Other Side of Midnight*.

"And she said how, to her surprise, she had enjoyed almost every page of each book. She compared it to having a bowl of ice cream with chocolate syrup and sprinkles: perfectly harmless, almost like a reward for your diligence to 'good' eating. Well, I tried out her recommendations – Susann, Sheldon, Jaffe, Robbins – and I ate it all up, just like she did. Of course, I still did plenty of my usual kind of reading, but after a few chapters of David Halberstam or the latest *New York Review of Books*, next time I'd settle in with *The Carpetbaggers* for a bit."

Alena paused, looked a little self-conscious, then continued.

"The thing is, I came to realize that I needed to do this in other areas of my life: Stop being so darn serious, so purposeful, all the time. It's OK to be silly, to be lazy, to just *be*. And you know what? That was such a relief. I felt so much better, more relaxed. Then I started to seek, and create, those kinds of situations with other people."

She stopped again, caught her breath a little, and her voice became shaky. "I hadn't realized how much of my life I'd spent alone. But that's in the past now. I'm not that person anymore."

Alena flicked a tear away, sniffled a little, then sat down and was embraced by the woman sitting next to her. The applause was more robust this time, with a few cheers and whoops as well.

Bradley, a stocky, solidly built man well into his 50s, stood up, looked down briefly at the smiling lady in the next chair, then moved his feet slightly.

"Well," he said in a gritty, tough-guy voice, "I originally came here under false pretenses. I thought it was gonna be fun."

A number of people laughed, and he smiled somewhat ruefully.

"Some of you probably know the score. You raise your kids, they grow up, they leave, and then it's just the two of you. And I thought, 'OK, just the two of us, peace and quiet at last.' So, I'd go off and watch the Dodgers game on TV, or putter around in my workshop, stuff like that, and I thought everything was fine. I mean, we had our health, our kids were doing good out on their own, so what was there to worry about?"

Bradley looked down again at his wife (I figured that's who she was); she still smiled, but looked more reflective.

"And then, a few years ago, out of the blue, Gail comes to me with this Toward Transformation thing: 'Irene went there and said it was great,' she says, and starts talking about it, and I kind of nod along, not really listening. I just thought it was some different kind of vacation place, you know? And I figure, well, Gail really wants to go, maybe it'll be fun, and hey, getting out to nature doesn't sound bad. Especially if there's electricity and running water."

There was a little laughter at that.

"Anyway, we're here, and Gail says 'OK, it's time to go to our Transeminar.' And I thought, 'Huh? What kind of place is this, anyway? ' But she prods and pulls me along and we're sitting in a room with seven, eight other people. And so this gal Sheila gets up and says, 'We're going to talk today about communication in marriage' – oh swell, I think to myself. I figure it's gonna be about couples who fight and argue all the time, and what's that got to do with us?

"So Sheila explains that with communication, it's not only what you say and how you say it, it's what you're *not* saying. She asks us how often we have actual conversations, not just talking about the weather's going to be like tomorrow or what we should get at the supermarket this week, but about who we are as a couple, what we've experienced, that sort of thing. I have no idea where she's going with this.

"Then Sheila says, 'We're going to do a little exercise. Go off with your spouse to a private spot. Decide on an event that you agree was very important in your relationship, whether before or after you got married. Then talk about how you remember that event – what are the important details?'

"It all sounds pretty nutty to me, but I figure, well, we're here, so we might as well. And Gail and I decide to talk about the day I first met her parents."

He waved his hand dismissively.

"I'm not gonna go into all the details, but I was amazed at how different our memories of that day were, and that there were things which had, to be honest, kind of bugged me – or bugged her – that we'd never really talked about. As it turned out, I had some parts wrong, and she had some parts wrong. At the end, Sheila says, 'Just because you've been together for a long time doesn't mean you know everything about each other. Keep talking to each other – and I mean really talking to each other – and see what you find out.'

"So we're walking back to our cabin, and I'm seeing my wife in a whole new light, you know? And we talked a lot during the rest of that Transformation, and a lot on our way back from camp, and we just kept talking. Oh, sure, we still go off in our separate corners – you're not gonna keep me away from watching the Dodgers – but we make the time to just sit and talk. And I mean really talk."

He looked at Gail slyly.

"Of course, sometimes the talk leads to other things."

Gail blushed, gave him a soft slap on the arm, then stood up and hugged him. Somebody shouted, "Geez, take it outside, will ya?" and everyone laughed and applauded.

After breakfast, I found out my camp assignment, which was to work in the kitchen two hours each day; some days it was in the morning, others the afternoon or evening. That day, my shift wasn't until around dinnertime, but I figured that introducing myself beforehand to Bill and Tess was probably a good, responsible, grown-up type of thing to do, and it was. They came across as very friendly and said they'd try not to run me too ragged.

"If we do," said Tess, all rosy-cheeked and cherubic, "just remember it's Bill's fault."

"If it's my fault," said Bill, with thinning hair and a little pot belly, "there was probably a good reason."

We all laughed. Tess slipped me a brownie that was to be the dessert for lunch.

That afternoon, as Mom and most of the other adults went to the first round of Transeminars, I set out to find the other kids. It took a little while, but I finally came across them hanging out at the row of bathhouses adjacent to the lake's designated swimming area. (I observed that their method of operation was to migrate continuously to areas of the camp where there would be little or no activity – since the "camp swim" schedule didn't start until a little later, the bathhouses were a good place to be for the moment.)

"Oh, there you are," said Rafe. "Thought you had gotten kidnapped by bears or something."

"There are bears around here?" I asked, a little surprised that nobody, not even Marcus, had mentioned this before.

"Eh, probably," he replied, then added casually, "Which might explain why I haven't seen that kid from Mendocino this year..."

"Rafe!" said Diana sharply. She looked at me kindly. "He really likes being an asshole sometimes."

"'Sometimes'?" said Funk.

Rafe ignored them and asked me what I thought of the Transtestimonials. I replied cautiously that they were "interesting."

"Oh yeah," said Rafe derisively. Then he stood up straight and affected an earnest expression. "Before I came to Transformation, I didn't know my ass from my elbow," he intoned solemnly. "Now, I get it right almost 50 percent of the time."

"Laugh track!" said Funk.

"Jesus, Rafe," growled Diana.

"What?" said Rafe. "Did you hear Bradley going on and on? It's honestly just embarrassing."

"Look, you know that Bradley and a lot of men in his generation aren't always good at the interpersonal stuff," said Diana. "That took a lot of guts for him to get up and say that, even among people he knows. Don't be such a shithead."

Rafe shot her a glance, then rolled his eyes. He looked around at everyone and rubbed his hands together ceremoniously. "So, we gonna do the thing?"

The five of them started to get up and head toward the lake.

"The 'thing'?" I asked as I walked along with them.

"Yeah, just something we like to do to celebrate another year of Transformation," said Rafe.

We moved in the direction of the beach area, and the edge of the water, but then veered off onto a little path that took us out of sight of the camp. After walking about another 50 yards, we reached a spot that was entirely in shade, and Rafe said, "OK, this looks perfect."

He and the others kicked off their sandals and flip-flops and gingerly entered the water. Grace halted and looked at me expectantly, so I shed my footwear and went in. The water felt quite chilly, and I rather hoped that whatever it was we were going to do wouldn't take very long.

Finally, when we were about thigh-deep, Rafe had us form a circle facing each other.

"All right, Seth," he said to me. "What happens is, when I count to five, we all fall over backwards, and then stay in the water as long as possible."

He looked at everyone. "Ready? Everyone put your arms out."

They extended their arms to the side, and I followed suit. Rafe counted, "1, 2, 3, 4, FIVE!"

I'd had the suspicion that this was a set-up, that they'd keep standing up while I plopped in the water by myself, so I paused for a second to see what would happen. But all five of them fell over into the water, so I did, too.

It was absolutely freezing, but I was determined to stay there however long the five of them did. I wasn't sure how many seconds passed – maybe 15? – until I'd had enough and stood up gasping.

I was alone.

I instantly thought of my dream, wondered for just a second if I were hallucinating.

Then I realized I wasn't alone: The other five were already moving along the shore, hunched over from cold and clutching at themselves. I ran after them and caught up where they had collapsed onto a sunny patch of grass. I flopped down likewise, and we all lay there breathing rapidly as we basked in the sun's warmth.

At length, Rafe managed to say to me, "You did pretty good!"

I briskly rubbed my arms and said, "What, did you guys just get right back up and come out?"

Rafe smiled. "Oh, yeah. Who the hell wants to stay in fucking cold water?"

Mishy, Funk, Grace, and Diana all laughed.

I suppose I could've been mad at them, but it's not like they had deliberately played a prank on me. Actually, it had been refreshing, even stimulating, in a way – not that I was in any hurry to try it again.

Gradually, we all sat up. Grace was wearing a white T-shirt

that was now soaked and practically transparent, her bra showing right through it. I realized I was staring at her just as she returned my gaze, raising her eyebrows slightly. At least she didn't appear to be offended.

"So," I said to no one in particular, "what the hell was that all about, anyway?"

Rafe shrugged. "It was just something we started doing several years ago. A couple of the older guys – juniors, seniors in high school – thought we all should 'baptize' ourselves to start another year of Transformation. You know, clean away all the bad stuff we'd accumulated over the previous year and begin anew. Some crap like that."

"Except that they were pretty serious about it," said Diana.

"They actually called it 'Transbaptism,'" put in Funk.

"Yeah, we just kept on doing it because it was fun," said Mishy. "A little crazy, but fun."

"Plus," said Funk, "it's interesting to see what happens when a new person joins in. I don't know of anyone who stuck it out as long as you did."

"Hear, hear!" said Diana, and raised her hand toward me in an imaginary toast. "Welcome to Transformation, Seth!"

They all imitated Diana, repeating "Welcome to Transformation, Seth!" more or less in unison.

"And stop looking at Grace's tits," added Rafe.

Seth and Mom (Continued)

"Hey, Seth?" said Mom, quietly and tentatively.

I put *Welcome to the Monkey House* face down on my chest, so I wouldn't lose my place, and looked over at her.

"Yeah?" I tried to sound halfway between annoyed and tolerant.

"Um, when I was talking with some of the other parents today, they told me about this one thing which was helpful when they'd first started coming here as a family: a kind of a 'check-in' with each other at the end of the day," she said, making little semicircular hand motions, which she always did whenever she felt nervous about what she was trying to say. "Like at dinner time, or in the evening sometime, or just when you're getting ready to go to bed."

"A 'check-in'?" I said, obnoxiously imitating her gestures for a few seconds. The little lamp on the night table next to my bed made grotesque-looking shadows of my hands on the cabin wall.

She frowned.

"Well, really, it's just talking about – I don't know – something you saw, something you heard, something you experienced during the day that was interesting to you. You don't even have to explain why it was interesting, although of course that would be nice. I guess the idea is that you capture these little, uh, slices of life or whatever, so they're kind of reference points for your stay here. Like maybe you start noticing things around you, or about you, that you hadn't before?"

I didn't say anything, but I already knew what her next sentence was going to be.

"So I'd like to try that," she said, sounding more forthright.

"OK," I sighed. I figured it couldn't be too horrible. "But you go first."

"Sure," she said, and thought a moment. "Well, let's see: I was walking through the picnic area, and I saw these two little girls, maybe six or seven years old, and they were playing a hand-clapping game – you know, 'Miss Mary Mack'? And, I don't know, it was just kind of comforting, somehow. I mean, here we are in this unfamiliar place, we don't really know anybody, and here are these kids doing the same thing I used to do when I was their age. Maybe that seems a little silly, but I felt good about it."

Mom smiled a little, then nodded at me.

"Your turn."

I briefly thought about having seen Grace's bra through her soaked shirt after the little ceremony in the lake – something I'd replayed in my mind's eye quite a bit in the hours afterward – but that was obviously not what Mom would want to hear. However, I saw no reason why I couldn't give her the gist of what happened.

"...so I guess they do that every year, even though the water is freezing cold," I concluded my retelling.

Mom chuckled a little.

"That's sweet. People really like their little customs and rituals, sometimes, even if they don't know why."

I dog-eared the page I was on, closed the book and put it on the nightstand, then turned out the lamp.

"Night, Mom."

Walking
with Grace

Even after the "Transbaptism" in the lake, I still felt wary about the other kids. It was all going too smoothly. (Good thing for me the teens-at-summer-camp wasn't a horror movie genre yet, or I might have been really worried.) I couldn't shake the feeling that there was a shoe yet to drop, that they would find a way to put me in my place as the interloper and deny me genuine inclusion into their sphere of fellowship.

I had assumed that this group of kids was like any other I'd come across before: those who exclude or ostracize because they see their social collective as a precious commodity whose access should be as limited as possible – or just because they can. I didn't grasp, at least not then, that this zealousness took a level of energy and focus the kids in Transformation, even if they felt that way, simply weren't interested in putting forth.

More importantly, the kids were in their own way aping the Transformation philosophy that each new arrival brought with him or her the potential to enrich and perpetuate the community. Rafe, Diana, Grace and the rest, including the kids who'd been their age when Transformation began, had over time formed a community *within* the community – quirky and capricious in its youthfulness, of course, yet possessing a bond whose strength they themselves didn't necessarily appreciate.

This revelation still lay ahead for me. But I was about to take a big step down that road.

Standing in line for breakfast on Sunday, Grace asked casually if I'd like to have a tour of the camp and its immediate surroundings. I quickly accepted the offer. She suggested we go in the afternoon.

The first part of the camp tour was boring and conventional, making the rounds of the various common buildings and areas, and Grace apologized for it. "But we have to start somewhere, right?"

Grace tended to be on the laconic side, but we made small talk quite easily. She had this funny little drawn-out burr in her voice whenever she started to speak, like an engine warming up until hitting its full cycle.

We walked among the cabins, including some that were built to accommodate families of as many as five. She took me by buildings on the outer periphery that I hadn't seen yet: one that was the recreation center and another for arts and crafts activities. These were set aside for larger Transeminars, she explained.

Then we walked along the shores of Lake Hilltop, which looked serene in the afternoon sunlight. At one point, she paused and gazed out onto the water.

After about a minute or so, I asked tentatively, "Are we looking at something in particular?"

"Nope," she said, slowly. "Just really pretty here."

I tried to match her appreciation for the scenery, but wound up feeling self-conscious. Still, she was right: It was really pretty.

We moved away from the lake, toward what appeared to be a dense clump of trees. As we got closer, though, I could see a little path winding through it. We went about 30 yards until we came to a small clearing, and Grace pointed at a small embankment that was all grassy.

She sat down and settled back against the embankment. She patted the spot next to her, and I joined her. It felt very comfortable, like sitting in a soft lawn chair. Grace told me she and her friends referred to it as "The Sitting Woods."

"This is a great place for when you want to get away for some quiet," she said.

"'When you want to get away'? You mean, it's inevitable?"

Grace looked at me sardonically.

"Sixty adults and kids in one place?" she replied. "How can you *not* want to get away?"

We left The Sitting Woods and began climbing a hill that got progressively steeper. When I stumbled slightly, Grace grabbed my elbow to steady me, and held on for a few extra seconds. Our eyes met, and then she turned her gaze frontwards again.

"Where are we going?" I asked.

"My favorite place."

We continued on until we reached a small plateau and traversed it until we came upon a small outcropping of rocks. Grace climbed up on it and sat down, and motioned for me to do the same. From where we were, we could see almost all of the camp below us; I looked for the dining hall to orient myself, and saw where our cabin was. There were various people walking around, some of them holding towels and headed to the lake, others strolling together more leisurely. A few little kids frolicked on the large green near the rec center. There was a lot of activity, but the sound didn't carry to where we were.

"So, you go to that other place for when you want some quiet," I said. "What do you come to this place for?"

She gave me a look that was surprisingly gentle, almost vulnerable.

"To remind myself why I like being here."

Grace put her arms out slightly to the back so she could

lean on them.

"Down there," she nodded in the direction of the camp, "are the people I've probably been the closest to since I was a little girl. I've loved them, gotten angry at them, forgiven them, loved them all over again. I just like being able to see all of them, and this place, all at once, without them knowing. As if I was floating over everything."

I couldn't help staring at her as she spoke. Gone were the short, terse sentences, and her voice sounded purposeful, practically lyrical.

She shifted her position until she was facing me, sitting closer.

"So," she said, "when did your parents split up?"

I almost did a cartoon-style double take.

"How did you – I mean, what makes you think—"

"Well, you came here just with your mother," she said. "I mean, all the way from wherever that place in Oregon is, with *just* your mother. So that was a clue. Mainly, it was recognizing little signals here and there – takes one to know one, right?"

Early on, during our small talk, I'd been taking stock of things we seemed to have in common, like coming from a small town, books we had liked, being an only child. This new revelation went to the top of the list.

I gave her a short version of the story.

"And you're sure they're going to get divorced?" said Grace when I'd finished.

"At this point, I'd be shocked if they didn't."

She nodded silently.

"How about you?" I asked.

Grace frowned, closed her eyes.

"I was nine. As for the how and why? She was a bitch. He cheated on her. Which happened first, which was more important? You'll have to take that up with them."

The bitterness in her voice was abrupt. She paused, then shook her head. She turned to look in the direction of the camp.

43

"There were maybe two months or so left in the school year when they told me they were splitting up. I thought that our lives must've been too full of unhappiness, so I decided that I would do all I could to make everything perfect and free of stress."

Grace turned back toward me.

"That's apparently a common reaction among kids when their parents plan to get divorced," she said, with a slightly forced grin. "I read about it when I was in junior high. At least I knew I wasn't crazy.

"Anyway, I didn't just pick up my room every day, I vacuumed and dusted it. I insisted on washing their dishes, glasses and utensils after dinner, not just mine. If there was a mess anywhere in the house, even if I hadn't made it, I cleaned it up. And you better believe I was the best student in my class – the whole school."

She smiled sadly.

"When summer came, I begged for them both to take me to Transformation. I was convinced that this would be the final touch to the big reconciliation. We'd all have the best time ever at camp, and then they'd forget about the whole divorce thing.

"So what happened? First, there was a massive traffic jam on the way, and we didn't get in until about 9 the first evening. Then we found out there'd been a mix-up and we'd been given the wrong cabin, so there weren't enough beds for the three of us – I told them it didn't matter, I could just sleep on the floor. I did everything I could think of to make sure they were enjoying themselves – I even stood in line at the dining hall to get them their food – and spent the rest of the time worrying that I'd forgotten something."

"God, you must've been exhausted."

"Oh, yeah. I think it was maybe the fourth day. I was running from the rec center" – she pointed at it – "to get to my cabin, because I wanted to make sure their beds were made. Can you believe that? Anyway, I tripped and fell flat on my face. It didn't hurt, not really at all, but I just started bawling. I realized right then and there that, here we were, supposed to be having the time of our lives, and I was fucking miserable.

"Fortunately, Diana and Mishy, and Jana – another, older girl – happened to be passing by and saw me. They took me off to Jana's cabin, and I broke down and told them everything. I think I must've cried on Diana's shoulder for a good half-hour. She actually carried me back to my cabin, tucked me into my sleeping bag, and stayed with me while I slept. And Jana and Mishy found my parents and told them what was going on with me.

"The next day, I felt better. My parents tried to convince me that we should just leave, forget about Transformation, but I talked them into staying. It went a lot better, and I was able to enjoy myself without worrying about my parents.

"Of course," she added, shrugging, "when all was said and done, they still got divorced. But" – she held up her index finger and smiled proudly – "at least I got a big concession: They take turns coming with me to Transformation each year."

"That's great," I said. "So things got better?"

"Yeeeahhhhh," she said. "Time certainly helps. They did get their shit together. I'll give 'em that."

"Well, maybe they can talk to my parents, then," I replied frostily.

Grace drew even closer to me.

"Hey Seth?" It was the first time either one of us had addressed the other by name.

She put her hand on my arm.

"Do yourself a favor? Don't push your feelings deep down inside or anything like that, but watch it with the self-pity, OK? It really doesn't do you much good."

"All right," I said, taken aback by her directness.

We were silent for a few minutes, and she shifted back to her former position, watching the camp in the distance.

"It's just that," I began, stopped, then tried again. "I mean,

45

at least I know I'm not responsible for their happiness and all that. But how do you just throw away, like, 20, 21 years together, 18 of them married? Do you just stop loving, just like that? Is there something wrong, I mean really fucked-up, with them?"

Grace turned to look at me. "You're worried about them," she said, softly.

"Well, yeah," I said. "But I also have to wonder, is that's what gonna happen to me, too, someday? I'll fall in love, get married, and then just decide, 'OK, I'm finished'?"

She thought for a minute before answering.

"It would be worse if you didn't care – about them, or about yourself."

"Why?"

She put her knees up, folded her arms on top of them, rested her head on her arms and gazed at me kindly.

"Because then you wouldn't be the nice guy I thought you were."

I didn't answer, just looked at her.

Suddenly, she snapped her head back up.

"Oh, wow, what time is it? You probably have to start your shift soon. We should head back."

We scrambled down the hill carefully, and within minutes were walking into the camp. When we got to the dining hall, she reached for my hand and squeezed it.

"That was nice," she said. "See you at dinner."

At dinner that evening, Rafe and Funk talked about a mutual acquaintance of theirs and his adventures at a Grateful Dead concert. The volume and volubility of their conversation was such that it overrode anyone else's attempts to talk, so Diana, Mishy, Grace and I just listened. Under the table, Grace felt for my hand and held it for a few minutes, until she went to get more lemonade.

After dinner cleanup was over, somebody set up a projection screen on the other side of the room and a film projector on the other; apparently, he was in the audio-visual business – even taught film classes part-time at a college – and had a personal collection of, or access to, all kinds of movies, which he brought with him to Transformation every year. That night, he screened Charlie Chaplin's *Modern Times*.

By the time Chaplin's Little Tramp had met Paulette Goddard's urchin, Grace was holding my hand. She didn't let go until the final scene, when the two of them are striding down that long road together.

The next morning, we lingered over breakfast. It was, to my memory, the first time I ever had the conscious sensation of lingering over a meal. This felt like a very adult thing to do.

Grace had her own camp job to do shortly, cleaning up the women's bathroom. I had lunchtime kitchen duty that day, so the upshot was we wouldn't see each other until early afternoon.

I walked her to the bathrooms, and when we'd finished saying "Later" to one another, she took my face tenderly in her hands, drew me toward her, and I wrapped my arms around her shoulders, and our lips touched firmly and gently.

I suppose we could've chosen any of a number of more picturesque locations than a campground bathroom facility as the setting for our first kiss, but I don't think either one of us regretted it.

Seth and Mom (Cont.)

Mom caught up with me one evening, as I was getting a cup of coffee (although I hadn't yet acquired the taste, I relished the opportunity and freedom to get one whenever I liked).

"Well," she said, blithely, "you certainly seem to be keeping a lot of company with that girl – what's her name? Greta?"

I knew Mom was fishing, but I played along.

"It's Grace, Mom."

"Oh, that's right. Well, she seems very nice."

"Yeah, she's pretty cool," I said, in the same tone as I might comment on a US Treasury report.

"Good," she said, smiling as if she'd cracked a top-secret enemy code. "Very good."

Peers

It's certainly true that Grace occupied the lion's share of my thoughts from then on. But I did pay attention to what else was going on around me at Transformation, filing away various items of interest, some of which I didn't quite appreciate or fully understand at the time.

Predictably, most of my time with Grace was spent in the company of Rafe, Diana, Mishy and Funk, or some combination thereof. ("Funk," as it turned out, derived from his last name, which was "Funkowicz." His first name was Tim, but I was given to understand that he didn't use it, and strongly preferred others avoid using it as well.) I tried not to begrudge her this: They were her friends, after all – she obviously considered them as such – she'd known them far, far longer than me, and Transformation was a special opportunity for her to be with them.

Mornings tended to go by fast. If I didn't have to work in the kitchen, I usually went to breakfast a little on the late side, since I knew Grace would most likely be there, as would the four others. We'd kill time in the dining hall until whoever was cleaning up that morning shooed us away, and then some or all of us might go to one of the Transeminars.

And then it would be lunch, and after that we were into the afternoon. Invariably, the six of us would gather at some point, wherever we could find at least some privacy, and hang out.

What would we do? Sometimes play Frisbee, if we could find a big enough open area that wasn't in use; and sometimes we'd go swimming, if there weren't too many little kids around ("Don't wanna say anything that might disturb their delicate little minds, after all," sneered Rafe). Mostly, we'd just sit and talk about anything that came into our teenaged minds. Music. Movies. TV shows. Books. What you hated about school. What you liked about school. Dumb things you did as a kid. Dumb things other people did as kids. Dumb things adults did. What you would do if you had a million dollars. How one might actually get a million dollars. Where you would want to live when you were an adult, out on your own. Whether there was life on other planets, and what it would be like. The times we got away with murder. The times we didn't get away with murder. How we would get away with murder next time.

During one of these discussions, I happened to find out that Funk, like me, was a fan of *Star Trek*; one of the TV stations in our area used to broadcast the reruns regularly, and I had watched them several times over. For the most part, the show was absolutely ridiculous: the acting, the production values, the so-called special effects. But I found myself drawn to it, and no, not just because of the short skirts or other alluring outfits worn by the women. For all the drama and adventure in encountering the strange and exotic, you got the sense that serving on the Enterprise was a job, with work shifts and daily routines, downtime, perhaps even occasional boredom. Somehow, the future felt familiar, even accessible.

Since I seemed to be the only one in my town who had seen *Star Trek*, I was glad to run into someone else who knew the show. I came to realize that *Star Trek* was a way for Funk to externalize his scientist/intellectual self and have fun with it at the same time; he knew people considered him an egg-head, and he appeared to revel in this perception.

Funk and I talked about our favorite characters and the most memorable episodes, of course, and it didn't take long before I realized that Funk was serious about his fandom: He would point out incredibly trivial details about the show, like how certain scenes were filmed, or recreate dialogue between two (or more) characters. And not only had Funk collected *Star Trek* magazines and posters, he had even planned to go to New York for a *Star Trek* convention a few years ago, only to find it was sold out.

"You wait and see," he said, when I expressed surprise that such events existed. "They'll be all over the country, and probably the world, before long."

And sometimes, there was simply nothing to talk about, so we just sat, until we decided it was time to move somewhere else.

Occasionally, there would be a bottle of wine – at least that's what it said on the label – or a joint to share among us. We made sure to find a well-hidden spot, usually far off into the Sitting Woods, tried to pace ourselves and make whatever it was we were indulging in last as long as possible. Rafe was almost exclusively the supplier, not only of the weed and booze but the chewing gum and the eye drops we used to mask our activity; I guessed he'd probably packed a whole suitcase just for the contraband. And he got ample satisfaction out of providing all this, as if he was possessed of the highest order of benevolence ("Not to worry, guys! I've got some strawberry apple wine to save our afternoon.").

This was not a completely new experience for me. Back home, I'd known the thrill and satisfaction of sneaking off with a friend or two to some remote place in the neighborhood to share a bottle of beer, a cigarette or two, some tokes of a joint, and get away with it (not without some degree of paranoia beforehand, though – "Do I look high? Do I? Am I acting weird or anything? AM I?"). OK, this happened maybe five times in the space of three years, but my friends and I were convinced we were the epitome of errant, disaffected, alienated youth.

Well, until we got home, anyway.

But at Transformation, there was a kind of solemnity along with the surreptitiousness. Going off to drink or smoke felt like some duty we were expected, even obliged to perform. And the care and vigilance that went into it belied the whole image of reckless, rebellious teenagers. We were like a subversive 1950s educational film come to life, "How to Have Fun at Your Teen Party – and Not Get Caught!" All we needed was the authoritative-sounding narrator and zippy background music:

See how Diana takes only a very small drink from the bottle before she passes it on to Mishy? See how Mishy does the same thing before she gives it to Funk? This way, everybody gets about the same amount of wine – and no one drinks too much!

Well, it was a fun party, but now it's over, and it's time to clean up! Make sure you take the empty bottle with you and place it carefully in the nearest trash can; hide it underneath the trash that's already in there so nobody sees it! "That's right, Seth," Rafe says: "Don't leave any food or snacks or garbage behind, either!"

Before you leave, have one of your friends help you check your appearance: Did you spill anything on your shirt? Do you look disheveled in any way that might look suspicious? "Hey, Grace!" says Rafe. "Keep your eyes open!"

Now say something in your regular speaking voice. Are you stumbling over your words? Do you sound like you're trying too hard to talk normally? "Careful there, Mishy!" says Funk. "No need to give a speech!"

"And don't laugh," Rafe says to Seth: "Maybe you should go hide in the bathroom for a while."

Rafe and Diana were the dominant personalities in our group. Rafe would take the lead, and Diana would either affirm, elaborate on, or contest his pronouncements:

Rafe: *"We should definitely go play Frisbee by the lake!"*

Diana: *"You know that's where Elliott holds the tai-chi session."*

Rafe: *"Aw, c'mon, we won't get in their way."*

Diana: *"No, it's just plain rude. We can go to the rec center field."*

Rafe: *"...and then I told him where to get off!"*

Diana: *"That's ridiculous. You know he wasn't really going to stop you."*

Rafe: *"Yeah? What makes you think that he wasn't gonna come down on me like a ton of bricks?"*

Diana: *"Because he said, 'Whatever you want to do, Rafe, I don't care.'"*

Once, when Grace and I were alone, I asked her what seemed to me an obvious question.

"Have Rafe and Diana ever been, you know, a couple?" Grace shrugged.

"They tried a few times, I think. It didn't take."

"Well, what about Funk and Mishy?"

"Mishy's had the same boyfriend since, I don't know, eighth grade. Funk? I'm not sure he's ever bothered with girlfriends."

"Oh."

But there were others in our midst. Transformation was like one of those watering holes in the African wilderness you see in documentaries, where different kinds of animals come together to drink and bathe but don't necessarily interact with one another, at least not all the time. For instance, if we hung out in a high-traffic area, there was a group of boys in the eight- to nine-year-old range who might congregate nearby, although they hardly acknowledged our presence.

There also was a quartet we all referred to as The Girls: Dee, Zoe, Min, and Lily. They were on the 11- to 12-year-old cusp, that age when kids sometimes don't realize how much more space they're suddenly taking up. At first, I had trouble remembering which one was Zoe and which one was Dee; they had similar features – dirty-blond hair a little longer than shoulder-length, knobby knees, long torsos – but Dee was taller, and Zoe had a little button nose. Recognition wasn't a problem with Min, who was Korean-American, and certainly not with red-haired Lily, who although the most diminutive of the four was unquestionably the leader.

They seemed drawn to us enough to want to be in our orbit – if, that is, they didn't have anything better to do – so they'd often materialize some yards away, writing or drawing in the notebooks they kept in the little backpacks they carried around, gradually moving closer to where we were clustered. If we were doing something they thought was interesting, they'd lobby for us to include them, which we sometimes did, if possible.

For instance, our Frisbee-tossing session would be adapted into a game where we older kids would take turns tossing the Frisbee as high and as far as we could, while The Girls would vie with one another to catch it; the one who caught it the most times was the winner. Since none of them were adept at catching a Frisbee consistently, Rafe suggested a point system: five points for an outright catch; four points for a catch on a first bounce; three points for picking up the Frisbee if it hit the ground and rolled on its side.

This nonetheless left plenty of room for disputes, many of them quite spirited, although these stopped before anyone's feelings were irretrievably bruised. I think we were all impressed, as well as amused, at the level of effort and passion The Girls put into the game.

Hey, it helped us to kill the time.

But for the most part, they were content to sit and scrawl

in their notebooks, which often seemed to be a coordinated rather than random activity. When I happened upon them once in the sheltered picnic area, they hurriedly closed their notebooks and looked at me with a combination of defiance, annoyance, and contrived nonchalance.

I decided to try and be disarming. "Good day, ladies! Whatcha working on there?"

Lily gave a furtive glance at the other Girls and replied indifferently, "Nothing. Just having a little fun."

I smiled effusively, leaned forward a little and pointed at her notebook.

"Is that about me?" I asked in a stage whisper.

Their eyes all widened simultaneously for a second.

"Everyone *always* thinks it's about them," said Dee, summoning up as much scorn in her voice as possible.

"*Especially* boys," said Lily, picking up on Dee's tone and narrowing her eyes at me.

"Well, don't let me interrupt your fun," I said blithely, strolling away.

The Girls scrutinized me as I left, and when I was a couple dozen yards from them, opened their notebooks again. I could hear them tittering.

One afternoon, the six of us were hanging out in a semi-sheltered picnic area. Rafe was in his familiar spot, sitting on top of a picnic table with his feet resting on the bench. The Girls approached warily, Lily in front. The other three stopped about 15 feet away from Rafe, but Lily kept going until she was right up close to him.

The scene looked like something out of a throne room, the supplicant begging a favor from the king. Except that Lily more resembled a Celtic warrior princess out to negotiate a pact with a neighboring kingdom. In this case, her request was for the use of something called the Lone Cabin, an abandoned hut that sat on the adjacent property just a few yards over the line from Hilltop. The Hilltop owners had intermittently sought to acquire the parcel of land, including the cabin, I found out from Rafe, but negotiations always seemed to bog down. In the interim, though the Lone Cabin wasn't part of the camp, older kids at Transformation had long made use of it – discreetly, they bragged.

("Why 'Lone Cabin'?" I asked Grace.

"I don't know. Maybe like 'Lone Ranger'? Look, it's not as if anyone strains their brains for catchy names around here.")

The first cohort of older kids at Transformation had unilaterally decreed that the Lone Cabin was accessible only to those of high school age, and Rafe – who had been about to enter his freshman year at that time – had since taken it upon himself to continue enforcing this edict.

So Lily, hands pugnaciously set on hips, addressed Rafe, whose stature was magnified by his perch on top of the picnic table.

"We want to go to the Lone Cabin," said Lily, nodding backwards in the direction of Zoe, Dee, and Min.

"I see," said Rafe, in his best authoritative voice. "And why is this?"

"Well, we want to do this special art project for our parents, you know? And we want to do it in private, where no one can see, so it'll be a surprise. We can't use the arts and crafts building, because the little kids are always in and out, and they'll mess it up or tell somebody what we're doing."

Rafe nodded. "Very commendable. But I'm afraid it's impossible. You are not of age yet."

Lily eyeballed him, trying to keep a poker face. "We're not going there just to play with Barbie dolls or something," she said, evenly. "This is for a very good, important reason. And I don't get why we have to wait two years before we can use Lone Cabin. What, we're magically going to grow up just because we're 14?"

Rafe crossed his arms and maintained his gaze on Lily. "It is a well-known scientific fact that the human brain, upon passing the age of 14, acquires a certain maturity and sophistication it has previously lacked. My learned colleague, Dr. Funkowicz, who will be studying at Cal Tech in another year or so, can verify this. Dr. Funkowicz?"

He extended his hand in the direction of Funk, seated at the next table. Funk closed his eyes and nodded slowly and sagely.

I expected Lily to scream, shout, throw a tantrum, but instead she folded her arms in front of her and continued to lock eyes with Rafe.

"That," she said quietly, "is such bullshit."

"Lily!" said Diana, reprovingly.

Lily looked at her, irritation starting to percolate.

"What? He says that all the time," she said, pointing at Rafe. "In fact, just about everything he says is bullshit."

Rafe sighed melodramatically. "It is sad," he said, affecting a David Carradine/"Kung Fu"-like voice, "when the children do not respect their elders."

"Truly, this is so," Funk said with similar diction.

"Well, that doesn't mean you have to say it, too, does it?" said Diane to Lily, and then adopted a more soothing tone. "Look, you can use my cabin. My parents won't mind. And we'll make sure your stuff is in a safe place."

Lily scowled, looked at her three partners then back at Diana, and shrugged. "OK," she said, retaining defiance in her voice.

I had to use the bathroom just then, and realized it was about time for me to report for kitchen duty. When I passed by the picnic area several minutes later, I saw Lily straddling the bench of the picnic table where Rafe was. Diana was directly behind her, braiding Lily's hair, while Lily carried on an animated conversation with Rafe. I couldn't hear what they said, but it was easy to see that this was a friendly argument. The rest of The Girls sat at a neighboring table, looking on with fascination and glee.

Besides The Girls and us high schoolers was an odd couple, in many senses of the word.

Patrick had just turned 13, with soft features and curly, bushy hair, and a placid demeanor that made you wonder if something was wrong with him. He hardly spoke at all, and if you tried to engage him in even the most rudimentary conversation, he would more likely as not mumble one- or two-word answers.

Funk told me that he had come up with an idea for a game: How Many Words Did Patrick Say Today?

"Obviously," he explained, "it's based on casual observance, depending on how frequently you encounter him during the course of the day. But in any case, yesterday I heard Patrick say 'Hi,' 'Yes,' 'No,' 'Maybe' and 'Bye.'"

"He actually said a two-syllable word!" said Rafe. "Amazing. Well, I also heard him say 'Please' when someone asked if he wanted syrup for his pancakes, and 'Thanks' when they gave it to him. So that would make seven."

"You guys are mean," said Diana. "He can't help that he's shy. Have you ever tried talking to him – I mean, like having a conversation?"

"Well, once I tried to have a discussion on philosophy with him," said Rafe. "I asked him if he believed there was such a thing as free will, and he said, 'I guess so.'"

"A three-word sentence!" said Funk. "That's astounding. He must've been exhausted afterwards."

Diana looked away in disgust.

I decided to see if I could reach Patrick. This was only his third time at the camp – maybe he'd open up a little to someone who was even newer to Transformation than him. So when I happened to see him reading the list of Transeminars posted on the bulletin board in the dining hall, I eased up to him.

"Hey, Patrick!" I said, jovially. "I'm still trying to decide which things to go to today. What looks good?"

Patrick looked at me expressionlessly, slowly raised his finger and pointed it at one title.

"That one," he murmured.

He turned away and shuffled out the door.

And then there was Morgana.

She was almost 14, and easily the most conspicuous person of any age at Transformation. Part of the reason was her appearance: very pale, with an unruly mane of white-blond hair that hung down almost to her waist and framed a still very childlike face and a pair of wide blue eyes that, I swear, almost never blinked.

But more than that, Morgana seemed consumed with absolutely boundless joy, taking delight in everyone and everything. She would express this exhilaration in speech, song or movement, often all at once: a soliloquy or ditty excerpted from any number of sources or from her own imagination; dance steps that might've originated in classical ballet or some bizarre folk tradition.

When she introduced herself to me – sooner or later, I was told, she would introduce herself to everybody in camp she didn't already know – and I told her my name, her response went something like this: "Seth! Like in 'breath'! A breath of fresh air! The air all around us here!" (She paused, closed her eyes and inhaled mightily.) "Doesn't this air just make you feel brand new? What is it they say – 'Out with the bad air, in with the good air.' Oh, this is the best air there is, isn't it? I hope it will make you feel as good it as makes me feel!" Her voice was chirpy but cultured, vowels and consonants perfectly formed and enunciated.

Then she sprang upwards, legs akimbo, and romped around

me. She wore a purplish-blue tie-dye T-shirt – her favorite outfit, as it turned out – that had likely once been big enough on her to serve as a dress but now barely reached mid-thigh; her movements continually exposed her underwear, and I felt embarrassed and looked away.

Morgana moved, in every sense of the word, among all the various coteries of children. She would happily play with the toddlers and pre-schoolers, as well as the younger school-age kids. From there, it got a little tricky. The older elementary school-age boys, for instance, would have nothing to do with her, although that had more to do with male solidarity than Morgana herself. The Girls liked her well enough, but regarded her as some odd cousin whose presence you tolerated, politely, until you made up an excuse to go somewhere else, which they would do. The kids in my group tended to keep her at arm's length, not excluding her from conversations but not particularly engaging her, either.

"Oh, she's a sweet kid," said Mishy, when I told them about our introduction. "She hasn't got a mean bone in her body."

"I just find her draining to be around," said Diana. "For God's sake, nobody can be that happy all the time, can they?"

"Not without drugs," muttered Rafe.

I looked at Grace for her comment.

"The first few times she sang 'Amazing Grace' at me were kind of cute," she said. "After that..."

Maybe it was just because I hadn't been around Morgana as long as the others had, but I found it hard to be down on somebody who seemed so blissful about the world. So I would humor her, even tease her.

For instance, I noticed that when she came upon any collection of people numbering at least two, she would greet them with an enthusiastic "Hi, everybody!" Once, when she did so to Grace, Diana and me, I replied blandly, "Hi, everybody."

Morgana stiffened and struck an artificially affronted pose.

"*I'm* not everybody," she said with concocted haughtiness.

"Well," I said, "neither are we."

She laughed out loud, almost bending over with merriment, and smiled effusively at me.

Over the next few days, it became our ritual: She would say "Hi, everybody," and look at me expectantly; I couldn't bring myself to disappoint, so I gave the responses. Later, I heard her coaching the younger kids to say it, too.

"Oh, Seth-as-in-breath. What in hell have you done?" Grace joshed me, after the umpteenth time Morgana had said the magic words.

One afternoon, I decided it would be nice to have a little time all to myself, so I hiked to The Sitting Woods, eased into the grassy seat, closed my eyes and let my mind wander. I hadn't been there for a few minutes when I heard someone coming up the path.

It was Morgana. Her face brightened when she saw me, and she rushed over.

"Hi, Seth!"

I was a little surprised, but grateful, that she hadn't given the usual greeting.

Morgana sat down next to me, very close by. The phrase "personal space" hadn't yet come into vogue then, but it was one more thing of which she seemed to have little awareness.

Nonetheless, I was determined to be sociable.

Noticing that she was wearing a purple T-shirt and shorts, I said, "Hey, no tie-dye dress today?"

She giggled a little. "No. I would have, but I promised my parents I would wear something else every once in a while."

Then Morgana gave a little sigh, which seemed genuine rather than for dramatic purposes.

"Oh, my parents," she said, a little sadly. "How I must exhaust them so."

"Really?" I said, actually curious about her choice of words.

"Yes," she sighed again. "It's just that, well, I can't seem to make them understand how I feel about some things."

She leaned back against the embankment, her shoulder touching mine.

"I wore that dress the very first time I came to Transformation, when I was a little wee lass. And it was as if it absorbed everything that's special about being here – the love, the spirit, just the whole atmosphere – and transferred that all to me, through my skin. I thought it was just my imagination at first, but I could really feel it, practically in every part of my body."

She paused, as if savoring the memory.

"So I've always worn the dress as much as I can, especially when I'm here. And you know what, Seth? That feeling hasn't gone away. It's stayed with me, and it's gotten even stronger! Especially the last couple of years."

She clutched my arm.

"I've tried to explain to Mom and Dad what it's like. How, sometimes, no matter where I am, I can feel the sun like when it's directly over Hilltop, or those little breezes from the lake, or that moment in the morning after a cool night when the air first becomes warm."

Morgana's face was flushed with excitement, but her voice had a hint of desperation to it. She tightened her grip on my arm.

"You know what I mean, don't you, Seth? Aren't those wonderful things? And I let these sensations just, just BE inside me, and they build up and up. Then suddenly there is this absolutely glorious feeling I have, which I can't even describe."

Her voice started to quaver, and her eyes were suddenly moist. She stopped to catch her breath, let go of my arm, and leaned back against the embankment.

"When it's over, I feel – just for a second – a kind of tiredness, but it's a delicious kind," she said, quietly. "Oh, Seth, it's so, so good. But Mom and Dad...well, they just don't understand."

She looked at me tenderly.

"I hope you can experience something like that here, Seth. I think you really need to have something positive happen in your life – don't ask me how I know, I just do. Maybe that something will be here."

Morgana touched my shoulder lightly, then got up and sprinted exuberantly back down the path.

I wasn't certain why, but I suddenly felt sorry for her; it seemed to me that underneath all that *joie de vivre* lay something not a little disturbing, which she didn't fully understand. I decided right then and there that I would continue to be friendly to her as I had been – but that I didn't want to be alone with her.

Seth and Mom
(Cont.)

"You know," I said to Mom, "I don't see you much anymore."

Mom looked up from the magazine she was reading.

"Oh?" she answered, with a sly smile. "I'd have thought that would make you happy."

"C'mon," I said, then I sighed before continuing. "OK, I'm sorry I was such a pain in the ass about coming here."

"That's OK," she said, breezily. "Are you ready to say the magic phrase?"

"What 'magic phrase'?"

"'Mom, you were right, and I was wrong.'"

I smirked. "Don't push it."

In plain fact, though, my encounters with Mom seemed few and far between, because she had clearly thrown herself all the way into Transformation. She went to at least one, if not two, seminars each morning, and a couple more in the afternoon.

So I'd been doing little things like sitting with her in the dining hall for at least part of a meal, or maybe if she happened to be there having a coffee break. We'd kept up our little end-of-the-day "check-in" ritual, she talking about having gone along this or that trail, or seeing that incredible sunset the other day, and I talked about how I liked swimming in the lake and hanging around with the other kids.

"Like Gertrude?" she'd ask, arching her eyebrows just a little.

"Grace, Mom."

"Sorry."

I asked her this time about the Transeminars she'd attended, since those were apparently the most demanding in terms of time and energy.

"Well," she said, cautiously, "there's one about...relationships."

"Oh? Relationships like dating? Marriage?"

"Yes," she said, "but also family-type relationships. Or friendships. Even work relationships. Whatever relationships we deem important to our lives."

I blanched a little at her last remark, because it sounded too much like Marcus.

"So, what else are you taking?"

"'Taking'?" She laughed a little. "You make it sound as if we're in college, comparing our class schedules."

"But Joanne," I said, trying to match Rafe's imitation of Marcus. "This isn't a *school*. We're here to expand our awareness and knowledge of the *world*."

Mom stuck out her tongue at me, then continued.

"There's this other seminar that's for women like me who are, you know, getting towards middle age. It's really more of a discussion group. We talk about, oh, common experiences – like what a pain-in-the-ass it is to have kids."

She smiled mischievously.

"But we also talk about, um, how we've changed, what we see differently now as opposed to when we were just starting out in the world. Things like that."

I nodded. Then it hit me: I hadn't thought of my mother – either of my parents – as anywhere close to middle age. I knew, of course, that they were right around 40, but until then it hadn't registered as anything significant. They were still pretty much the same as I'd always known them, right?

I looked at her. I mean, I actually tried to assess her, evaluate her, as if she weren't the woman who'd made me peanut butter sandwiches for lunch or driven me to Little League games. Her face was a little broader, a little more lined than when I'd been in elementary school, I conceded, the hair a little grayer, maybe the voice a little more full-bodied. But was she middle-aged? I just couldn't see it. Maybe that said more about me than it did about her.

Camp

I never had the intention of being a teenage informant on camp gossip, but that's how it turned out.

I discovered that the dining hall, since it was open all day long for meals or coffee breaks, was often a forum for informal discussions among the adults. And whether I was in the kitchen chopping up onions or wiping down tables in front, it wasn't especially difficult to overhear a lot of the dialogue. Even when I was fairly close by, nobody seemed to pay attention to me; I think my apron must've made me invisible. Most conversations were general state-of-the-nation or world, how's-the-family type exchanges, but others were quite compelling.

For instance, there was the matter of one couple, Joe and Denise, who had brought along an au pair that year. They'd hired Therese, the 20-year-old daughter of one of their neighbors, for the summer, and decided she should go with them for Transformation; they rented a separate cabin for her and their twins, Curt and Claire. I'd glimpsed her a few times: She was tall, with short, wavy black hair, and seemed devoted to the kids. I wondered how anyone could have a problem with her, so I lingered just within earshot as I refilled the salt and pepper shakers.

The people I heard talking about this had objections along two fronts. First was the philosophical: Transformation, they said, was meant to be experienced as a family, especially if you had young children – if you weren't attending Transeminars, the argument went, then you should be interacting with your kids, playing games with them, taking them swimming, going on hikes and so on.

This led to the second point of contention: Few couples at the camp could even afford to hire an au pair to look after their children. So Joe and Denise were not only flouting the spirit of Transformation, in the eyes of these adults, they were giving themselves a benefit that no one else had.

"You bring this girl along, so that you can do whatever you want all day long while she looks after your kids," said one woman. "What the hell's the point of even taking your kids here, then? Why not leave them with your parents or someone else and just go by yourselves?"

They fell silent. I finished refilling the shakers and began putting them on tables.

"Geez, if I had the amount of money it took to hire someone as an au pair and pay her way here," said one man, somewhat morosely. The others waited for him to finish the sentence, but he didn't.

"So that's who she is," said Diana thoughtfully, after I related this to the others. "I thought it was kind of weird that she was always around Curt and Claire. Now I get it."

There followed several minutes of criticism aimed at Joe and Denise, who apparently had a history of flaunting their high-income lifestyle: a new car practically every year, top-of-the-line leisure clothes, and other summer getaways to places like Maine or Baja.

"And the thing is," said Mishy, "they used to live a lot simpler, from what I know – they had this little apartment in San Joaquin, drove a VW that had been around since, like, Eisenhower. Then I guess Joe got into this computers thing several years back and now they're rolling in it."

The speculation began about Therese, and how she was

probably some spoiled rich kid, and – this from Rafe, naturally – maybe even getting it on with Joe.

"You know," I finally said, "I feel kind of bad for Therese." There was silence from the others.

"Oh, it's not like anyone put a gun to her head and made her take this job," I continued. "And I'm sure she's getting paid well. But she shouldn't get grief just for doing what she was hired to do. What did she know about this place? I'm sure Joe and Denise didn't bother to think about the consequences of bringing her along, or if they did, they didn't care. But that's not Therese's fault."

"Hmmm," said Grace. "I guess you're right. She's probably kind of lonely, too – I mean, for people more her age."

"We should definitely get her to hang out with us," said Rafe.

"Yeah, you just want to get into her pants," smirked Funk.

"You think she's exotic or something because she's an au pair," teased Mishy.

"Well, she certainly does have 'a pair,'" said Rafe, in a vaude-villian voice.

"Laugh track!" replied Funk. This was, as I discovered, a longtime running gag between Funk and Rafe, whenever one of them said something intended to be outrageously funny.

"Shut up, Rafe," said Diana.

We decided we should invite Therese to hang out with us. As it happened, Joe and Denise had planned to let her have free time that evening, so after dinner, Mishy led her to our gathering place at the edge of the woods, just out of sight of the camp. We all introduced ourselves.

We asked Therese about being an au pair for Joe and Denise, and she said it was really going well: She'd known them since she was in junior high, and had already been babysitting Curt and Claire for years.

Rafe – who made sure he sat next to her – lit a joint and offered it to her, and she took one quick drag and passed it along.

"Thanks," said Therese. She had one of those convivial voices that work well with people of any and all ages. "I don't want to get stoned or anything. I have to be back at the kids' cabin in about an hour-and-a-half for their bedtime."

"So you have to go to bed when they do?" said Rafe, quite deliberately leaning close to Therese. "That must be a real drag."

Therese smiled, not seeming to mind Rafe's proximity. "Oh, I don't mind. And I don't really go to bed. After they fall asleep, I just switch on a little reading lamp and do some work."

"Work?" asked Diana.

"It's this project I'm doing for college. I've been helping a professor with her research on linguistic development in Central Europe during the Middle Ages." She went on to describe the reading and writing she had to do for the project.

Rafe seemed dumbfounded, and I caught him giving Diana a look that said, "I don't have a shot here, do I?"

"You never did, you idiot," Diana's replying glance said.

Diana and Mishy told Therese a little about Transformation, past and present. Rafe had inched a little farther away from Therese, who looked interested and appreciative as she listened.

"So, how do you like being here?" I asked her. "Are people being nice to you?"

"Oh, yeah!" she said brightly, but then furrowed her brow a little. "Well, the thing is, there've been a few times when I've been watching Curt and Claire while they play, and a mom or dad comes along with their kid. And then the kids are all playing together, you know, and the parent says, 'Hey, I'll be right back,' and they're gone for 20, 30 minutes? It's like they just assume that, since I'm minding one pair of kids already, no big deal for them to leave theirs.

"But see, I'm being *paid* by Joe and Denise to watch Curt and Claire. So these parents must figure they can catch a free ride, you know? As I said, they don't go away for very long, but it's just kind of annoying."

I wondered if these same parents were bad-mouthing Joe and Denise for having an au pair, even as they used her services for free.

"Have you told Joe and Denise?" I asked.

"Well, no," she said, apologetically. "I don't want to cause any trouble or anything."

"It's really unfair of those other parents to do that," declared Diana. "You shouldn't be put in that position."

"I guess," Therese said, looking down for a minute. "Maybe I'll talk to Joe and Denise about it later."

"Yeah!" said Rafe, throwing his fist into the air. "Fight the power!"

Therese looked at him, somewhat puzzled. Diana closed her eyes.

There were other discussions in the dining hall I'd overhear, about what people at Transformation believed about the future. Some of their predictions proved quite interesting in retrospect.

One person declared Carter would easily get another term ("Who's going to beat him? Bush? Reagan?") and after him would come eight years of Mondale. Two years later, the morning after the first election I would vote in, about every other student at my college walked around with an expression of shock and disbelief at Reagan's victory.

Another said The Beatles would get back together "in just a few years," with a big reunion tour starting at Madison Square Garden and a new album that would be the biggest seller ever. Not long after the 1980 election, I was at a bar with some friends watching the Patriots-Dolphins game when

I heard Howard Cosell – of all people – announce that John Lennon had been killed.

One discussion about the Cold War yielded a prediction that in about 10 years, the USSR would collapse. ("Do you really think the Soviets can hold together all those republics, with all those different religions and ethnicities? And all that business going on in Afghanistan – they're going to get their heads handed to them. I give it another 10 years or so, and the whole thing's going to collapse.") Eleven years later, my friend Fredrich, who had fled East Germany as a young boy with his family, would weep on my shoulder after finishing a bottle of wine and seeing clip after clip of the Berlin Wall coming down.

Sometimes, people would talk about sports, and one guy thought OJ Simpson going to the 49ers (he'd just been traded before camp started) would be "the best possible thing" both for him and the team; OJ would not only help establish the Niners as a model franchise, he said, but would become a big part of the community – maybe even a political force. On the day of the White Bronco Chase 16 years later, I would be at home sick, and unable to bring myself to turn the channel from the never-ending TV coverage.

But the most interesting discussions involved Jerry and Marcus, who at some point always wound up having coffee together during the day.

Although Marcus, when he had first met my mother and me, had tried to make it sound as if directing Transformation was a group effort, it was pretty obvious that he and Jerry were the ones in charge. And they presented a contrast in leadership: Marcus was all about grand, sweeping visions and philosophy. Jerry was the one who made sure the bills got paid.

In any case, when they sat together in the dining hall, invariably they were joined by other people who had complaints or suggestions about the camp.

One, Howard, tried to pitch them on inviting an acquaintance of his to give a seminar on investment strategies. But there was a wrinkle: The acquaintance, it turned out, did this for a living, with a ready-made presentation and program that people were supposed to follow. Moreover, it would be unrealistic to expect him to do this for free.

"But," said Howard to Jerry and Marcus, "I think Chuck'd be willing to lower his price for Transformation. So if you just add maybe three, four bucks to the fee for next year, and figure on, what, about 50-60 people coming? That would probably more than cover it."

Marcus smiled his unctuous little smile across the table. "Howard," he murmured. "Thanks so much for passing this along to us. It's very interesting, and I'm sure Jerry and I, and the other organizers, will give it a lot of thought."

Ten yards away, as I got the coffeemakers cleaned and ready, I wondered why someone hadn't strangled Marcus by now. What did people see in this guy?

Jerry shook his head slightly. "I don't know, Howard. I'm happy to bring it up for discussion, but something just doesn't feel right about this. Transformation's always been about people who want to *share* their knowledge and skills, not sell them."

"C'mon, Jerry!" said Howard. "Don't you agree that providing information on investments would be valuable for everyone here? And I'll tell you, Chuck is as savvy as they come on the subject."

"I'm not disputing that one way or the other. And yes, I know in the past we've reached out to people we think would be a good fit for Transformation. But this would be hiring someone to come here to do a job, not inviting them to be a participant in the camp."

"Geez, Jerry," groaned Howard, clearly getting irritated. "How long do you think you can keep this thing going the way it is now, a little cutie-pie summer camp where everyone talks about stuff like marriage and relationships? Urban history? Educational games for kids? I'm talking investment strategy here, something that's really useful for people. So you bend the rules – or whatever you call it – to get Chuck here. I'm telling you, it'll be worth it! And you know, in time Chuck could wind up being a real draw for the place. You could get double, maybe triple the attendance, and it'd more than pay for itself."

Marcus spoke up again, his smile less pronounced but still pasted on his face. "OK, Howard, you've made your point. You've given us all a lot to think about. Looks like it's getting close to lunch, so we'd better clear out so Tess and Bill and the crew can get the place ready."

When I heard Marcus say that, I instantly turned my back completely to them and tried to make it seem as if I had made dining hall preparation the center of my world.

Howard got up, started to leave, and turned back again to Jerry. "Look, Jerry," he said in a quiet voice. "I didn't mean to fly off the handle, but I just think you've got to face reality. Another five, 10 years, it just won't be the same here: You've got people who'll be retiring, or their kids will be adults, and they'll have a different outlook on life than now. So, give it some thought, that's all I'm asking."

He gave a little wave and walked away.

Jerry slumped a little, shook his head, looked at Marcus.

"Most damn ridiculous thing I've ever heard."

"Howard actually suggested that?" asked Diana when I reported my observations later on.

"Are you really surprised?" said Rafe to her. Then he spoke to me. "Howard always seems to be, I dunno, working some angle. One year, he brought along these boxes of peanut butter cookies from some company he'd put money into, I guess, and he somehow talked Bill and Tess into putting them out with the coffee and tea. And he made a little sign that he put next to them, 'Want more? Talk to me!' I tried one, and it was awful; I couldn't spit it out fast enough. If more than a dozen of those cookies got eaten, I'd be surprised."

"I bet he has some sort of stake in this investment strategy guy," said Funk. "You know – get him a gig, and Howard gets a cut of the fee."

"Wow, that's really kind of sad," I said, stroking Grace's hair as she lay with her head on my lap. "It's like he sees everyone here not only as a friend but as a potential customer. Or maybe *just* a potential customer."

With that, Rafe sang a few lines from "Keep the Customer Satisfied." He had quite a good voice.

On another day, as I was setting up the coffeemakers again, I noticed Jerry speaking with a small-framed woman named Marilyn, who looked mid-40ish.

"...and as you may know," she was saying in a very evenly modulated voice, "during the past couple of years I have accepted the Lord as my savior."

Jerry cleared his throat and looked a little uneasy as he fumbled around for a reply. "Uh, yes, Marilyn, we did know that, and, uh, we're certainly happy it's made such a difference in your life."

"Well, Jerry, I would now like to make a difference in my friends' lives by preaching the Lord's work here at Transformation."

I suddenly felt this irresistible urge to sing something from *Godspell*, like "Day by Day." Did Marilyn like that song? Maybe she would ask us to sing it with her at breakfast? That might not be so bad.

Jerry opened his mouth to speak, closed it, tried again. "Do you mean, like through a Transeminar?"

Marilyn smiled beatifically and nodded.

"But isn't that something you could just do on your own, whenever you want?" said Jerry. "I don't know why you feel you need to schedule a seminar."

"Quite frankly, I think that our community's spiritual life is something that hasn't been addressed sufficiently. If I remember correctly, the only time that's happened is when Gwen led sessions on transcendental meditation. So I feel the Christian religious tradition could, and should, also be represented at Transformation."

Jerry raised his eyebrows. "Well, I'm not all that familiar with transcendental meditation, but I don't think it has much to do with religion, per se. It's, uh, supposed to be a way to relax, look within, so that you attain some greater insights into yourself and the world, and self-improve. Right? So Gwen was teaching the techniques to help people get the most out of TM."

Marilyn nodded slightly. "Yes, but praying to the Lord is also a way to relax and gain insight, and so on. Not everybody understands the beautiful, wonderful simplicity of that, though, and this is what I'd like to share."

Jerry squirmed a bit in his seat. "Marilyn, I believe we've offered Bible classes a couple of times in the past, but they weren't really very popular—"

"Ah, this is not 'Bible study,' Jerry, although certainly the Bible would be an important part of the Transeminar. No, this is more of a personal conversation, from me to my dear friends, on how crucial it is to accept the Lord and to let Him be your strength. It's something I would, in particular, like to make available to the younger people in Transformation, this being such a critical time in their lives."

Marilyn turned toward me, caught my eye, and smiled with an almost demonic serenity.

"OK, let me think about it," said Jerry, in a not particularly convincing manner.

"Oh, no, not Marilyn," sighed Mishy. It was just before dinner, and we were sitting in the arts and crafts building. Rafe and Funk were idly cutting up pieces of paper and gluing them together, with no discernible artistic effect.

"Yeah, last year she started talking to me about pop culture and how it harms my soul," put in Rafe. "She asked if I listened to KISS, and did I know that their name stood for 'Knights in Satan's Service.' I said, 'Don't worry, I don't listen to KISS. *My* favorite is Black Sabbath.'"

"Laugh track!" shouted Funk.

"Will you two shut up?" grumbled Diana.

One morning, as I gave the dining hall the once-over, Jerry came in and greeted me, then sat down at the nearest table. He looked at me expectantly, which I took as an invitation to join him.

"I always like to just see how new folks are doing here – meant to do it earlier with you, but it's been pretty busy," he said, contritely.

I wondered if he'd spoken already with my mother, who'd perhaps let on that I was unhappy about having to come. For all I knew, Marcus also might have said something to Jerry about my surliness with him. So maybe now everyone was watching me, in case I did something rash. And here I'd been eavesdropping on people while doing my kitchen and dining hall chores. Had they noticed?

But I didn't get that sense from Jerry. He actually seemed to be glad to talk to me, instead of dealing with more complaints about the camp or suggestions for improving it. I just made some innocuous comments about how nice and welcoming people had been, like Bill and Tess, and that I was glad to have found kids to hang out with.

"And I have to say I'm pretty impressed that you guys have been doing this for 10 years," I said grandly.

Jerry nodded. "Yeah, it's been quite a run," he said, mildly.

Then I said, "Think you can do it for another 10?"

He chuckled. "Ten? Heck, I'd take five." He smiled quickly, as if to counteract that little edge of sarcasm I detected in his voice.

I could have just let it go, but I just felt I had to continue.

"So, what's the hardest part about running Transformation?" I asked, and added, "I know you don't run it all by yourself, of course."

Jerry was thoughtful for a few moments.

"Well, you know, there's getting all the registration done, and making sure the arrangements are in place for food, sanitary supplies, that sort of thing. And getting the right number of people for the right number of chores, of course."

He sighed a little.

"But I'll tell you, Seth, sometimes I think the hardest part of running Transformation is trying to get everyone to remember why we hold it in the first place."

I looked at him in some surprise. He suddenly caught sight of his wristwatch and stood up to leave.

"Sorry to cut this short, pal," he gave me an affectionate pat on the shoulder. "Duty calls."

Grace & Seth

It must've been pretty obvious that Grace and I were taken with one another.

At first we were intuitively surreptitious about it around others: the hand-holding, the kissing, even the physical distance we kept between us.

But it didn't take long before we began showing our affection for one another in public. Obviously, we didn't stand up in the dining hall and announce it. Nor did we scratch our initials on a tree or on a bathroom wall.

It was, suddenly, OK for both of us, and we just knew it.

And, of course, we didn't tell our parents. But even they picked up on some of what was going on. Mom certainly had, even if she kept on apparently forgetting Grace's name and calling her "Greta," "Gertrude," "Gillian" and so on. I began to suspect she was doing that to get a rise out of me.

Grace's father was with her this year. As she explained, her dad tended to be more easygoing and somewhat less vigilant than her mom, although that didn't necessarily stop him from making awkward appearances every now and then. Sure enough, Grace and I were having dinner when we heard a "Hi, hon!" behind us. I turned around to see a wiry, medium-height man, his hands on Grace's shoulders.

"Hi, Daddy," she said, with patient warmth.

He affected some surprise at seeing me – not very convincingly – and to me said, "Oh, don't believe we've met? I'm

Grace's father. But just call me 'Todd.'"

Funny enough, I hadn't actually gotten around to asking Grace's last name, so I couldn't have referred to him as "Mr. _____" anyway.

"Hi, Todd," I said, shaking the hand he proffered to me. "I'm Seth."

"Ah, that's right, you and your mom – Joanne? – are new-comers, right?"

And so on.

When Grace and I ran into Todd, he always made a point of putting a hand on my shoulder at some point in the conversation.

"At least he seems to like you," said Grace, after one encounter.

"Are you sure he's not trying to give me a Vulcan nerve pinch or something?"

"A what?"

"Never mind," I muttered.

Among our gang – that was the word Mom always used ("How are things with the gang?" "What did you and your gang get up to today?") – the acknowledgement of Grace and me as a couple came in various ways.

Funk had little or no reaction.

Mishy clearly thought it was all wonderful, as if I was a newly adopted family member.

Diana was very hospitable to me, but there was something in her manner suggesting that, if I were ever to cause Grace any kind of physical, mental or emotional harm, the consequences would be dire.

Rafe seemed to accept my presence, not being especially warm but at least including me in his pronouncements, observations and bon mots: "Hey, Seth – what's the most shit-faced thing you've ever done?"; "Seth, tell me if I'm wrong: The only experience you've had with drugs was listening to Cheech and Chong, right?"

The Girls, although technically an auxiliary to our "gang," I suppose, also weighed in on Grace and me. Or at least Lily did.

From conversations with Grace and the others, I'd gotten to know a bit more about Lily, notably the fact that she'd been quite a legend at the elementary school from which she'd just graduated. As a kindergartener, she let it be known early on that, despite her small size, nobody was going to push her around. When school ended the following spring, the word had gotten around: Watch out for That Little Redhead. By third grade, she'd moved beyond self-defense and began sticking up for friends and classmates she felt were being victimized. Among their ranks was Zoe, who at that time had a lisp noticeable enough to put her in the crosshairs of two fifth-grade boys.

So it was that, one afternoon, when the two had cornered Zoe in the hallway and were teasing her ("Haw! Say 'sarsaparilla soda'!" "No, say 'She sells seashells by the seashore'! Haw haw!"), one of her tormenters happened to look up and see Lily – barely taller than some of the kindergarteners – advancing on them. She didn't run, didn't yell, just walked steadily and methodically; her face was not some mask of rage, but etched with a determined, well-tempered ferocity.

She'd gotten within about 10 yards when one of the boys whispered loudly to the other, "Oh shit, it's That Little Redhead." They set off down the hall, walking quickly rather than running, thus preserving at least a shred of dignity. The kids who'd been watching spontaneously burst into applause.

Anyway: One afternoon, Grace and I were in the semi-enclosed picnic area, sitting on one of the benches and being thoroughly oblivious to the rest of the world, exchanging the kind of cutie-pie banter that tends to make everyone else give you a thoroughly wide berth. We'd kissed a few times in quick succession, closing our eyes as our lips met and then opening them.

"Oh, God," said a little voice with disgust.

We turned, and there were The Girls, a few benches away. They'd entered unnoticed by us and settled in with their little backpacks. Lily, per usual, stood a few feet ahead of them, looking at us with considerable distaste.

"Do you two *have* to do that?" she said.

"No, Lily, we don't *have* to," I answered, softly. "We *choose* to. And that's what makes it so beautiful."

Grace and I kissed again, barely containing our mirth.

"Oh, please," said Lily. "Couldn't you do it somewhere else, at least?"

"Lily, c'mon," said Grace, teasingly. "There's just no resisting a sweet face like this." She chucked me lightly under the chin and scratched the tip of my nose.

Lily scowled, but her cohorts – although equally appalled as she – couldn't quite repress their smiles.

"You know," I said to Grace, "I'll bet that, back home, the boys are absolutely drooling over Lily."

Lily folded her arms over her chest in indignation and took a few slow steps toward me.

"Of course," I added, "I wouldn't be surprised if Lily isn't drooling a little herself over some guy. I'm sure there's a great love story just waiting to be told."

Zoe, Dee and Min sniggered at that. Lily stepped forward, hauled back and punched me hard in the shoulder. I recoiled – I don't know where her strength came from, but her blow actually hurt.

By reflex, I looked at her challengingly, and she redoubled the glare she'd been wearing.

I suddenly thought of those two fifth-grade boys.

Then, without moving my head, I looked in Grace's direction, and affecting a high-pitched, timorous voice, squeaked,

"Grace? She's gonna beat me up!"

Zoe, Dee and Min broke into full laughter. Lily tried to sustain her fierce expression, but a grin spread across her face, and she slapped me on the same shoulder – feather-soft in comparison to her first blow.

I gave a horror movie monster-type roar, picked her up by the waist and slung her over my shoulder; she was incredibly, impossibly light. Lily feigned outrage, howling and giving me little love taps on my back as I waltzed her around the room, vowing to dunk her in the lake. Finally, I halted and shifted her around in front, supporting her in my arms.

"You know, I don't think I'd want you as a boyfriend," said Lily, throwing her skinny arm around my shoulder. "But I kind of wish you were my brother."

"Lily, I'm afraid your parents couldn't afford me," I said.

This immediately sparked a discussion among The Girls which became high-pitched and rapid-fire: Maybe I could be Lily's secret brother, and she could keep me in the basement, or out in the garden shed, or in the woods behind her house.

"I wish he was *my* brother!" said Dee.

"You already have a brother," retorted Lily. (Aaron, the brother in question, was on some work-study program at college this summer, and thus absent from Transformation.)

"Yeah, but he's just a big jerk-off," Dee grumbled.

"Dee!" said Diana.

"What if all of us had him as a secret brother?" said Zoe excitedly.

"Oh, yeah!" said Lily, squirming in my arms.

I put Lily down and she scooted over to the other three, and they reached into their backpacks to pull out pieces of paper, pencils and crayons, and began to scribble furiously.

Grace and I left, completely unnoticed.

A couple of days later, I found on my cot a large manila envelope. Inside was a piece of paper that contained four separate drawings: They were representations of me as the "secret brother" for each of The Girls. All of the artwork was by Min – as the accompanying note mentioned – and I was blown away at how good it was, how accurate the likenesses were. In one panel, I was depicted as a pet of Lily's, complete with a collar and leash, and food and water bowls marked "Seth"; in another, I was out in the woods, sitting in front of a shelter made of sticks, with Zoe bringing me food; for Dee's panel, I was shown dancing in a Travoltaesque disco outfit, and Dee admonishing me ("Keep it down! Do you want the whole neighborhood to hear?"); and for Min, I was a life-sized, living doll that her cartoon self hugged, with an audience of clearly offended other dolls looking on.

I showed it to Grace, marveling at their imagination. "Good God," I said. "Who *are* these kids?"

Grace laughed softly and cozied up to me. "Well, they clearly have good taste in fantasy big brothers."

I kept that drawing for years, and may in fact still have it somewhere – I'll even frame it should I ever come across it. I don't know if I'll ever have kids (it's not too late, I suppose), so that may end up being the only child's picture I possess.

One other thing I noticed once Grace and I had become close: Morgana was keeping company with, of all people, Patrick.

About every time you looked up, she was leading him somewhere by the hand. Or you might pass by them, sitting at a table or under a tree, Morgana leaning in close as she spoke to him. Patrick looked as placid as ever, but he evidently didn't object to Morgana claiming his time and space.

Whenever Grace and I encountered the two of them, Morgana gave a glance that suggested we consider her and Patrick as our peers in romance.

I pointed this out to Grace during one of our visits to her favorite spot (I suggested we call it "the Place of Grace"; she gave me a mild smile of acquiescence).

"I guess our little girl is growing up," she said with a shrug.

I smiled. "Maybe they'll ask us out on a double date."

Grace gave me a blank look that slowly transitioned into one of mock horror.

"Yeah," she replied, with absolute dryness. "Then you'll find out how fast I can run."

Mom

As consumed as I was with all these new relationships and experiences, I did try to keep an eye on Mom. The so-called daily check-in was actually rather useful that way.

Since my anger about having to go to Transformation had dissipated pretty dramatically, I felt some remorse about having been so short with her earlier. Of course, there was still plenty of unresolved anger left from these past several months, but I'd concluded this would have to be dealt with later.

From what Marcus had told us, and from my own observations – the cars I saw in the parking lot, the clothes people wore – I knew you didn't have to be rich to go to Transformation. But I realized that, still, Mom had probably spent quite a bit of money to bring us here, and although I hadn't been asked my opinion about it beforehand, now that I was in fact enjoying myself I should perhaps make a point of being gracious.

That being said, I didn't want to go too much in the other direction and be incredibly nice. I was sure she would find this reversal peculiar, maybe even suspicious, and it would make her wonder what I was up to. Since I wasn't sure myself what was going on, that would have made the situation even more complicated.

Something else occurred to me. I'd noticed, several times, Marcus in close conversation with Mom – at the dining hall, walking around camp, standing beside the lake. Maybe he was evaluating her, too?

I found this disconcerting. There was something about Marcus that had just rubbed me the wrong way, right from the start. It felt as if he spent most of his time and energy trying to ingratiate himself to you, getting you to trust him. What did I even know about him?

So, after that conversation with Mom, when I was hanging out with Grace and the others, I asked, "What's the deal with Marcus? Has he ever been married or anything?"

"Sorry, Seth," said Rafe, peeling an orange. "He's not your type."

"Jesus, Rafe," sighed Diana. She gazed at me with some concern. "Why do you want to know about Marcus, Seth?"

I told them.

"Well," said Mishy, looking uncomfortably in Grace's direction, "there've been some rumors about Marcus..."

Grace closed her eyes and sighed.

"Yeah," she said. "The summer after my parents divorced, and Mom and I came to Transformation, he kind of attached himself to her. I'm pretty sure nothing happened, but it was all just kind of creepy."

"If there's a single woman – someone who's divorced or otherwise unmarried – he does seem to home in on her," said Funk. "I bet if you asked him, he'd probably say that he was just being friendly, didn't want her to feel alone, that sort of thing. Funny enough, though, you never see him do that with a single *guy*."

Seth and Mom (Cont.)

The following day, right before dinner, I stopped by the cabin to get a long-sleeved shirt. I was surprised to find Mom sprawled across her bed, looking up at the ceiling.

"Oh! Hi, dear," she said, sitting up. Her eyes looked a little puffy, and she seemed kind of tired.

"Everything OK?" I asked, trying not to sound too worried.

"Yes! Yes, I am," she said, a little too quickly. "It's just that, uh, well, the session today was kind of intense, I guess. There was some real catharsis."

I don't think I'd ever heard her use the word "catharsis" before, and it sounded odd.

Mom patted the bed beside her, and I sat down.

"Are *you* OK?" she said.

"What do you mean?"

"I mean, are you doing OK?" She let the question hang.

Ironically, this was the conversation I had wanted months ago. Now I simply wasn't in the mood for it. But I realized I couldn't let the opportunity go by completely.

"Yeah, I guess," I said carefully. "I haven't felt like calling the suicide hotline lately, if that's what you mean."

"Seth..."

"All right, I'm sorry. No, actually, I'm not sorry. I mean, I got up every day and went to school. I did what I was supposed to do."

"That's true. You did."

"And I just have no clue what the hell has been going on. Or what's going to happen next," I said, in about as savage a voice as I ever remembered using.

Mom closed her eyes and nodded. She sat up straight and put her hands over her knees, as if following some kind of safety instructions. Then she visibly relaxed.

"I understand. I do. The scary thing, Seth, is I'm not sure I know what's been going on, or where it's going to lead."

"So, what, you and Dad wake up one day and say, 'Let's split up'? Just like that?"

"But see, it wasn't 'just like that.' Do you think breakups are always heated arguments behind closed doors, knock-down-drag-out fights in the living room? Sometimes, it's a lot of actually quite civil conversations that slowly become more strained, more tense, less productive..."

She made those small circular gestures with her hands, then stopped.

"...and sometimes it's the conversations you never have."

Mom looked down at her lap for a second, then back to me.

"Seth, I'm sorry neither Dad nor I have had answers for you; it's because we haven't had answers for ourselves. But we both should've been doing a better job of checking in with you, making sure you were all right."

She took my hand.

"When we're back home, I want things to be different. We'll figure it out, OK?"

"OK," I muttered.

We hugged for a few seconds. I think it was the tightest embrace I'd ever gotten from Mom.

I decided to be conversational again.

"So, are you going to the movie tonight? I think it's a Marx Brothers film."

"Oh, that's nice," she said, then added demurely. "But actually, Marcus and I are going to split a bottle of wine and then do some stargazing."

A little later, Grace and I were sitting alone by the bathhouses, watching the sun go down.

"I'm sorry about Marcus," said Grace, softly.

I shrugged. "You shouldn't feel you have to apologize for him," I grumbled, and instantly wished I hadn't.

"I'm not. I'm just saying I'm sorry that he's freaking you out."

I nodded.

Grace licked her lips tentatively. "You know, there's really not much you can do about it, right? I sure didn't like it when he came onto my mom. But she was an adult, after all, and she had to work the situation out on her own."

"Yeah, well, this is *my* mom," I said sharply, "and I just don't want her to seriously screw up whatever chance there might be for her and Dad..."

I stopped, let out a breath.

"Shit," I mumbled. "Our first fight."

Grace leaned her head against my shoulder. The sun was almost completely gone now. I wondered if Mom and Marcus had set out on their walk yet.

"Parents," she said. "You can't live with 'em..."

"...and you can't live with 'em," I interjected.

The next morning at breakfast, I saw Mom sitting and chatting with Marcus again. I thought about coming up with some pretext – some question I could ask her – to interrupt them, but I couldn't, so I just watched from a distance. Then Mom got up and, from what I could gather, said something like "See you later" to him and walked off.

Instead of looking at her, I kept my eyes on Marcus. At this angle, I could see his face, but he was unaware of my presence, mainly because he was watching Mom. And something about his expression was vaguely unnerving. It wasn't just that he, quite obviously, found my mother attractive; there was a smugness about him, as if he had decided there was something he wanted, and that he knew he would get it.

Transeminars

In the lobby of the dining hall was a bulletin board, taking up most of one wall, on which was posted the lists of Transeminars. These were nothing fancy: plain white sheets of paper, with the title, day, time and location of each, plus the name (first name only) of the person or persons leading them. If you were interested in attending, you simply signed your name. As Grace explained, in the mornings were mostly one-time-only programs, each about an hour long; those in the afternoon were multiple sessions over a period of days – some almost the entire two weeks – and of longer duration.

Seminars that were one-day-only were grouped on the left-hand side of the board; those that comprised multiple sessions were on the right. (Bill told me that the Transformation organizers sent out to the camp mailing list a rundown of seminars that had been suggested; a seminar made the cut if at least five people indicated they would consider attending.)

Some had a formal title: "Proposition 13: The Good, The Bad, The Ugly" (Tuesday, 11 a.m., Rec Center, Alice and Ken); "Why Computer Science Will Be THE Most In-Demand College Major in the 1980s" (Wednesday, 10:30 a.m., Reading Room, Lawrence); "Join the Convoy: CB Radio for Everyone" (Thursday, 1 p.m., Arts and Crafts Room, Terry). Others didn't: "Organic gardening" (Thursday, 1:30 p.m., Outside Dining Hall, Wyatt).

One on the right-hand side caught my eye: "Relationships and How to Survive Them" (Mondays, Wednesdays, Fridays, 2:15 p.m., Annex, Toby and Kira). I noticed that among those who'd signed up for them was a "Joanne" – that was my mother's handwriting, no question.

I wasn't terribly motivated to go to any of the Transeminars, but remembering what Diana said – and trusting that she knew what she was talking about – I decided to see what they had to offer. As Diana had noted, there were some that actually sounded kind of interesting: "What Comics Tell Us About Society and Culture," for example, or an overview of film musicals from the Ziegfeld Follies to Ken Russell's version of "Tommy."

I decided to go to the one about comic books. For a few years running, back around junior high, I was a pretty regular reader of Superman, Batman, Spider-Man, The Avengers, Iron Man and the like. I guess it hadn't occurred to me that there was any kind of societal significance to them, so I thought maybe I'd learn something.

The seminar took place in the Reading Room, a small building in back of the last row of cabins; there were a couple of couches, a medium-sized bookshelf that was about half-full, and a rack with various newspapers and magazines (most of which were at least a year old). Ten folding chairs were set up facing the rear of the building, where a projection screen was set up. In back of the chairs was a tall, friendly looking man in his early 30s, fiddling with a slide projector, who introduced himself as Rick.

When he judged it was time to start – all 10 of the chairs were occupied – Rick talked a little about his experience with and interest in comic books, which he'd started reading and collecting when he was 10. At one point, he paused and smiled: "By the way, I think most of you know this already, but I am actually gainfully employed and happily married, and am raising two very active small children – and no, I don't let

93

them touch my collection." We all laughed.

To be honest, I didn't pay a lot of attention to the first part of the seminar. Rick talked about the origin of comics and comic books and how they became part of pop culture, and so on. At various points, someone would ask or debate Rick about a particular detail, or else just reminisce on, for example, buying a comic book at the corner store for a nickel or the mayor of New York City reading the Sunday comics over the radio.

My interest started to pick up when Rick got to the 1960s. I recognized the artwork on some of the slides Rick showed, and themes and topics he mentioned sounded familiar. For instance, he talked about how one Iron Man storyline (in which Iron Man took on the Crimson Dynamo) was an example of anti-Communist sentiment widely prevalent in the US at the time, whereas in a few short years the character the Black Widow – a one-time Russian spy – had changed from a villain to a heroine (she later wore a very skintight black jumpsuit, something that had been of considerably more interest to pubescent me than her sociopolitical background). He also noted how toward the end of the '60s student demonstrations – often typecast as subversive or Communist-driven – were depicted sympathetically in issues of Spider-Man or Captain America.

There were other indicators related to social changes in America, he said, like the emergence of Black superheroes – such as the Black Panther, whose name Marvel Comics briefly changed to "Black Leopard" so as not to suggest any approval of the Black Panthers; nobody, readers or staff included, liked the idea, so Marvel restored the original name. Returning to Iron Man, Rick noted how Iron Man's alter ego, industrialist Tony Stark, had originally been a weapons manufacturer, but in the early 1970s began to question his priorities and shifted to other areas.

Rick then described how in that same period, Spider-Man featured storylines involving drug abuse, and as a result the Comics Code Authority refused to put its seal of approval on the cover. I actually remembered that series very well.

A slightly older man in back of me grumbled a bit and then spoke up.

"See, Rick, that's where I get really uncomfortable," he said. "Why should kids have to read about stuff like drugs and politics and things like that in comic books? Far as I'm concerned, the best comics were the ones where Superman managed to outwit Lex Luthor, or Batman saved Gotham City, or Captain America beat up on the Nazis. Those were good, simple stories and kids learned basic values about good-versus-evil from them.

"Look," he added, "you can call me old-fashioned. Fine. But damn it, kids grow up so fast nowadays. Take a look at what's on TV or in the movies. Shouldn't there be something for them to enjoy that's wholesome and positive? I just don't understand how anyone could think that having stories about drug abuse or whatever in comic books is a good thing."

Rick nodded patiently while the man spoke, then replied. "A couple of things, Len. First, comic books – at least the kind we've been talking about, for the most part – aren't produced just for kids. They never have been, even though we might think otherwise.

"And that leads to the other point, the one I've been trying to get at here: how comic books reflect the issues and concerns – and the general characteristics – of a particular era. Captain America first came out just before the US entered World War II, which of course was very much on the minds of Americans. He was supposed to represent all the good qualities of our country, right? So you could say Captain America was a source of reassurance as well as patriotism at a time when Americans were confronted with a clear-cut threat to national security and our very way of life."

Rick looked at Len, who seemed to signal agreement.

"Now, look at Captain America in the 1970s. He starts to feel unsure about his place in modern American society, and is troubled by social and political unrest – yet he also states his belief in the freedom to protest. And then at one point, Captain America renounces his identity because of a major political scandal that's left him disillusioned with the US government; this change took place in the wake of Watergate.

"Now, Len, you may not like it, but these were things a lot of us were thinking about during that time. Sure, comic books have a lot of fantasy to them, but it's also important for them to have at least some kind of anchor to real life, so readers have a point of reference. Do you see what I mean?"

"Yeah, yeah, I get it," Len said, somewhat impatiently. "But it's one thing for kids to read about beating the Nazis and winning the war, and another thing when they're reading about how confused everyone is about America and what's right and what's wrong. What do they get out of that? How does that help them become good citizens?"

Then Len looked in my direction, and back at Rick.

"Maybe this nice young fella here has a thought on the subject." He turned to me again.

I wasn't necessarily averse to being called on in class, but I hadn't expected to have it happen here. And then I found the words coming out of my mouth almost before I realized I was going to say them.

"Well," I said, "I guess to me it's kind of funny how much adults believe they know about what's on kids' minds."

I looked at Len.

"No disrespect meant."

"None taken," said Len, politely.

"I mean, we're not stupid. We see things. We hear things. We know things, even when adults don't think we do – or don't want us to."

Except, of course, little things like your parents' marriage falling apart, I thought to myself, fleetingly.

"What is it that adults tell us from practically the first day of school? 'OK, you're a big boy/girl now. Time to start growing up.' So adults should just be straight with us about what's going on. Reading about drugs or political corruption or sex in a comic book? Who cares? We're gonna learn about these things somewhere – might as well be from you. And, OK, you might not have all the answers. Maybe that's where we're supposed to come in – figure out the answers for ourselves, you know?"

I wasn't expecting applause, and I didn't get any. Which was fine with me, really.

A few minutes later, when Rick had finished and was packing up the slides, Len came over to me and shook my hand.

"Hey, kid, I didn't mean to put you on the spot like that," he said in a friendly tone. "It's just – aw, I don't know. Sometimes I feel like we've gotten in way over our heads, and hardly anyone gives it a thought. I just think things used to be a lot simpler, and it was better for everyone, including kids.

"Guess that puts me in the minority around here, doesn't it?" he added, lowering his voice.

He chortled to himself.

"Of course, when I was your age, there were probably plenty of old coots around who were saying the same things I am now."

Len gave me a pat on the shoulder and started to leave.

"Take care of yourself, kid. You may have to."

There were a few other seminars I attended, including one about volunteer and travel opportunities for "young people" (college-age or a little older). The best was "The 1980 Election: What to Look For," given by Ralph, who was a high school civics teacher. Given that it would be the first election I would ever vote in, I decided attending might be a good idea – perhaps even my duty.

Ralph put up a big map of the US and briefly described what some of the most important social and political factors were likely to be in certain states or regions – every so often, he slipped in a disclaimer, like "In my humble opinion" or "Just my educated guess." I had a hard time following a lot of what he was saying, but some of it was interesting.

About a half-hour or so in, a thin, intense-looking woman a few seats away from me piped up, "OK, Ralph, let's hear your prediction."

Ralph looked a little surprised. "My prediction? For the election?"

"Yeah, c'mon, give us your 'educated guess,'" chortled the man sitting next to her.

Ralph frowned a little. "Well, I'm not sure I feel comfortable doing that." Then he chuckled. "Oh, what the heck: We're all friends here, right?"

He paused, seemed to collect his thoughts.

"Hmmm. All right. I'll say the Democrats keep the Senate and the House, although their majorities in both might not be as strong. And, of course, Carter wins a second term, pretty easily, too."

There was a silence. The thin woman spoke up again.

"Who's he gonna beat, Ralph?"

"Oh, probably George Bush—"

"Huh? What about Reagan? He damn near beat Ford in the primaries."

"Yeah, but that was just a one-time thing. Bush is the Republican Party chairman, he's been an ambassador to China, director of the CIA, which are pretty high-profile roles – and he's got a lot of support in the party establishment. It's his 'turn.'"

The man next to the thin woman spoke up again.

"Ralph, you're crazy if you think the Democrats are still going to be in control after 1980."

"Why do you say that, Al? Carter's the incumbent, and it's pretty rare for one to lose."

"Well, Carter will," Al replied. "Yeah, I know the economy's better – a little better – than what it was a couple of years ago, but he completely screwed up on energy reform. And that's gonna bite us in the ass sooner or later, especially if the Middle East goes bonkers again, and you know it will. You think he's gonna be able to deal with it? Not a chance."

"Geez, Al," said a short man with thinning dark hair and a mustache sitting in the front row. "I didn't know you were so down on Democrats. Didn't you vote Carter *and* Tunney in '76?"

"Stupidest thing I could've done," shot back Al. "Thank God Tunney lost, at least. No, I'm done with Democrats. We gotta cut taxes, build up our military, and just get the government the hell out of our way – I was so happy when Prop 13 passed this summer. Yeah, I hope Ronnie gives it another shot in 1980. He's got my vote."

This touched off a loud back-and-forth between Al, the man with the thinning hair and several other people. At first, it all seemed like a generally friendly argument. But you could see people's faces hardening, and amidst the chatter you could hear phrases like "Goddamn liberals" and "Republican fascists" tossed around.

Ralph stood there watching helplessly.

I waited a few minutes to see if things would settle down. When they didn't, I left. I could still hear their voices as I made my way to my cabin. I looked back at one point, and I saw Ralph stalking away.

Dinner that evening was strange. Word about the big blow-up had evidently gotten around, and you could see some people clandestinely eyeing one another now and then across the dining hall. It was hard to tell if they were angry or ashamed about what had happened, but you could sense the discomfort.

Morgana certainly did. She sat at the table with Grace and me, and the rest of the older kids, and for once she was almost as quiet as Patrick, who was next to her. I saw her gaze off in the distance with some concern, then look down at her plate.

"Something wrong, Morgana?" I asked.

She started a little, her eyes wide as ever.

"I don't know," she said, trying to force a smile. "Maybe just my imagination."

Seth and Mom (Cont.)

As I approached the cabin to begin getting ready for bed, I was a little surprised to see Mom coming from the other direction; up until now, she had always been the first one in for the night.

"Hi!" she said, sounding very chipper.

She gave me a big hug. I hadn't the slightest idea why.

"Let's not go in quite yet," she said, and sat down on the front stoop of the cabin, then patted the spot next to her. "It's such a nice night."

I sat down and looked at her suspiciously. If I had thought of it then, I'd have tried to smell her breath (that would've made for a good story).

"So what's got you in such a good mood?"

Mom just grinned and shook her head a little.

"Oh, I don't know. Just hung around with Marcus and a couple of other people by the lake, having a little wine. Marcus was telling some stories about the early years of Transformation and – oh, I can't even begin to tell them like he did."

The last thing I wanted was to hear about The Great and All-Powerful Marcus, so I tried to think of a way to change the subject. I'd been musing about the Transeminar on politics that had ended in chaos, so I figured that was as good a diversion as any.

"Hey, Mom," I said, trying to put into words what had been

going around in my mind. "Have you ever been friends with someone, and then you got into a really bad argument about something, and then you weren't friends anymore?"

Mom looked a little taken aback.

"Not that I can think of," she said. "Sure, I may have gotten mad at somebody, but I don't remember ever simply dumping them because of a disagreement. Did you have a problem with someone in school or—?"

"No, no, it's nothing to do with me." I gave her a little recap of the Transeminar.

"Well!" she said. "That sure sounds like a helluva an argument. But you know, Seth, politics can be that way. I've seen friends yell at each other about this issue or that candidate, and half an hour later they're having coffee as if nothing happened."

"Maybe, but it's just that some of the people were really taking it seriously, you know? Like, they were saying things that, well, maybe you can't take back. I just wonder if this is the sort of the thing that might cause problems for the camp."

"You mean like, people would stop coming here because they disagree with one another? Oh, hon, I don't think so. I'm sure that there've been plenty of spats and disputes over the years at Transformation. It's the nature of people, you know?

"Besides," she added, "I'm sure Marcus would know how to fix things."

It's taken a lot of years, but I no longer shudder at the memory of her saying that. Not so much, anyway.

Bill and Tess

I was still thinking about all this the next morning while working in the kitchen. This time, Bill and Tess had me chopping up some vegetables for a stew that would be served at lunch.

By now, there was a certain routine: I'd do my job while Bill and Tess would try to give me insights into the culinary world; inevitably, they'd end up chatting, arguing and reminiscing, and almost completely forget about me.

On this occasion, Bill had been ruminating on different kinds of stews he'd learned to make over the years, and Tess would interject every so often about whether the recipe had called for so many cups of sage or tablespoons of oregano (or vice-versa – I couldn't keep it straight half the time), and so on.

"...but Brian said he always liked to put in some olive oil, didn't he?" said Bill, and then acted as if he'd said a swear word.

There was an uncomfortable pause.

"Brian," sighed Tess. "Don't get me started."

I looked at them.

"What?" I said.

"Brian was someone who used to come here – he and his wife Cary," said Tess, softly.

I waited for her to continue.

"They first came in, what, '73?" continued Tess, looking

over at Bill, who nodded. "Their son had been killed in 'Nam about two years before – barely 20, for God's sake. They had been having a real tough time, and someone told them about Transformation, so they decided to give it a try, see if they could find a way to cope."

Tess paused to dip her finger in the broth Bill was stirring, brought it to her lips, and gave him a slight shake of her head.

"Anyway," Tess went on while Bill tended to the broth. "That was the year, you know, that the US pulled out of Vietnam. If you did a survey, you'd probably have found that most of the people here were against the war by the time it ended; some had been against it practically from the start, others had been supportive but changed their minds over time. So now, it was over – well, it was 'over' for the US – and we were trying to sort it all out: What had happened and why? What should we do now? That sort of thing.

"So that's what was going on when Brian and Cary came here. And you could see they really were having problems, and I mean with each other. Brian seemed to want to move forward, I guess. He would talk with people who had been anti-war, to try and make them understand what he'd been going through, but also to see what their points of view were. Cary, though, she couldn't do that. She was still too sad, angry even. She didn't want to hear anything about Vietnam being a mistake, or whatever."

Tess dipped her finger again into the broth and tasted it, gave Bill a long look and a nod of approval.

"For the next three years, they kept coming back, and you could just see this problem between them getting bigger. It's not that they argued or were unfriendly with each other – at least not that anyone could see – but you just knew, somehow, this wasn't going in a good direction. Got to the point where Cary would hardly associate with anyone; she'd go to a seminar here and there, and spend the rest of the time off by herself.

"Last year, they didn't come, and we guessed why. During the presidential campaign, there had been talk about pardoning the draft resisters, and that obviously wasn't going to sit right with Cary. Brian, though, he seemed OK about it, not really in support but not wanting to fight it. So when Carter gave the pardon, right on his first day in office, we figured that must've been too much for Cary. And sure enough, later that year we heard they had split up."

Tess gazed at Bill and touched his shoulder lightly.

"We kind of hoped Brian would show up this year, at least. He seemed to get on pretty well here, and Bill liked to talk stews with him. But..."

She shrugged and threw up her arms.

"I don't know," she said, sighing again. "I kind of feel, somehow, like we – Transformation, I mean – failed them."

Bill stopped stirring and shook his head.

"Hon, we've been through this," he said. "Transformation doesn't come with a guarantee. That's why there's a 'Toward' in front of it, right? Hopefully, you start down the road at least, and then you'll find the rest of the way. It just depends on what you're looking for. Cary and Brian didn't know what they were looking for, not as a couple, anyway: For him, being here was probably enough, but she clearly wanted something else."

Tess frowned. "I know, Bill, I know. I just wish somebody could've helped Cary think about what that something was."

"Maybe what she wanted was to not be with Brian anymore," I said.

Bill and Tess stared at me, and I felt a stab of regret for my remark.

"Geez, I'm sorry," I said, hurriedly. "You know them way better than me. I have no idea what I'm talking about."

I handed Bill the vegetables I had been chopping, and he poured them into the pot.

"Seth, don't worry about it," said Bill. "You may be right.

That's probably about as good an explanation as any."

Tess stood watching Bill stir the stew.

"I don't know," she mumbled. "I don't know."

Diana

The morning had been cloudy, cool, just a hint of damp in the air, but sometime during lunch the skies cleared, the sun came out, and when I left the dining hall, the temperature had warmed up considerably.

I was at a loose end. Grace had decided to go to a seminar, which I said was fine with me ("Not that that should matter, right?" I'd asked; "Well, should it?" she replied), and so I walked around to see where everyone else had gone.

I ended up down by the lake, and walked along the trail we'd all taken that first day. I rounded a bend, and sitting on a large rock was Diana, her face lifted in the direction of the sun, her eyes closed. I was debating whether or not to disturb her when she happened to turn in my direction.

"Hi, Seth," she said, her smile radiant. "Come sit down."

My throat went dry. OK, yes, Grace and I were in some kind of relationship, but there was something about Diana that seemed to draw me. The fact that she was gorgeous probably had something to do with it. So was the fact of her being Black, though it embarrasses me now to acknowledge that awkward-white-kid mindset. There weren't very many Black kids in my town, let alone my school, so I guess a part of me felt that getting to know Diana would be a broaden-your-world type of experience.

I climbed up to where she was and sat down next to her.

She continued smiling at me.

"I didn't mean to disturb you or anything," I said, haltingly. "I was just – I didn't know where everyone was. Except Grace. She's at a seminar."

"Oh," she said. "Well, Rafe and Funk are up at the Lone Cabin, and I don't want to think what they might be doing. And Mishy – I think she's doing her job."

Diana turned back toward the sun and closed her eyes. "Me, I'm just enjoying this," she said, her voice low and airy.

"Yeah, it's nice," I said, trying to sound casual. "Prrrretty good shit."

I felt a sudden stab of panic, and blurted out a hurried "Oh! I-I'm sorry."

Diana looked at me with some bewilderment.

"For what?"

"Um, bad language. I guess I've been getting a little careless."

She seemed confused, and then she understood what I'd apologized for, and laughed lightly. I hadn't really heard her laugh up to that point; even her laugh sounded gorgeous.

"Oh, Seth, don't sweat it," she said, and laughed again. "I must come off like some crotchety old schoolmarm, huh?"

I laughed, too, somewhat cautiously.

Her laughter subsided, and she looked a little wistful. "I guess I take after my Gan. My grandmother, on my mother's side. Not that she was an old prig – well, she was old. She wasn't exactly a prig, not from what I know about her, according to Mom. But when she came to live with us in Modesto after her husband – my Gandad – died, she had to become a different person."

Diana sighed a little.

"See, my older sister Daphne – she's 10 years older than me – was going through a real tough time: sex, drugs, butting heads with our parents, all that stuff. I was eight, nine years old, and it was like overnight someone had stolen my family and left me with a horde of crazy people. And Gan hated it. So when there was an argument at the dinner table – and it seemed like there was always an argument at a dinner table – and Daphne would cuss out Mom and Dad, Gan would jump down her throat. But the thing is, when Daphne wasn't around to listen, she'd get on Mom and Dad, too.

"You can bet I found this very confusing. I remember when I was 10, and this had been going for a year, and there was one week when it was just really, really bad. I was sitting on the porch by myself, trying to read, but basically just wanting to be by myself. And Gan came by and asked me how I was doing. I exploded at her, said I was tired of her yelling at everyone, and asked why she hated Mom and Dad and Daphne. This lasted maybe about a minute, but it felt like an hour, a day. And when I was done, I felt ashamed about it."

Diana was silent for a moment. However beautiful I'd thought she was until then was nothing compared to how she looked now.

She started up again, her voice soft but resolute.

"Gan nodded and said she understood. 'I know you're up-set, and you have every right to be,' she told me. 'But I don't hate anyone, least of all your parents and your sister. I yell at them not out of hate or anger, but love. I love them so much, and what I hate is the things that get in the way of their love for one another. And it's words, hateful words, they use that are part of what get in the way. That's what I try to tell them, and I guess I think the only way they'll listen is if I yell at them. I don't like doing that, but I don't know any other way.'"

Diana was quiet again. I didn't want to push her, but I felt like she really wanted me to know the rest of the story.

"So what happened?"

"In a month, Gan was dead. She had a heart attack – may-be it was stress, probably it was just old age. As far as I was concerned, though, our family situation had caused her death. So from then on, if there were any arguments and harsh words between Daphne and our folks, I was the one who spoke up and told them to cut it out."

"Hadn't you started going to Transformation by then?" I asked, after doing some calculations in my head.

Diana took a breath. "Yes. But Daphne never came with us; she stayed home the first couple of years. Then one day she was gone. Just packed up what things she could and took off."

"Did you guys get any, I don't know, advice here on what to do?"

She looked at me thoughtfully.

"Transformation isn't a magic act, Seth. It's not like you get a set of instructions and then WHAM! Everything's fine. It was months before we knew whether she was still alive, and more months before she even would talk to my parents on the phone. Finally, finally, about four years ago, she agreed to at least come back to California. We met her at a restaurant about 40 miles from where we live – that was as close as she was willing to get – and got to talk with her for, oh, I don't know, maybe an hour. It was...OK. There've been a couple of letters since then. Not much, but more than what we had before."

I couldn't think of anything to say. I remembered what Bill had said to Tess: Transformation doesn't come with a guarantee.

We just sat there, gazing out at the lake for a little while. Finally, Diana spoke again.

"I guess I'm conditioned now to jump in like that when I hear people I love talk nasty to one another, even if they're just kidding. I can't help it."

"People you love?"

"Yes. I love Grace, of course, and I love The Girls, and Morgana, and Mishy, and Funk."

"And even Rafe?"

"Yeah, even Rafe. That fucking asshole."

"Diana!" I said, mimicking her disapproving voice.

She seemed startled for a second, then laughed heartily. I

laughed with her, and our laughter seemed to reach clear to the other side of the lake.

"Yeah, I guess I do get on Rafe in particular. It's probably because I know him so well."

Then we were quiet. I felt an urge to ask about her and Rafe, but instead I swerved to another Rafe-related topic that had been on my mind.

"Say, Diana, about Rafe."

She looked at me expectantly.

"This whole thing with him, I don't know, laying out the rules and telling people what to do – like with the Lone Cabin. I mean, who put him in charge anyway?"

Diana gave a slight smile, as if I were a little kid asking about the birds and bees.

"Well, Seth, he pretty much put himself 'in charge,' as you call it."

"But doesn't that get kind of annoying? Why do you guys put up with that?"

"Because Rafe really, really likes being in charge."

I waited for her to elaborate, but after a few moments I realized she wasn't going to say anything more. She leaned back a little and gazed at me.

"Look, Seth, it's just not that big a deal. Most of what he talks about is stuff we were going to do anyway. If he wants to act like our leader or something, who cares?"

She shrugged, looked away, looked back at me.

"Besides," she said, and here her voice became softer, "if he ever really got out of line, I could put him straight."

I knew she was serious. My admiration – looking back now, I think that's the best way to describe it (and certainly better than just lust) – for her increased, but so did the vague sense of intimidation I felt in her presence.

In a few moments, though, this jumble of feelings passed. It was a lovely afternoon, and I was in a quiet, picturesque place with a beautiful girl.

We watched as, far off in the distance, a hawk circled toward the mountains. I realized then that I had never seen a hawk out in the wild.

The Lone Cabin

I was surprised when Rafe showed up at my cabin on Tuesday afternoon, just after I'd arrived from the dining hall to get some sun lotion.

"Knock, knock!" he announced genially, then came through the screen door.

"Hey, man, I came because—" he broke off when he noticed the case in the corner containing the guitar I had very grudgingly brought along. "Whoa! You play guitar? Shit, you should've told me! We gotta get together sometime and jam."

"I don't really play—" I started to explain, but he waved me off.

"Naw, we definitely should play. But that's not why I'm here. You and me, we got business to transact."

"Oh?" I found this interesting and unsettling at the same time.

"Yeah, it's about you and Grace. I know you two have been getting close, and well, let's just say I think you're gonna get even closer, and soon."

"How so?"

"Because Grace just talked to me about wanting to take you with her to the Lone Cabin tomorrow. And that can only mean one thing."

He gave me a leer.

It took me a few seconds, but I realized what he was talking about. I think my mouth must've gaped some.

"I guess I ruined the surprise, huh? I thought she'd have already talked with you about it. Sorry, man."

He smiled gracelessly, but it was pretty clear he wasn't that sorry at all.

"I don't understand," I said. "Are you in charge of the Lone Cabin or something?"

"Not really. I just kind of keep track of who wants to use it, and when, so there's no conflict or overlap. And, if there's some kind of problem with the place, we'll know – more or less – who was there when it happened. You know?"

He clapped his hands together.

"Anyway, we need to get you ready for this great event, and that's why I brought these with me."

He reached into his jeans pocket, and with a flourish, pulled out a roll of what turned out to be condoms.

My mouth dropped lower.

"Don't sweat it, man, just looking out for the two of you. But" – he held up a cautionary finger – "we have to negotiate a little."

"Negotiate?"

"Yeah, I ain't giving these away for free."

"Well," I tried to think, my mind racing, "I didn't bring any money with me, so I don't know…"

"Aw, it doesn't have to be money. In fact, I'd rather it not be money. I like doing trades. So, whaddaya got?"

I looked at my stuff, and my eyes fell on the briefcase housing my cassette collection. Rafe saw it, too.

"Ah-hah! I think we might be onto something here. Let's have a look."

He picked up the case, sat down on my bed, and began browsing through the tapes.

"Wow, Mott the Hoople? The Tubes! Not bad. Any Tull? Oh yeah – hmmm, already got that one. Stones, Bowie – Mahavishnu Orchestra? Geez, kid, you jump around a lot, don't you?"

"Well, I saw them on *Don Kirshner's Rock Concert* once and thought they were pretty good."

He shrugged, skimmed some more, then stopped and pulled out two cassettes.

"OK, now we're talking."

He showed me the two he'd selected: the Jimi Hendrix *Band of Gypsies* album and Cheap Trick.

"These two," he said, and in his other hand held up the roll of condoms, "for four of these."

"Fucking Rafe," Grace growled when I told her that afternoon.

She looked at me entreatingly.

"I didn't say that was why I wanted us to go there, you know. I mean, it's just a really nice place where we'll be all alone, but we don't have to..." Her voice trailed off.

I stroked her shoulder.

"Look, don't worry about it. Let's go there. I really want to see what the fuss is all about with this cabin, especially with you. We'll see how we feel when – when we get there. OK?"

She smiled at me, took my hand that had been on her shoulder and held it against her stomach.

"OK," she whispered.

At dinner, Grace seemed distracted. When someone spoke to her, it seemed to take her an extra several seconds to realize it, and then she would make a short, almost dismissive reply.

Rafe, meanwhile, pretended that we were not sitting almost directly across from him, and continually looked or talked past us. But at one point, he gave me a quick suggestive glance, winked and went back to chatting with Funk.

I felt compelled to ask Grace if she was OK. She said "Oh yes!" as if she couldn't imagine why I'd be asking her such a question.

The evening's movie was *Willy Wonka and the Chocolate Factory*, and Grace and I opted to stay and watch it. We helped move tables and chairs, and settled in toward the back. We were flanked on one side by The Girls and on the other by Morgana and Patrick.

The Girls laughed at almost every other scene. After Augustus Gloop was dispatched, Lily remarked, "Oh, my God, I never realized how creepy this movie is. When I saw it as a little kid, I was always too busy thinking about all the candy."

"I know!" said Min, joyfully scandalized. "It's like Willy Wonka *wants* all these terrible things to happen to the kids."

Meanwhile, to Grace's immediate left was Morgana, trying to snuggle with Patrick, who sat upright stiff and unyielding; she might as well have been cozying up to a stone statue. Nevertheless, Morgana was evidently enraptured by the movie, and when Gene Wilder sang "Pure Imagination," she hummed along and softly sang a few of the lyrics here and there. Grace looked up at me with a pained expression, and I nodded sympathetically.

Finally, as the Oompa-Loompas appeared following the horrid ordeal of Violet Beauregarde, Grace squeezed my hand, whispered "Let's go" in my ear, and all but yanked me out of my seat. The Girls were laughing about Violet and didn't notice our departure, but Morgana appeared a little surprised as we left.

Grace pulled me along, out of the dining hall, in the direction of the Sitting Woods. There was a full moon, so the way there was quite well illuminated. As we got closer, she began skipping; I matched her pace, and from some uniquely shared moment of inspiration we broke into "We're Off to See the Wizard!" until we collapsed in laughter near the path. Grace seized me and practically ground her lips into mine.

We went on in this manner for a little while, and I placed my hand on her stomach, which elicited a contented sigh from her.

116

This wasn't the first time I'd been in these circumstances; in fact, there had been two occasions prior to this when I had been in an amorous embrace with a girl, to the extent that hands – hers and mine – had wandered and explored.

So by now, I had more or less developed a strategy, which I employed as Grace and I continued to kiss. My hand crept upward – roughly at the rate of maybe an inch per every minute spent with lips locked – until I knew it was right below her breast. With base camp established, I sent out my thumb for reconnaissance, just barely brushing her, but enough to provoke another sigh. Emboldened, I brought the thumb in at a sharper angle, and this time made significant contact – she gasped into my mouth. And then Grace took the initiative from me, along with my hand, which she placed squarely on her breast.

We stayed this way for an exquisite if brief interval, and then she fell back a little, catching her breath. It was time for us to head back to the camp. In the moonlight, her face was luminous and utterly beautiful.

"OK," she said, a little tremulously. "About tomorrow?"

"Yes?"

"I want to," she said, and she fairly beamed at me as if she were the moon. "I *want* to."

I didn't sleep very well that night.

Obviously, my insomnia was due mostly to building anticipation over the very real possibility I would be losing my virginity in a matter of hours. Yet part of me also tried to suppress this expectation: Grace might change her mind, after all, and I was determined that if this happened, I would not let disappointment overwhelm me and make her feel bad.

Then again, I also had to consider that I might be the one to balk, and Grace the one dealing with disappointment. Would she be as understanding as me – or rather, as I believed

I would be?

It felt surreal having this internal conversation while my mother slept a few feet away. At our check-in earlier, she had been going on about a recipe one of the other campers had given her, and how anxious she was to try it when we got home – I couldn't even recall what the recipe was for, whether it was something you ate at breakfast, lunch, dinner or for dessert. Had Mom not noticed that my mind was clearly elsewhere? It's funny, but I think I actually felt a little annoyed at her for seeming so oblivious to my distractedness.

Then again, she hadn't been particularly big on delving into personal matters. It's not that we absolutely never had these kinds of talks: I remember at the very beginning of sixth grade, I felt a strange sense of insecurity, because so many kids in my class suddenly seemed taller or more mature than me; in this case, Mom picked up on my angst and when I told her what I was feeling she pointed out that I'd grown three inches since fifth grade, and said she kind of missed my "little-boy voice." I felt much better.

But such conversations just had not been part of our day-in/week-out family life, which made our so-called daily check-ins at Transformation feel unnatural – even though part of me kind of liked them. Still, I didn't intend to initiate a discussion about my upcoming introduction to sex.

However sleep-deprived I felt when morning came, I wasn't about to forego the trip. When Grace and I set off, shortly after lunch, I was in fact quite happy to be going, even just for the prospect of having a few hours alone with this girl whom I hadn't known existed a week ago, and now seemed to be at the center of my existence.

We followed the route we'd taken to Grace's favorite spot overlooking the camp, but when we got to the plateau, we headed in another direction and shortly thereafter began climbing another hill. It leveled out into a small meadow, and just ahead of us arose another hill, this one engulfed by a dense-looking forest.

"Let's catch our breath for a minute," said Grace, who, like me was a little winded. "Turn around."

I did so, and the sight before me was magnificent. From this height I could see more of the valley, and even the ocean far off in the distance. The hills and trees we'd passed through obscured the camp from our vision, although I could still see some of Hilltop Lake.

We continued on and entered the tree line. Grace directed me to walk behind her, since the trail we were following was barely visible, at least to me, and not very wide. I marveled at how she appeared to know where it was.

About 10 minutes later, she called my attention to something on the ground: a dinner plate-sized stone, half of it painted green, the other red – the green portion was closest to us.

"What's that?" I asked.

"It's kind of a trail marker and an early-warning system," she said, smiling at my question. "If the green side is pointing at you, that means the cabin is 'available'; if it's the red side, you should go back to the camp."

"I get it. If you're going to the cabin, you turn the marker to red; if you're coming back from there, you turn it to green, right?"

"Exactly."

"But what if someone forgets?"

"Well, nothing's foolproof," she said drily, picking up the stone and turning the red side so that it faced the trail.

We took a more diagonal track after passing the marker. I still could barely detect any trail, but Grace still walked on ahead confidently.

"How many times have you been to the cabin? You only turned high school age last year, right?"

"Well, let's just say it got a lot of use last summer," she

drawled. "Diane and Mishy each took me a couple of times, and all three of us had brunch one morning; and then another time Funk and Rafe came along, too. I'm not saying I could find it in the dark or with my eyes closed, but..."

Grace pointed to a phalanx of trees so close together that they acted as a curtain, shutting out any glimpse of whatever was behind them. As we drew near, I spotted a similar stone marker as the one we'd seen earlier – again, half green, half red, the green closest to us.

"That the fail-safe?" I asked.

"Huh? Oh, yeah, I guess you could call it that." Grace picked up the stone and reversed it, then dropped it back down. "Hopefully, if the first one didn't work, this one does."

"Um, not to be a blasphemer or anything," I said. Grace looked at me. "But is this whole thing really necessary?"

Grace shrugged. "There used to be a lot more kids our age here – I guess there were maybe a few...misunderstandings in the past? So it can't hurt. Rafe certainly feels it's a good idea."

"Just seems like Rafe gets off on having all these rules and regulations, like he's the one running the camp."

Grace gave me an appraising look, then extended her hand to me.

"We're here. Shut up and come with me."

I laughed at her directness. I took her hand, and she led me through all the brush and tree branches, and when we emerged on the other side there was the cabin about 10 feet away. It looked the same style as the ones at Hilltop Camp, but a little larger; the stairs leading up to the door were wider, as was the front stoop. The outside was definitely on the worn side, but not markedly so.

Beyond the cabin was an expanse of meadow, and a distant mountain range.

"Wow," was all I could think of to say.

As soon as we entered the cabin, Grace unlatched the wooden panels that covered the windows, which were screened, to let in some fresh air – it did feel pretty stuffy. The room was horizontally oriented, wide rather than deep, and there was an alcove on the right-hand side that appeared to be what passed for a kitchen area – there was a small sink against the wall. In the middle of the room was a shabby mattress on top of an equally shabby box spring; on the right-hand side, a Naugahyde recliner.

"Naugahyde!" I exclaimed. I turned to Grace. "I'm not a fan of Naugahyde or anything. I just like saying the word."

Grace nodded absently.

I noticed that the cabin was largely clear of debris, like leaves or discarded beer cans, although it could've used a good sweeping. I remarked on this to Grace.

"The idea is, you don't leave the place any worse than you found it," she explained. "If you don't clean up the mess you make, then people will know someone's been here. But if you do too good a job of cleaning up, same problem. Know what I mean?"

Grace tried to sound casual and chatty, but it was obvious she was nervous. I went up to her, put my hands on her shoulders, touched her face.

"OK, I'll shut up now. Promise," I whispered.

She shivered a little and smiled gratefully. I embraced her and kissed her with absolutely all the tenderness I could muster.

Grace stepped back, took off the green backpack she'd carried, and out of it drew a sleeping bag that she unrolled, unzipped, and spread on top of the mattress. She looked at me for a reaction, and the only thing I could think of to do was nod approvingly. With that, she began to unbutton her shirt.

I wasn't completely sure about protocol, but I thought that I should reciprocate, so I also started to undress, putting my clothes on top of the Naugahyde recliner.

Over those past couple of years, as I started to contemplate the whole idea of sex and what it involved, I'd wondered and speculated what it might be like to see an actual naked girl in person. I only had purloined adult magazines and PG or R-rated films to go by for reference, but I understood innately, somehow, that what they showed was probably not what I should expect in real life.

It had never occurred to me what frame of reference the girl in question, whoever she might turn out to be, would have about sex. Maybe she would half-expect a bolt of lightning from above, punishing her for her transgression.

All that fell away, though, when Grace and I faced one another, our clothes shed. To put it mildly, I rejoiced at the sight of her. I took her expression to mean she felt the same.

Grace grabbed my hand and started to draw me to the bed. I stopped suddenly, reached with my other hand to the Naugahyde recliner and rifled through my pants pocket until I found the condoms. I placed them on top of the mattress as I lay down with Grace. We looked at each other, almost in disbelief that this was happening.

I thought kissing her breasts might be a good start, and I was right.

We lay enmeshed, tension drained and passion sated. Sometimes we both dozed, sometimes one of us – I'd open my eyes to see Grace gazing languidly at me, or I'd watch her as her eyelids fluttered and closed. Then a brief gust of wind came through the windows and revived us. Grace untangled herself from me, got up from the bed, and padded over to a door on the left-hand side of the room. She opened it, then leaned on the doorjamb as she surveyed the scenery outside. She turned to look at me and motioned with her head to join her.

There were no stairs outside this door, just a short drop to the ground. But we were more interested in what stretched out beyond us: the mountains shining in the sun, a cobalt blue sky behind them. It was utterly silent. I stood behind Grace, enfolded her in my arms and drew her to me. The sensation was like nothing I could've imagined. She angled her head toward me, kissed me deeply, and we moved back toward the bed, not bothering to close the door.

It was getting near dinner when we returned to camp. The seminars had ended, and many people congregated near the dining hall, idly chatting, some holding glasses of wine or cans of beer. I saw Mom talking with Marcus, and when she saw me she gave a quick wave. Grace's father spotted us, came by and exchanged a brief greeting, squeezing my shoulder as usual.

Then from behind: "Hi everybody, where have you been?"

"Hi, everybody," I said to Morgana, her face animated and eyes sparkling as she held onto the hand of Patrick, who stood stock still and displayed no emotion whatsoever. Instead of waiting for her ceremonial response, I continued. "We just went for a walk. A very nice long walk."

"How lovely!" Morgana declared, then began singing to a meandering, uncertain melody. "How lovely to take the pleasant air, observe nature in all its charms, to take one's true love in one's arms. Isn't it, Patrick?"

"Yes," said Patrick.

PART TWO

BEING THERE

Questions
for Grace

Grace and I continued our liaisons in the best tradition of fu-
tile teenage love.

There were leisurely hours in the Lone Cabin, and more
furtive, hurried, passionate couplings just beyond the bathhouses, or behind trees and bushes within eyeshot of the
camp. Once, not five minutes after one of our trysts, I passed
Todd on the way to the bathroom; per usual, he gave me a
squeeze on the shoulder, asked how I was doing. *Just great*, I
thought to myself, *thanks to your daughter*.

Rafe's condom supply came in handy, but we discovered
that judicious use of hands, fingers, lips and tongues could
also make for an equal amount of pleasure.

Yet there was more: We walked with one another, talked
with one another, laughed with one another, laughed *at* one
another. And tried not to think too much that the days we'd be
together were dwindling.

I had things I wanted to know.

"Why me?" I asked her one afternoon as we sat at the
Place of Grace. She rested against me as we surveyed the camp
beneath us.

"Why *me*?" she said, laughing a little. "You make it sound

like you've been singled out for torture."

I didn't answer, and by way of reassurance she kissed my cheek.

"Why you," she said, introspectively. "I guess, because you're here?"

"Huh?"

"Oh, I know how that sounds. No, I don't mean simply because you're...'available.'" She trailed off and gazed at me, eyebrows arched slightly. "You are, right?"

"Um, yes. And I assumed the same about you."

She made a face somewhere between amused and surprised. "Um, yes? I definitely am. Have been for a while."

"So, let's get back to the question: Why me?"

Grace resettled herself against me.

"OK, this is what I mean by 'because you're here': If we were in school together – mine or yours – do you think we would've found each other?"

"I think so. How should I know? Neither of our schools is particularly big, so I'm sure our paths would've crossed."

"Yeah, but here, they crossed much quicker – in a lot of ways. That's what I mean by 'because you're here.' Transformation made it possible."

I pondered that for a moment or two, as we watched The Girls, far below and far away, scurry toward the bathhouses.

"Yeah," I said. "But what you're talking about is more the 'how.' I'm talking about the 'why' – why me?"

"Well, the 'why' is connected to the 'how.' You realize that I've known most of the people here, kids included, for nearly half of my life, right? And that's outside of Transformation, too: We've gotten together with Mishy's and Diana's families, even Funk's, from time to time over the years. But it's funny: I like seeing them, of course, it's just not the same as when we're all here. The vibe is just different – I think there's something about being away from our familiar places and routines. We're better with each other here, somehow? More honest, more loving."

She saw that I didn't understand.

"OK, what I'm trying to say is, stuff happens here, for whatever reason, and it can't be easily explained. You feel things, you do things that ordinarily you might not.

"So, on that first day, I see this cute guy I'd never met before walking from the parking lot on that first day, and it made an impression. Why do you think I followed you to the cabin, anyway?"

"Aha," I said. "So you didn't like me just for my mind."

She smirked and looked at me out of the corner of her eyes.

"As for the rest of it," she said, taking my arm and wrapping it around her, "you stood out in other ways that meant a lot. I knew you were trying to hold it all in, not make a big deal, but I could tell you were in some pain – and it was a familiar kind of pain to me. It's not that there haven't been other kids here whose parents split up, but I don't know, you carried yourself differently – maybe because it was still so fresh.

"And there was more. Even though you were new here – or maybe *because* you were new – you didn't just follow the easy path and do everything like the rest of us did. Like how you are with Morgana. We've always kind of skirted around her, did the whole smile-and-nod business. Instead, you made a point of being nice to her. You may live to regret it" – she laughed at that – "but for whatever reason, that was your decision. And the way you spoke up for Therese. I like how you're your own person, and I like the person you are."

She pulled my arm around her tighter. Below, a woman was dragging a very resistant and aggrieved young child across the center green.

I thought of another question to ask her.

"So you've never had a camp romance here before? Nobody who turned your head?"

She curled her lips and scowled, leaned her head back against my shoulder.

"Yeeeahh," she said, tentatively. "The summer I was 13, there was this new boy, Mario, and he was the only one at Transformation who was my age, so we got close, at least for a little while. It was all so very clumsy, though. One evening, we were out by the lake, and he turned to me and kissed me, and we kept at it for several minutes. And then he starts feeling me up, not that there was much for him to feel. I think it suddenly hit us what was happening, and we simultaneously freaked out. So we hardly went near each other after that. And he hasn't been back here since."

"And there have been no other guys here you felt attracted to?"

She uttered a reflective little "Hm," then continued. "Like I said, everyone here has become so familiar, it would be kind of like, I don't know, going out with a cousin. But I will say that, when I was 12, I did find Rafe sort of...intriguing?"

"Rafe?" I said in astonishment. "You had the hots for *Rafe*?"

She pinched my arm.

"No, not exactly. It's just that, well, I don't know how it is for boys, but when girls are that age, sometimes we get a little attached to guys who are older, unattainable – they're kind of 'safe,' if you get what I mean."

Her eyes twinkled. "Actually, if I had to guess, I'd say that's probably what you are for Lily and the other Girls."

"Are you serious?"

"C'mon! You didn't notice?" Then she shook her head slowly and said, as if to herself, "Guys never notice."

"Guess I didn't," I conceded, then added in gushingly romantic tones. "But then, I'm usually too busy looking at you."

"Yeah," said Grace, sardonically. "When you're not too busy ogling Diana."

I was about to protest, but I knew Grace was needling me. At least I hoped she was.

"Anyway," she went on, "that particular summer was one

of the times when Rafe and Diana were trying to be a couple, and I guess it started me thinking about relationships. I always thought Rafe was fun to be around, and he treated me nice enough even though I was some little kid.

"So seeing Diana with him, as his 'girlfriend' or whatever, I'd wonder what Rafe was like that way – would he be the same fun person, or would he be more serious, and would I feel differently about him?"

She shrugged. "Obviously, I got over it."

We were silent again. We didn't see any movement in the camp.

I asked the other question – or rather, I tried to.

"Am I the only one, um, I mean, was I the, uh—"

"The first? Yes, you were. Not that there weren't others who might have been, or almost were, the first. But yeah, you're in my history book."

She looked at me for my reaction. I kissed her.

"And?" she asked. "Am I in yours?"

"Oh yes. But I also have to say that I wasn't exactly inexperienced—"

"So I gathered."

"Thank you."

A slight breeze kicked up, ruffling her hair.

"Do you think it's odd," I ventured, "that we're only just talking about this now?"

"I don't know," she said, crinkling her brow. "When should we have talked about it, do you think? Before we hiked to the Lone Cabin? Or maybe when we were finished..."

"Maybe."

"But it was nice just to lie there and be quiet, not have to think of what to ask and what to say, wasn't it? Just let everything be?"

I thought back to that afternoon, only a few days ago. It occurred to me how little I really knew this girl, who could be so economical with her words yet sometimes so eloquent. But how much more did I really need to know?

Finally, I said, "I suppose so."

The breeze picked up a little. I wondered if a storm might be coming, but didn't see any clouds.

Then she sat up, turned around, and took my face gently in her hands.

"So now do you understand 'why you'?" she said, and there was a subtle firmness in her voice.

"I do if you do."

For a few moments her face was dead serious. But then I smiled, and so did she.

For one of our trips to the Lone Cabin, we brought along a near-empty bottle of some cheap, god-awful fruity wine Rafe pressed on us ("No charge," he said, winking at me). We each took a few slugs and could hardly keep from spitting the stuff out. And we laughed uproariously as we undressed each other and sprawled onto the bed.

After our lovemaking, we dozed a little, partly from our exertions, partly from the wine, and also because it was a pretty warm day. I woke up needing to take a piss, so I carefully extracted myself from Grace's embrace, opened the side door and let it rip, looking again at the distant hills and mountains framed impressively against the clear sky.

When I was done, I turned back toward Grace, who was still asleep. The positioning of her body and the way her limbs were arranged reignited my desire, briefly, but her face was so childlike in repose that I couldn't bring myself to awaken her. So I padded quietly away from the bed, to the other side of the cabin. And here I wondered what the hell I was supposed to do now; it's not like I ever thought to bring along reading material on these occasions.

I noticed that there was a small chest of drawers in the alcove, and thought perhaps I might find an old magazine or abandoned book in it – something of interest. That's when I noticed that the wall above the chest was marked up, so I looked closer. There were scribbles in ink, or perhaps paint, and some letters that had been carved into the wood.

"D.A. '51" read one.

Just to the right: "Becky 8/10/61"

Then I heard a groggy sigh and a faint, puzzled "Hey?"

"I'm right here," I answered.

Grace lurched toward me, wrapped her arms around me and buried her head into my shoulder, groaning softly.

"Mmmm," she murmured. "That wine was maybe not a good idea."

I patted her back gently, and after a few seconds she raised her head.

"What are you doing here?" she asked, still looking a little woozy.

"Just checking this out," I said, angling my head in the direction of the wall.

"What *is* all this?" Grace asked. "When I hung out here with Mishy and Diana, I never really looked at this part of the cabin."

"It looks like stuff written by people over the years who have been here. Look at the dates: ''51,' 'July 1949,' '6/20/65.' Wow, it's like a time capsule."

"But who were these people? Were they from Hilltop?"

"Possibly. Marcus did say the campground was built in the 1930s. But this cabin was never part of Hilltop, right? So who knows? I guess it's been used quite a lot, for one thing or another, for a long time."

We examined the markings and writings: "TIM"; "kim-my"; "Joe"; a crudely drawn heart shape with tiny letters inside, "BK+RO."

"What kind of name is 'Kilroy'?" Grace asked.

"What? Where?"

She pointed at a clumsily scrawled "Kilroy was here!"

I laughed. "My uncle told me about this. It was a saying from World War II. I guess there wasn't actually a Kilroy, but American soldiers would write it all over the place, so the Germans might think he was some kind of super-spy, or that it was a secret code or something like that. And then everyone else started writing it, too, even after the war was over."

Grace gave a little shrug.

"So, I suppose," she said, "that kids our age have been sneaking in here for decades."

I nodded. "I imagine so."

"And probably some of them were here to, uh, you know—"

I looked at her in feigned horror.

"Why, Grace! Are you implying that" – I pointed to the wall – "'Bill 'n Rose' from 1953 had sex in this very place? Unimaginable!"

"What, you don't believe kids 'did it' back then?"

"I'm sure they were all too busy fighting Communism or whatever to have such dirty, impure thoughts."

Grace gave me a knowing glance.

"C'mon. You honestly think our parents didn't fool around when they were our age? Do you know for a fact that your mom and dad were virgins when they got married?"

I tried to remember details about my parents' teenage years – I knew they hadn't met until college – and whether either one had ever mentioned a significant other from that period.

"I-I suppose it's possible that one of them, or maybe both, were 'experienced,'" I said, slowly. "But it's just – I don't know."

She grinned wickedly as I fumbled for words.

"Well," I said, recovering, "what about your folks? Do you know what they got up to before they were married?"

"Not a lot, to be honest," she said. "But I guess if there's one positive thing that came out of the whole divorce business, it's that I realized they were more than just my parents. They had lives before me, and they carried things from those lives into their marriage, and maybe a lot of these things were good, but maybe some weren't. And that's how we got to where we are."

Her smile became a gentle one. The sunlight beaming through the alcove's small window fell upon her body in an incredibly rich, soft-hued fashion. I don't think I'd ever seen anything so beautiful.

But somehow, out of the corner of my eye, something caught my attention. I looked at the wall and saw it.

"RAFE & DIANA 75."

Grace saw where I was looking and gave a little expression of surprise.

"That's Rafe's handwriting."

"Well, you did say they'd been a couple," I said.

"Yeah," she replied, her eyes still fixed on the spot. "But..."

"And that it didn't work out, but they decided to stay friends."

"I don't know. They both – and Rafe in particular – always seemed to make like this was no big thing, just something casual, and so forth. Maybe he took it a lot more seriously than he let on."

"So do you think deep down Rafe still wishes they were together?"

"Not sure." She pointed to the words. "This was three years ago, after all. Looking at them now, I don't think you'd ever know they had been...close. I mean, you didn't, did you?"

"No. But there's just a hint sometimes – you know what I mean?"

She nodded, and was silent for several seconds before she turned and went to rifle through her little knapsack, uttering a triumphant "Aha!" as she lifted out a little black marker and brought it back to me.

Grace uncapped the marker, found a relatively clear space on the wall and scrawled her name. She handed the marker to me ceremoniously.

Underneath "Grace" I wrote:

135

"&
Seth
8-78."

We admired our work.

"So you're an ampersand kind of guy, huh?" said Grace.

"Yeah, I guess so. Just seems more..." – I waved my hands around as I tried to find the right word – "poetic than a plus sign?"

Then she fixed her gaze on me.

"I don't know what time it is, off-hand, but I bet it's getting toward midafternoon. And I seem to recall Rafe saying he and Funk wanted to hang out here later on."

She stepped toward me, touched my face, ran her hand across my chest.

"I think we should end our little art history lesson," she whispered.

Skinny Day

"'Skinny Day'?" I asked Grace. "What in hell is that?"

We were sitting outside the Reading Room, basking in the midafternoon sunlight, and waiting to go to a seminar on journal writing Grace wanted to check out. It didn't sound all that interesting to me, but I thought attending a Transeminar together was a good-boyfriend type of thing to do.

"It's the day we – you know, the older kids – go skinny-dipping at Far Pond," she replied. "See, on Sunday afternoon, there's a special meeting where all the adults talk about Transformation and its future. So it's a perfect opportunity to take off."

"To 'take off' in more ways than one, huh?" After she elbowed me, I asked, "But why set aside a special day for it? Couldn't you just go whenever you want?"

Grace shook her head. "Not a good idea. You never know if an adult might decide to go hiking around where the pond is, or see us going in that direction and ask what we're doing. This way, we know that all the adults will be in one place for most all of the afternoon."

She continued. "Thing is, we're expected to help look after the little kids. There's usually one adult, or maybe two, at all times to supervise; the rest of us take turns pitching in for maybe a half-hour or so. You do your shift, then you go off to Far Pond – or, of course, you can go early and then come back to help with the kids. But you really have to make sure you don't lose track of time."

"What's your preference?"

"Well, Rafe, Diana, Funk and Mishy like to go together later in the afternoon. I figured you and I could both do a shift early." She looked at me slyly. "That way, we might, uh, have some privacy when we get to Far Pond, at least until the others come."

A week earlier, the thought of being naked around anyone was both a disquieting and far-fetched notion. But now, I felt no qualms about the prospect.

Our child-sitting stint went quickly and without incident. Actually, it was kind of fun to play simple, repetitive games made up on the spot: I was The Monster who terrorized everyone but was ultimately captured and rehabilitated; at one point, I was surrounded by several kindergarten-age youngsters while I pretended to sob and plead for forgiveness. I happened to glance a few feet away and Grace, holding a shy but thoroughly engrossed little girl on her lap, was smiling at me tenderly. Soon thereafter, we had our beach towels in hand and were on our way.

Far Pond was a good mile or so from camp, near the top of a sloping hill surrounded by trees and other vegetation. Much like Lone Cabin, you really had to know it was there to look for it. I followed Grace through what passed for a trail, climbing and stepping over branches and bushes, until the ground began to level off and we emerged into an open space, where the pond lay before us.

As we'd started out, I asked Grace about the origin of "Skinny Day" – the phrase as well as the event.

"Well, it was before my time, you could say," she laughed. "But I guess it began the first summer Transformation took place here. The older kids who were here at the time just thought it was a good way to, you know, be outrageous. Or they just wanted to have a little fun. Who can say?

"But Rafe and Diana and other younger kids heard about this, and it became a sort of dare, you know? And when they got to be a little older, they kept up the tradition – which by then had its own name."

"But why 'Skinny Day'?"

She shrugged. "I suppose because if one of the adults ever happened to hear one of us say it, they wouldn't really know what we were talking about. And besides, it was just easier to say than 'Skinny-dipping Day.'"

We'd heard voices as we were getting near the end of the climb, and sure enough, about 20 yards away were The Girls, frolicking in the water. But as soon as they spotted us, they ran onto the shore, and a frenzied, comic mayhem ensued as they wrapped towels around themselves while simultaneously trying to put their clothes on over their wet bare bodies.

"Gee, don't leave on our account," I called out.

"It's OK," said Lily, shouting over her shoulder with her back to us as she hurriedly pulled underwear and shorts on. "We were gonna leave soon, anyway."

Finally, all four were dressed. Clutching their towels, they sped off to the opening we'd come through and were out of sight.

I nodded in the direction they had gone.

"How did they know about this? I thought Skinny Day was only for the older kids."

She laughed a little. "Remember what I told you? The younger ones pick up on this sort of thing – they hear stuff from older brothers or sisters, or they just do a bit of snooping. It's not incredibly difficult."

"Should we notify Rafe about it?" I said.

Grace looked at me quizzically. "Huh? What do you mean?"

"Well, they're not supposed to take part in Skinny Day, right? Isn't that against 'the rules' or something? Shouldn't

Rafe know about it so he can do, well, whatever it is he's supposed to do?"

Grace's expression changed to one of affection.

"You are just too funny," she said, softly.

Grace walked a few steps ahead toward the pond and turned back to me.

"So," she said, gesturing in front of us. "What do you think?"

Far Pond was bordered on the far side by a rock face that rose maybe 20 feet, the top of which was overrun with more trees and vegetation. A little stream trickled down the far right of the cliff, feeding into the pond. Several boulders of varying size dotted the water and shoreline.

"In case you're wondering, no, nobody jumps off the cliff," Grace said. "For one thing, there's probably all kinds of prickers and poison ivy and God knows what else up there. But the water's only about four feet deep at most, so you could really mess yourself up.

"Still," she said, "there are plenty of ways to enjoy yourself here."

She batted her eyes at me.

We unrolled our towels and spread them on the beach. As I stood up, I caught sight of movement in the bushes beyond us, and there was a quick flash of something red.

"Hey, uh," I said in a hushed voice, pretending to look somewhere else and affecting a relaxed expression on my face (you learn a lot of handy things by watching action-adventure shows on TV). "Don't look behind you or anything, but I think The Girls are spying on us."

"Oh?" said Grace, who was now wearing only her T-shirt. "Well, girls will be girls."

"But it doesn't make sense," I said, trying to maintain the illusion of detachment. "If they wanted to see us without clothes on, they could've just stayed on the beach, couldn't they?"

"It's more fun to make it, like, a forbidden fruit, you know?"

she said. Then she peeled off her T-shirt, kissed me decorously on the cheek, and headed toward the water.

I was momentarily annoyed, though also secretly a little amused, at being the object of apparent prurient pre-teen interest. Then I had an idea. I took off my T-shirt slowly, seductively, shaking my hair (which was moderately long at the time) dramatically as if I was some male model. I lowered my shorts and stepped out of my underpants, which I twirled around my fingers a few times and let fall onto my towel. Then I began to strike a series of classic muscle-man poses, or like an athlete out of the Ancient Olympics.

From behind the bushes came, in succession, a stifled laugh (sounding like something between a snort and an unsuccessfully rendered raspberry), a sharp "Ow!" and a "Shhh!"

"Hey, Charles Atlas!" called Grace, lolling on her side half-submerged in the water. "You gonna come in or just stand there and flex all day?"

"I'll be right in," I answered with an exaggerated volume. "I have to take a quick piss. I'm just gonna use these bushes..."

I started walking in that direction, and there was a flurry of motion, bushes and tree limbs shaking. Through the leaves, I could just make out Zoe's back as she followed the other Girls down the path.

"Well," I said with not a little satisfaction, turning toward Grace, "that's that."

Grace regarded me with about the coyest smile I'd ever seen.

"You're looking pretty good there," she said. "But I think you should come over here."

I strolled into the water and lay down next to her.

"I'm here," I said.

She gazed at me with absolute, supreme contentment.

"So, that whole thing with The Girls," I said. "Did you do that when you were their age? Did you hide in those same bushes to get yourself an eyeful?"

"Me? I was a good girl."

"Not like you are now."

"No, definitely not."

I was contemplating the idea of covering the entire upper half of her body with kisses when I heard voices behind us.

"Yo!" said Rafe.

He, Diana, Funk, Mishy and a guy I hadn't seen before made their way onto the beach.

"Sorry if we're interrupting," he said, dropping his towel and taking off his shirt. "Actually, I'm not sorry. This is a great day to be here."

He gestured toward the other guy, who had a trimmed beard and medium-length hair.

"This is Zack, who used to come here back when the camp was brand new. He just dropped by to visit for the day. He's old – like 23 or something – but we let him hang around with us. Zack, that's Seth, who's at his first Transformation. And you remember Grace, right?"

Zack waved. "Hey, Seth. Hey, Grace – looking good."

Grace reflexively began to cover up her breasts, stopped, nodded a little sheepishly, and mumbled a greeting.

Rafe looked over in my direction.

"Please don't get up," he said, mildly.

"Oops, never mind," he added quickly. "You already have."

I started to look downward without thinking, and Rafe winked.

"Laugh track!" he said.

The five of them undressed and walked into the pond several yards away from us. I tried not to gape, but I couldn't help but sneak a peek at Diana, who was as spectacular naked as I'd imagined. Rafe, meanwhile, was incredibly furry – the perfect wolfman.

But I didn't want to spend too much time looking at other naked people, when there was a thoroughly lovely one only inches away from me. I'd like to think of that as a sign of my growing maturity, but it's also true that Grace probably would've killed me if she caught me staring at Diana.

The afternoon eased onward. Trees blocked most of the sunlight from hitting us directly, but it was warm and comfortable nonetheless. A joint was passed around, and I took a couple of hits, as did Grace, but neither of us was particularly interested in smoking. The two of us lay on our backs next to each other in the shallowest part of the water. The water was lukewarm, yet still refreshing and comfortable. I couldn't remember the last time I felt this relaxed; the hard edges that I'd felt pressing in around me all these months seemed to soften and fall away. Grace's fingers grazed my arm as she felt for my hand and squeezed it. Yet I didn't feel aroused, just filled with a hazy sense of bliss. Maybe at least some of that was because of the weed and lack of adequate sleep the last few days, but I reveled in it nonetheless.

I thought of how extraordinary it was to be sitting around naked with this group of people whom I'd never even met more than a week ago. What did I know about them – or rather, what did I think I know?

I knew Rafe clearly relished asserting his presumed authority as the oldest of the Transformation "children," even though he might play it for laughs. I knew Diana had a maternal-like penchant for keeping discipline and harmony. I knew Mishy was more the Earth Mother type than Diana, showing an abiding, unconditional affection for everyone in our circle. I knew Funk seemed to enjoy being in our company, if nothing else because we provided a stimulus-response dynamic for him (he would probably put it that way, too).

And Grace.

I knew lots of important things about her, or that which she'd chosen to tell me, anyway. But sometimes when we'd been together, there were those intervals of silence in our conversations. I'd glance over at her and see a distance in her gaze, somewhere far from here. And that had made me wonder: Where was she? What was she thinking about?

And at that moment, she squeezed my hand again. And I wondered how long it would take us to get dressed, leave the pond, and find a nice, quiet, private place where we could get undressed again.

I became aware of a conversation Rafe and Zack had been having. Zack, it developed, had had a similarly unfocused post-high school experience as Rafe, but eventually went to a community college and later settled into working for a non-profit. He and Rafe were going back and forth about it, and there was some increasingly notable tension in their voices.

"Still just doesn't make sense to me," said Rafe. "Sitting in an office all day, calling people or writing letters to try to get money? Doesn't that make you feel, like, pathetic after a while?"

"No, man," Zack answered. "Not if you really believe in what you're trying to raise money for. And you often wind up having some pretty good conversations."

"C'mon, Zack. Do you really think the money you're asking for actually gets used for what you tell people it's supposed to be for? You know the guys running the show are taking it for themselves."

"No, that's completely wrong, Rafe. I can't explain it in so many words, but the way things are set up, they can't touch the money. Everything is legit. You're just looking for an excuse to run down what I'm doing because you're too chicken-shit to get your life together."

"What? Just because I didn't go right into college? You didn't, either—"

"But the difference is, I didn't just sit around at home. I tried things out, and yeah, some didn't work. But you can't hide out from the world, you know? I mean, what have you got going for yourself, other than being the top dog of the Transformation kids?"

"Don't, OK? Really, just don't, Zack. I'm serious. I don't need that shit, not from my parents and not from you. Not from anyone. So you figured it all out. Great. Yay, Zack! I probably don't deserve to be in your almighty presence..."

"Rafe!" said Diana, with some alarm. "Where are you going?"

"Rafe, Rafe, don't go, man," said Zack. "C'mon. I'm not trying to put you down. You know that."

There was a pause. I opened my eyes and looked in the direction of the voices. Rafe was standing several yards away with his back to everyone else, breathing hard. Then he slowly turned around and sat down again.

"It's cool, man," he said to Zack. "I didn't mean to unload on you. I'm happy for you, really."

He exhaled and shook his head, then looked toward the pond. "I dunno. It's hard to think there could be anything much better than this."

A short time later, we all had decided we were ready to leave, and got dressed. As we finished, we heard someone approaching.

"Hi, everybody!" said Morgana, running up to us and instantly looking in my direction.

"Hi, everybody," I said resignedly, but not without warmth.

"I'm not everybody!"

"Well, neither are we."

And once more, Morgana laughed as if she were hearing it for the first time. Then she came toward me.

"Seth, how did you like your first Skinny Day? Isn't it wonderful, I mean, just absolutely wonderful, to be free and naked in such a lovely place?"

I searched for some kind of answer, but it didn't matter, because she went on.

"I remember my first time here – it's hard to believe it was only last year."

Morgana turned to Grace. "Remember how much I begged you and Diana to let me go with you, even though I was a bit 'young'?" she said merrily.

"Gosh, Morgana, how could I forget that?" said Grace with sarcastic blitheness, completely lost on Morgana.

Morgana turned back to me.

"And yes, I was uncertain about the whole thing at first, but once my clothes were off, I felt so exhilarated, so alive in a way I hadn't been before!"

She paused, lifted her eyes skyward, and then began striking a series of artistic poses: a dancer; an orator; a nymph.

"When I'm naked, I feel sometimes like a statue, or a sculpture, come to life. Maybe when I'm older, I'll be an artist's subject. Wouldn't that be thrilling, to be a work of art?"

"Morgana, sweetheart," I said, deadpan, "you're already quite a piece of work."

Grace looked away to try and keep from laughing.

Morgana beamed at me gratefully. Then something caught her eye off to the side, and she opened her mouth wide in unbridled joy.

"Patrick!" she cried.

It was indeed Patrick, trudging down to the edge of the water, wearing orange swim trunks that looked about two sizes too big for him.

"I didn't think you were coming!" said Morgana, and she kicked off her sandals, quickly stripped off her T-shirt dress and underwear and dashed over to him.

"You guys gonna come along?" said Mishy, hanging back a little while Rafe, Diana, Funk and Zack walked up to the path. "Or are you going to watch the world's greatest love story unfold?"

"Right behind you," said Grace.

I looked back to the water. Morgana was in front of Patrick, talking and gesticulating excitedly, throwing in an occasional pirouette or other dance move. Patrick watched her with eyes wide open, trying to be as composed as is possible when you're a 13-year-old boy and there's a stark naked girl only a few feet away from you.

For the rest of that day and most of the next, if I happened to be in proximity to The Girls, they watched my every move, their faces masked in faux innocence. All I had to do was feint at flexing an arm muscle, and they collapsed into snickers, then quickly pretended to be engaged in something else.

"You're so mean," said Grace as she watched one such incident.

"But so desirable," I replied huskily.

Grace gave me a light bop on the head, then led me away.

Rafe

I'd been putting off the jam session with Rafe ever since he'd first suggested it. I hadn't even wanted to bring along my guitar to camp in the first place, but Mom had practically put it in the car herself.

The fact was, I had barely touched the guitar in almost three years. Before that, there'd been a period of several months where I fully immersed myself in it. I'd worked out chords and learned quite a few songs, mostly in what I suppose you'd call the folk-rock genre: Crosby, Stills, Nash & Young, America, and especially Cat Stevens. I enjoyed playing for its own sake, in the privacy of my own room – I let only a very few of my friends hear me.

And then, one day I put the guitar in its case and just left it there. I was simply taking a break, I told myself, and would get back to playing in a few days. A few days became a few weeks, and then a couple of months. Ultimately, it became easier to just not think about the guitar. And that's how matters stood until this day.

But I had vaguely promised Rafe to get together and jam, and it seemed important to him, so I resigned myself to what would hopefully be a quick, relatively painless interval of attempted music. After that, the guitar would go back in its case. Maybe, once I got home, I'd sell the thing – or just give it to someone who really wanted it.

Rafe had said to come to his family's cabin, so at the appointed time I lugged my guitar to the appointed place. As I neared the row where Rafe's cabin was, I heard angry voices, and I paused to look around the corner. Rafe was standing outside the cabin, arguing with two people I assumed were his parents: The man was a smaller, less hirsute version of Rafe; the woman had the same sort of medium-dark complexion as Rafe.

"...totally ridiculous," said Rafe's mom.

"Ralph, you can't be serious about this," said Rafe's dad.

"I don't get what the problem is," said Rafe, spreading his hands outward. "I'm just going to go back with Funk and hang out there a couple of days. No big deal. Then Funk will drive me home, or I'll catch a bus. Or I'll just hitchhike. You don't have to do a thing."

"That's not the point, Ralph," said his mom. "You know you've got to get your application in very soon if you want to enroll for this fall."

"Hey, I'll do it, don't worry! I'll still have plenty of time when I get back."

"Ralph," said his father, trying to strike a calmer tone. "You've been putting this off for weeks now. We agreed to take you here this year if you would get down to it right after we got home."

"And you said you would go to hear Frank and Lori's seminar – and you didn't even do that," his mother put in.

"But—" Rafe started to reply, but his mother cut him off.

"No, that's it! No more excuses. You are *not* going to Tim's house. Period. You can make plans with him the second after you put that application in the mail. Understand?"

His father looked at his watch. "Hon, we've gotta go." Just before they started to walk away, he turned to face Rafe, seemed about to say something, then gave up and headed off.

Rafe noticed me lingering and nodded at me. I walked over to him.

"'Ralph'?" I said, trying not to sound too derisive.

He glowered. "Yeah, it's my slave name." (I gathered from that remark he must have watched "Roots," too; I sometimes wonder if he ever held up his guitar to the heavens and intoned "Behold the only thing greater than yourself.") Then with forced cheeriness he said, "Hey, c'mon man, let's play! Glad you came!"

We went into his cabin, and he offered me a chair while he sat on one of the cots. I put my case on the floor, opened it and took out my guitar. Rafe looked it over and I handed it to him.

"Nice, nice. That's a pretty good brand, from what I've heard." He ran his fingers over the strings. "Oooh. Think it's been a while since you've changed these. Or tuned 'em."

He spent a few minutes fiddling with the tuning heads until the guitar sounded much better, then handed it back to me, talking about string gauges and which ones he preferred – all pretty much unfathomable to me. But the tension he'd been carrying was gone now, and for that I was glad.

Rafe took out his own guitar, which had the look of an instrument that had been cared for and adored.

"Wanna try something? Here, play this." He showed me a progression of chords with a very bluesy feel, and after repeating it a few times, nodded at me to join him. We ran through it three times, and toward the end he said, "OK, keep going." I continued with the chords while he soloed, and quite impressively, too.

Then, giving me a smile, he rejoined me on rhythm and began to sing:

> *Oh, that lady of Modesto*
> *She's sweet as sherry wine*
> *Oh, that lady of Modesto*
> *She's sweet as sherry wine*
> *Don't you touch that lady of Modesto*
> *Someday I'm gonna make her mine!*

He played another solo, sang another verse, and as I got to the end he gave a quick nod with his head that I took as a signal I should stop; when I did, he gave a final little flourish and let the last notes resonate.

Rafe grinned at me. "I wrote that one," he said, with pride.

"Autobiographical?" I asked, remembering that Diana was from Modesto.

"Ahhh," he cocked his head back and forth a couple of times, "yes and no."

Before I could inquire further, Rafe broke into another song, which turned out to be something by the Grateful Dead. I was able to pick up on the chords and join him for the last three-quarters of it. He led me on a couple more songs, the last of which transitioned into a free-form jam I thought would never end.

"All right!" said Rafe, when we were finished. "Let's hear you do one."

"Ummm," I mumbled.

"Hey, c'mon, don't be shy. I know you haven't played in a while. Just give it a try."

I drew a blank at first, but then I moved my fingers across the fretboard experimentally until something clicked, and I found myself forming chords. At last, haltingly, I began singing "Peace Train."

My playing felt choppy and clumsy to me, but I saw Rafe nod his head vigorously and he played along, alternating between rhythm and lead. By the last chorus, he had joined me in singing.

"Man, it's been years since I played that! Not joking, either," said Rafe, with a big smile. Then he pointed at my guitar. "But that doesn't sound like a good key for you. Why don't you use a capo?"

I winced. "Because I don't have one?"

Rafe scowled. "No capo? Hold on..."

He opened his guitar case and rummaged around, then

151

held out to me a spring clamp capo. "Used to use a strap-on one, but I like these a lot better. Try it on, maybe, the second fret?"

I clamped it on, and tried playing the chords for "Peace Train," humming along. I had to look carefully where I was placing my fingers.

"How about we try it again?" said Rafe. "All right, from the top!"

He played the opening riff, and although I came in a little late, we were in synch from thereon in. This key felt a lot more comfortable for my voice, and the sound was brighter, too. I also was more confident in my strumming, so that it seemed like an actual song, rather than words fastened onto a melody.

When we had finished, Rafe chuckled and shook his head.

"Cat fuckin' Stevens!" he exclaimed. "OK, I have to tell you something, and you gotta promise you won't mention it to anyone, especially not Diana – she'd give me shit up one side and down the other."

I nodded, and Rafe leaned forward onto his guitar. "See, I started playing when I was 12, mostly did a lot of rock and blues. Then, when I was 14, I was hanging out with this guy a few years older than me who also played guitar, and he starts bragging about all the things being a guitarist got him, namely weed, booze and girls. And he says, 'You know what really turns on the chicks? Play some Cat Stevens. Drives them wild, because then they know that you're a gentle, sensitive kind of guy, y'know what I mean?'

"So I bummed 'Teaser and the Firecat' and 'Tea for the Tillerman' from someone, and I learned a bunch of songs – 'Peace Train,' 'Moonshadow,' 'Wild World,' stuff like that. And early in my freshman year of high school, I got hung up on this one girl, really tried to impress her, and of course I mentioned I played guitar. Finally, she invites me to come over and to bring the guitar along. When I get there, I take the guitar out, and I'm sitting right in front of her and looking into her eyes while I play..."

Rafe began strumming softly, and sang the first verse of "Wild World" in a theatrically sorrowful voice with a facial expression to match.

He stopped playing after the verse and continued: "I get to the end of the song, and I figure, 'Well, any second now, she'll tear off her clothes and jump on me.' And instead, she makes this disgusted face and says, 'God, I *hate* Cat Stevens! Don't you know any Black Sabbath?'"

Rafe laughed uproariously, and I did, too.

"But you know," he said, "I learned a big lesson from that: You can't do something just because you think people want or expect you to do it. You gotta stay true to yourself, right?"

He shook his head a little forlornly. "If I'd just kept on learning Black Sabbath, she'd have had me right then and there."

Rafe put his guitar aside and leaned back on his cot.

"Hey, man, I'm sorry about the shit with Zack at the pond the other day. And I'm sorry you saw that thing with my parents; that was pretty awkward. I just, I dunno, I get tired of people getting on me all the time."

I nodded. "What was this seminar your folks wanted you to go to, anyway?" I asked.

"Ah!" he said, smirking. "Frank and Lori have this talk – almost every year, it seems – called something like 'Things to Do When You're Stuck.' You know, if you've lost or quit your job, gotten divorced, just got out of college, or high school or" – he pointed at himself – "in general are in a rut and not sure what to do next. Frank and Lori go through a big list of suggestions and ideas. Like, OK, you can go to Alaska and work in a canning factory for several months, or join the Peace Corps, or participate in a bunch of different volunteer programs that last from two weeks to a year, and so on and so on.

"What my parents don't get is, I've heard all this before – from teachers, guidance counselors, practically every adult who knows me. It just washes over you after a while, you know?"

He held up his arms defensively as if he was being inundated.

"Why don't you do something with your music, then?" I asked. "You're really good."

"Oh, man, I'm nowhere near enough good to make it," he said, dismissively.

"So you could maybe go to music school, learn more?"

"Nah. I'm really just done with school. It was all I could do to get out alive, you know?"

He looked away for a minute, then back at me. "Besides, I don't want music to be my bread-and-butter, you see? I like playing music, but not enough to make it my job. Because if things started to go bad, and I couldn't get enough work, I'm afraid I'd start to hate it, right?"

There was a somewhat uncomfortable silence. I felt words ready to come out, and I said them before being conscious of them.

"You need this place, don't you?"

Rafe raised his eyebrows at that.

"I mean, it's not just that you like it here." I collected myself and continued. "All these rules, these rituals, whatever you want to call them, that you made up or that you enforce. They're the only things you can count on, aren't they? The only structure you have now. No wonder Transformation means so much to you."

I wondered if I'd said too much.

"So, am I way off base? You want to punch me out?" I spread my arms, as if inviting him to throw a roundhouse at me.

Rafe thought for a moment, laughed dourly, and then frowned.

"Yeah, you're right. Zack's right. About all I have in my life now is being the oldest 'kid' at Transformation. Big deal, huh? Hell, I should just leave it behind, leave everything behind, just get the hell out of California, maybe get out of the USA."

"Well," I said, "I don't know about that. Why does it have to be all or nothing? Look, you get a lot out of being at Transformation, and people like having you around here. I've seen it. But maybe you need to take a year off, do something else, and then come back to Transformation as an adult instead of a kid. Does that make sense?"

Rafe stared at me. "Huh. OK, I guess I could think about it," he said, half-dubiously. "Maybe being up in Alaska for a few months and making a shit-ton of money wouldn't be the worst thing. Yeah, and then when I'd come back here, I could pay for Mom and Dad *and* me; that would be hilarious. Yeah, I'll give it some thought."

I sensed our jam session was winding down, so I put my guitar back in its case.

"So," Rafe said, trying to sound as if this would be a casual question, "you and Grace? How's that going?"

It was my turn to think a little.

"Um, it's going...really well, I'd say."

He leered a little at me. "And you're making good use of the..."

"Yes," I answered quickly, "we are. Thanks."

Rafe suddenly looked curious. "Have you never played music for her?"

"Well, no. I mean, I hadn't—"

"Aw, man, you have to! C'mon! She'd love it!"

He leaned toward me, leering again. "And I bet she would *love* Cat Stevens!"

Heading back to my cabin, I happened to run into Diana. She was wearing a sheer, gauzy, ankle-length dress, the silhouette of her hips and legs quite visible in the sunlight. My mouth went a little dry as she greeted me and asked what I'd been up to. I told her about my jam session with Rafe, and she expressed approval.

Then I screwed up my courage. "Hey, Diana. I'm a little worried about Rafe."

Diana seemed taken aback. "Oh?"

"Yeah, we were talking about what he should do with his life and all—"

"Ah," said Diana. "That's always a fun conversation."

"—and I suggested he think about some kind of music school. I know he's not a good student, but—"

Diana stopped me. "He's what? 'Not a good student'?" She sighed. "Was this where he said something about how hard it was for him to finish high school?"

"Well, yeah."

She sighed again and rolled her eyes. "Oh, for God's sake. Seth, Rafe was a perfectly good student. He wasn't valedictorian or anything, and it's not like he won any awards for citizenship or whatever, but he was easily in the top third of his class."

"Then...why would he—"

"Because he tries to put on this act that he's some kind of rebel or misfit, so nobody will expect anything from him. Believe me, we've heard this all before."

She put her arms on my shoulders and smiled affectionately.

"You are a sweetheart, Seth, but don't worry so much about Rafe. He'll figure it out, one of these days."

She gave me a peck on the cheek and walked away. My legs felt like they were about to dissolve.

I sang the last lines of "Moonshadow," strummed the closing two chords, and let the sound fade as I gazed at Grace across from me.

She wore a slight grin. "That was really, very, very nice," she said, unable to completely remove the diplomacy from her voice.

"Oh," I said, a little deflated. "Not a big Cat Stevens fan, huh?"

"No," she said. "I remember when I was seven or eight, one of my older cousins was wild about him and played his records all the time. I couldn't see what all the fuss was about, frankly, so I never liked listening to Cat Stevens."

Her smile became more expansive and warmer.

"However," she added, "I like listening to *you* play Cat Stevens."

I had started to put my guitar away, but I assumed playing position again and started to strum the opening chords for "Wild World."

When I got back to our cabin later, Mom said that somebody had been by – "the boy with all the hair? Rabe? Reef?" – and left a package for me, pointing to a little brown bag on my bed.

I opened it (at first I wondered if he would have been stupid enough to leave me condoms or drugs), and found the Hendrix and Cheap Trick cassettes I'd given Rafe as part of our "deal." And there was the capo he'd lent me during our jam session.

Also included was a little note: "Keep the change."

Morgana, Lost and Found

During lunch the next day, a woman who I recognized as Morgana's mother approached our table. She had similar, although not perfectly identical, features as her daughter: You could see the likeness in her eyes, her youthful-looking face and her pale-blond hair.

"Hi, Elly," Diana said.

"Hello, everybody," Elly said. I think we all inwardly recoiled a little at her use of the now all-too-familiar greeting, but she was obviously unaware of its dubious significance. Besides, she clearly had something on her mind.

"Have any of you seen Morgana?" she said, her forehead wrinkling. "We haven't seen her since breakfast, and apparently she didn't come to lunch."

Now that Elly had mentioned it, I reckoned that something had indeed been a little different about today thus far. Usually, we would've had at least one gregarious visit, however brief, from Morgana by now.

We variously shook our heads, shrugged, said "No, sorry."

"I suppose I'm worrying for nothing," continued Elly, smiling with some effort. "It wouldn't be the first instance where she lost track of time. You know how she can be."

We all nodded in a comforting sort of way.

"But still, this is really unlike her. And I must say, she seemed preoccupied with something last night. I thought maybe she was just tired, but I don't know..."

"Don't worry, Elly, I'm sure we can find her," said Diana.

"Thanks, dear," Elly said gratefully, and gazed affectionately at all of us. "You're all such wonderful friends to Morgana. I'm sure she's off on one of her adventures and we've just missed one another somehow. Anyway, I appreciate whatever you can do to help."

After Elly left, Grace looked at Diana and said, evenly, "You volunteered us pretty quickly, there."

"Well, I guess I'd be worried, too," replied Diana, a little tersely. "Anything can happen. What if she was hiking around on one of the mountain trails and had a bad fall? Or, who knows, what if she ran into a bear?"

"If Morgana ran into a bear," interrupted Funk, "she'd probably convince it to take her back to its den, so she could play with the whole family." He made a goofy face, raised his arms, rocked back and forth, and affected a Morgana-like sing-song voice. "Oh bears, my big, bouncy bears, how I love to dance with you, my big, bouncy bears."

Rafe held up a hand. "No, Diana's got it right. We gotta search for her."

We stared at him.

"Think about it," he said. "If Elly doesn't find her, if she doesn't come back, then there'll be a whole bunch of people out scouring not only the camp, but everything around it. I dunno about you guys, but I'm not really comfortable with that."

I guessed what he meant: Maybe the adults would stumble onto the Lone Cabin and see that it was being used; or perhaps there were other camp secrets I didn't even know about yet that might be uncovered.

"That isn't why I said we should look for her," Diana said testily. "But thanks."

We finished our lunch and gathered near the bathhouses

to determine where we should look.

"Why do I suddenly feel like I'm in a Saturday morning adventure cartoon?" I whispered to Grace, who smiled faintly and softly elbowed me in the ribs.

"So," Diana said, "I guess if we want to figure out where Morgana might've gone, we have to think like her."

"OK," said Funk. "Hit me in the head with a two-by-four. That should help."

About a half-hour later, I was walking to the Sitting Woods – where Grace had first taken me that day, barely more than a week ago. I came to the clearing where the embankment was, and sat down against it to rest a little and collect my thoughts. I tried to think if there might be any clues in what I'd seen or heard of Morgana in the past few days. The last interaction I'd had with her had been at Far Pond, of course – and my last sight of her was her cavorting in front of Patrick.

Patrick. I realized I hadn't seen him today, either. But then again, he wasn't exactly someone you noticed – unless, that is, he was in the company of Morgana, which he usually was. So maybe it wasn't just her that was missing.

I'm not sure what led my brain to the next conclusion, but I rose up from the embankment and set off in the direction of the Lone Cabin.

Another half-hour or so after that, I was climbing uphill, struggling to remember where the path to the cabin was. I'd been there a few times now, but Grace had led the way. I tried closing my eyes and visualizing her walking in front of me, so that I might recall some kind of landmark or anything familiar at all. But my attention ultimately focused on this image of Grace, how confidently she moved through the brush and trees, the swaying of her jeans-clad behind...

No, this wasn't helping. It was just making me horny.

Wouldn't it be just swell, I thought to myself: Maybe Morgana and Patrick are already back at camp, and I'll be the one who never returns. What would happen then? (*"Parents Vow to Remain Together to Honor Memory of Son Lost in Mountains"*)

Suddenly, off in the distance, I heard a noise.

I stopped moving and listened.

There it was again. It was a voice, high-pitched and urgent, but I couldn't make out what it was saying.

I headed in the direction where it seemed to be coming from, trying to make my movements as quiet as possible so I could hear.

The voice sounded again, and it definitely seemed closer. I was able to catch a few words this time: *"sorry...leave...come back."*

Then up ahead I saw the marker stone, the red side facing me. I'd found the trail, such as it was. I moved a little faster.

I'd reached the denser part of the woods, and through the trees a few hundred yards away I thought I saw a figure, running carefully down the incline. I stopped and listened, and though I was pretty sure I heard distant footsteps, I couldn't see anyone.

I resumed walking, and in a few minutes I saw the big clump of trees that helped shelter the cabin. I spied the second marker stone, also with the red side facing toward me, moved around it, and through the assortment of vegetation I saw the roof.

I slowed my pace without exactly knowing why. If that had been Morgana whose voice I heard, was she in danger from someone or something? The door to the cabin was slightly ajar, and I crept up the steps and, holding my breath, gingerly eased inside.

"Seth?"

Morgana was sitting on the edge of the bed, barefoot, in

her T-shirt dress. She looked forlorn and a little rattled, but relief flitted across her face when she saw me. She climbed off the bed, ran to me, and gave a quick but powerful hug.

"Were you – were you looking for me?" she asked, in a tone of wonderment.

"All of us have been looking for you. Your parents were worried. What's going on?"

Morgana's eyes widened to maximum circumference, her mouth slightly gaping. She took my arm and led me to the bed. I sat down warily, and she scrambled up beside me, facing me at an angle with her legs tucked underneath her, her knees just touching the outward edge of my left thigh.

"Morgana," I said with more urgency. "Why are you here? Was there someone else with you?"

She opened her mouth to say something and closed it. She pursed her lips and then spoke haltingly, her voice the quietest I'd ever heard it. She looked so much like a little girl, nowhere near almost 14.

"Seth. I-I know about you and Grace." She lowered her eyes away from me.

"What about me and Grace?" I asked quietly.

"I know that you – the two of you – have had sex." She brought her eyes up again, locking them with mine.

"Oh, I didn't spy on you or anything, and Grace didn't tell me," she added hurriedly. "When I saw you at Far Pond the other day, there was something – I just could tell somehow."

Now it was my turn to be at a loss for words. Morgana was regaining her equilibrium as she continued.

"And I think it's beautiful, glorious, that you have these feelings for one another, that you act on them, that you can – can truly reveal all of yourselves to one another, be together physically as well as emotionally and spiritually."

She absent-mindedly reached over and picked off a little seedling that had gotten stuck on the thigh of my jeans. She picked at it and rolled it around in her fingers, and her voice became breathy and dreamy.

"That's something I've wanted – I want – to experience, to feel all of that joy. And Patrick—" She halted again, then resumed.

"Oh, Seth, he's such a sweet boy! There is so much about himself that he doesn't show, not even to his parents. But I can see, I can sense the beauty in him, and I know I can bring it out. And I know that we could have the special kind of love that you and Grace have."

I felt mortified, and even queasy, about what she was saying. But there was also part of me that pitied her at how she had created this fantasy world that was simultaneously childish yet tinged alarmingly with adult feelings she couldn't fully comprehend.

"That's why I was so happy to see him at Far Pond, and I thought that revealing myself to him, as I did, would help him see me as someone to desire. But I realized that we needed to be all alone, away from everybody else, so we could be truly free to share all of ourselves. So I brought him here – yes, I know I'm not 'supposed to,' according to Rafe. It's just that some things are more important than rules and regulations."

She looked down at the seedling, and cast it aside, bent closer to me. A tint of desperation came over her.

"But Patrick – I guess I must have scared him, upset him. He ran away. I begged him to stop, told him I was sorry. He wouldn't come back."

Morgana turned to face me, put a hand on my knee. Her voice became urgent.

"It's my fault! I don't know how this all is supposed to work! But maybe your coming to look for me is a fortunate twist of fate. You can show me what's supposed to happen. And then I'll know, and I can show Patrick!"

With that, she grabbed my hand, pulled it in the direction of her breasts, and her face filled with anticipation bordering on frantic.

Then a change came over her.

"No," she murmured. "No, no, no."

She let my hand go and I snatched it back.

Morgana slumped, hung her head, and closed her eyes. Her breathing became regular again.

"Seth, I – please, please forgive me," she said softly. "This was completely wrong. I don't know why I—"

A small tear trickled down her cheek.

I briefly patted her shoulder with great care and restraint.

"Morgana, you have to listen to me," I said, trying for the right mixture of firmness and tenderness. "I don't know how it's all 'supposed to work.' It's not like Grace and I suddenly became experts or anything. I can't explain what happened between us, or why. Somehow, everything came together in a certain way, and we just knew when we were ready – or felt we were ready, I guess – to take that next step."

Morgana's eyes were wide open again and earnest as she listened, sniffling a little every now and then. I kept my hands as close to me as possible, so there was no possibility that a physical gesture of sympathy from me would be misinterpreted.

"What I do know is, if someone's not ready, not truly ready, then there's nothing you can really say to make them think otherwise. Nor should you try to. You may not even be as ready as you think you are. Do you understand?"

She nodded, to my immense relief.

"I suppose I need to apologize to poor Patrick," she sighed, then smiled dolefully. "If he'll ever let me within 10 feet of him again, that is."

"Well, you're a pretty creative person," I said, reassuringly. "I'm sure you can come up with something. Maybe write him the best letter of apology of all time."

Morgana giggled at that, then suddenly looked at me with some trepidation.

"Please don't tell anyone about this?" she said. "Especially

Grace. I wouldn't want you to get into any trouble with her because she thought that something was, you know, going on with us."

I was baffled at this, but I nodded. That put Morgana at ease again, and she smiled affectionately at me, then reached over and began to lightly caress the back of my neck.

"She's very lucky to have you," she said. "You really are a gentleman of the highest rank."

Abruptly, she leaned forward and kissed me full and hard on the mouth.

Then she turned away, bent over, put her sandals on, stood up, smoothed down her T-shirt dress, moved toward the door, and faced me again.

"Oh," she said. "If we go back to camp together, people might get ideas, you know? Maybe you should wait a little while and give me a head start."

She blew me a kiss, waved cheerily, and left.

I exhaled, fell back onto the bed and put my hands on my face, still feeling Morgana's kiss on my lips; at least she hadn't slipped her tongue in my mouth. I hoped that 15 minutes would be enough lead time for Morgana, because I couldn't wait to be back with Grace again.

Keeping my promise, I said nothing to Grace or to anyone else about the encounter with Morgana. Everyone was so relieved at her return that they weren't particularly curious about where I'd been.

Morgana was definitely subdued the rest of that day and most of the next. She sat with us at breakfast, and only tangentially chimed in on conversations, instead spending a goodly amount of time looking over at Patrick, who was sitting four tables away with his parents and little sister.

"What's with her?" Grace asked after Morgana got up from the table.

"Maybe she's just tired or something," I replied with a deliberative carelessness. "Takes a lot of energy to be so happy all the time, y'know?"

That afternoon, Grace, Mishy and I decided to take up residence in the arts and crafts building. Morgana was there at one of the tables, writing away; there were several balled-up pieces of paper around her. She looked up in some surprise, then gave us a clumsy, toothy grin.

"Whatcha doing there, Morgana?" I said breezily.

"Oh, nothing," she said, a little too quickly. Then she gathered herself and continued. "It's an epic tale of, uh, betrayal and forgiveness, with love eventually winning the day. At least that's how I've planned it. But sometimes stories don't turn out the way you think they will, do they?"

"I, uh, guess not," I said. I could see Grace gazing at me with some perplexity.

As the three of us walked by Morgana, I stole a glance and saw "Patrick" in large, fancifully written letters at the top of the piece of paper on which she was writing. She caught my eye and looked apprehensive, so I smiled comfortingly.

Grace, Mishy and I pulled out various supplies – not that we had any real plans or designs in mind – and began sorting through them. When we looked up, Morgana was gone.

"Gee, not even a goodbye," said Mishy.

"What was all that business about stories not turning out the way you think?" said Grace, raising her eyebrows at me.

I suppose it would've been easy to just tell Grace – maybe not that moment, but later – what had really happened at the Lone Cabin. I might have even mentioned Morgana's kiss in some casual, lighthearted way. But I guess I felt like I not only had to protect Morgana, but also Grace: I don't think she would've appreciated Morgana's insight into our sexual relationship.

"Morgana moves in mysterious ways, I guess," I said, cutting up a piece of construction paper in random, haphazard shapes.

That evening, walking back from Hilltop Lake with Grace, we spotted Morgana and Patrick in front of the arts and crafts building. Patrick stood perfectly still while, several feet away, Morgana spoke to him from a stance that suggested extreme contrition.

"I don't know," said Grace. "I just don't know."

"Neither do I," I said.

The next morning, Morgana was keeping company with Patrick again. But although she spoke to him with the apparent ease and conviviality of before, she maintained a short but definitive distance, and made no attempt at physical contact. Reconciliation had been achieved.

Mom and Marcus

And then I saw the thing I least wanted to see.

It was afternoon, and I was at loose ends, because Grace and her father had gone off on an excursion – she did this at least once every Transformation with whichever parent accompanied her that year – and everyone else seemed to be elsewhere or dormant. I decided to stretch my legs and go to a part of the camp I hadn't really explored before, so I set out from the dining hall until I reached the outer row of cabins. Then, off to my left, I heard a door open and close, so naturally I turned around to see, and there was Mom, going down the steps from one of the cabins.

She was maybe 20 yards or so away, at an angle where I could see her, but she couldn't see me. She was walking at an easy gait, yet with a certain purposefulness in her step. I was about to call out to her, but something made me stop. And then, a second later, the door to the cabin opened again.

"Joanne!" Marcus called, a little urgently.

I ducked out of sight behind the nearest cabin, then peeked around carefully to see what was going on.

Mom pivoted to face Marcus, her face mildly quizzical.

"You forgot your jacket," said Marcus, who was barefoot, wearing only shorts.

Mom went back to the cabin steps, took her jacket, gave Marcus a slight smile and said, "Thanks" in a small, polite voice. Then she turned around and headed off again. Marcus stood and watched her for a few seconds until she was out of sight, then went back into the cabin.

I sank down against the outer wall of the cabin where I'd been hiding.

No, I thought to myself, and like Morgana the other day, I found my mind repeating the word. *No, no, no.*

It had happened. Mom had slept with Marcus. For all I knew, this hadn't even been the first time.

I'd let down my guard, gotten distracted with Grace, Morgana, Diana, Rafe. I realized that Mom and I hadn't done our daily check-in for what seemed like a long time.

Now, all kinds of scenarios started racing through my brain – so quickly that it wasn't until a little later that I really sorted them out.

So much for any hope that my parents would reconcile. We'd get home, and almost immediately Mom would head over to Dad's apartment to tell him about Marcus. This would precipitate a horrible argument – *At least I tried*, Dad would say, *but you were looking for any opportunity to run out* – and an equally horrible altercation that would end in homicide, and I'd be essentially an orphan.

OK, not that. My father would be devastated, though, and from then on when I visited him he would be withdrawn, sitting in the same clothes he'd been wearing for days, the lights off, garbage piling up.

Or maybe Dad would just get in his car – the cheap Ford he'd bought after moving out – and drive away, just keep going and going, and we wouldn't hear from him for weeks, even months. *Dear Seth, I'm writing to let you know that I have taken a job in the commissary of a salmon-canning factory in Alaska. Rafe says hello.*

Of course, by then, Mom and I would be long gone. Barely home from camp, Mom would start packing up things so we could move in with Marcus. When she wasn't doing that, she would be on the phone with him: *Oh, Marcus, you're so sweet, yes, everything will be wonderful – Oh, Marcus! (tee-hee)*

And so we'd abandon our home, head south to Marcus' house. I had no idea what his house was like, how big it was, how many rooms, but somehow I knew that I'd wind up living in the basement. *Look at all this space, Seth! Isn't it great? You can set it up however you like!* The only good thing about this would be that at least I couldn't hear them having sex in his room, which would undoubtedly be every night. All I could look forward to was going away to college in two years, assuming I got into one we could afford. Or maybe Marcus would somehow get ahold of the money that was supposed to be set aside for my tuition. I wouldn't have put it past him.

Wait. Grace.

I didn't know where she lived in relation to Marcus, but it certainly couldn't be that far. I'd get her address and run away there. Well, actually, I guess I'd have to choose whether to go to her mother's or father's house. I didn't know which one would be best, but I'd figure it out.

If, for some reason I couldn't swing that, maybe Mishy or Funk would help me out. I reckoned that things were too tense between Rafe and his folks to approach him.

As for Diana, I'd worry that I might tempt fate being under the same roof with her.

"Hey, Diana, can I come in for a sec?"

"Sure, Seth."

"I just wanted to ask if you knew where – oh, my God! I'm sorry! I-I didn't know you would be completely undressed!"

No, I shouldn't think about that, I told myself. The girl I most wanted to see naked (or clothed) was Grace.

But, OK, Diana was the only *other* girl I wanted to see naked.

Hell, maybe I'd take The Girls up on being their secret brother.

I think I just sat there for maybe five minutes or so. Then I got to my feet and found myself walking toward Marcus' cabin. I wasn't sure how or why this was happening, it just was.

When I first noticed Marcus' attentions toward Mom, I had a little fantasy about stopping him in his tracks. It had involved storming into his cabin, pushing him around and making threats on the order of "You stay away from my mother, you hear? Or else you're gonna be swallowing your teeth!" And Marcus would cower in abject humiliation, sobbing and begging my forgiveness.

Now I was actually at his cabin, knocking softly at the door.

I heard a rustling inside, and as the door opened, without looking up, he said, cordially, "So, did you change your mind—"

Then he saw it was me.

"Oh! Seth!" His voice was a blend of surprise with a hint of considerable discomfort. "Uh, good to see you, uh, is there something you need?"

I raised my hand slowly, as if I expected it to make a fist, but instead I pointed my finger at him.

"You," I began. "My mother."

I jabbed my finger at him.

"Just...don't. You understand?"

He gaped at me.

I turned around and stalked off.

Behind me, Marcus called out in a faltering voice: "Seth! Wait! I didn't—there's nothing—I..."

When I'd gotten about 50 yards away, I turned my head slightly enough to see him slouch back into his cabin and shut the door.

Grace was initially sympathetic that evening when I told her.

We'd been looking forward to watching *The Wizard of Oz* in the dining hall that night, but Grace could tell something was bothering me, and about halfway through she finally pulled me outside. We made our way in the moonlight to the

Place of Grace and settled down together. In the distance, we could hear people in the dining hall singing along to the "March of the Winkies" song.

"I'm sorry you saw that," she said softly. "I can understand how upsetting it must be."

I nodded. Grace looked out toward the lake and seemed to be mulling over something.

"Is it possible," she finally said, in a guarded tone, "that what you *think* happened might *not* have actually happened?"

"What, that Marcus and my mother had sex?" I replied harshly, without thinking. I softened my voice. "Sure, I suppose anything is possible. But you gotta admit, the evidence is pretty strong, isn't it?"

"I suppose so," she said, and pursed her lips.

I sighed. "I wonder how fast the divorce will come through."

Grace kept her gaze forward and frowned a little. She turned back to me.

"Do you really believe that this is it, the last straw? There's no way your parents can get beyond this?"

She held up a cautionary finger. "Assuming, that is, that what you think happened did happen."

She started to put her finger down, then held it up again.

"Actually," she said, with some assertiveness, "why would your mother even tell your father?"

"Huh?"

"Well, do you really think that all of a sudden she's now going to run off with Marcus? Maybe this was just a fling, and she won't give it another thought once you get back home."

I considered this and shook my head.

"No. I think she's just so vulnerable right now. She's been going to all these seminars here – who knows what kind of things she's learning? – and Marcus has been getting into her head. It just all adds up."

Grace seemed to take a deep breath and leaned a little away so she could look directly at me.

"Do you blame your mom for your parents' separation?"

"What? God, no! Why would you say that?"

"Well, just seems like you're putting a lot on her, like she's now the one who basically decides whether or not they're going to split up permanently. What about your dad? Don't you think he's 'vulnerable' now, too? Maybe he's had experiences like your mom's been having here."

She locked eyes with me and didn't let me go.

"I know one of the things that's been frustrating for you is not knowing why they arrived at where they did. So now, whatever happened before, if they do divorce you can point to your mom as the cause."

I began to sputter. "You-you make it sound like I *want* to blame my mom – or just blame somebody. I don't!"

I paused, caught my breath, then muttered, "I thought you were on my side."

Grace gesticulated in some exasperation. "Sweetie pie, there are no sides here. I hardly know your mom at all, and I know your dad even less. I'm just trying to make some sense of this so I can help *you* make sense of it. And I'm worried that this business with you going up against Marcus is you trying to take control of things that you can't, like I tried to do when my parents were splitting up. Do you get that? And do you get that I care about you?"

I actually felt a lump in my throat for an instant.

"Did you really just call me 'sweetie pie'?" I said, trying to suppress a grin.

"Yeah, I guess I did," she answered laconically. "Would you like it better if I called you 'shit head'?"

"Maybe a combination of the two?"

"OK, shit pie."

"I was thinking more of 'sweetie head,' but all right."

We heard applause from the dining hall. Dorothy had gotten back home to Kansas.

Seth and Mom (Cont.)

I half-expected to find our cabin empty when I got back, but I saw the light was on, and when I opened the door Mom was lying in bed reading. She smiled as I came in.

"Hi there, hon. Were you at the movie?"

I gritted out a smile as best I could.

"Yeah. Can't pass up *Wizard of Oz*, right?"

She chuckled sweetly. "Oh, I remember how terrified you used to be whenever the Flying Monkeys were on."

"Well," I said, "I think I'm over that."

I didn't see Marcus hanging around with my mother after that – not for the rest of the camp, as it turned out. Once more, I tried to stay with her whenever possible, keeping an eye out for him. But when Marcus was around, he hardly even glanced in our direction, nor did Mom look in his.

I wasn't comforted by this apparent change in behavior. I took it to mean that Mom and Marcus had simply decided to be more discreet in public, especially if I was in the vicinity. As far as I was concerned, the die was cast, groundwork laid, whatever dramatic phrase you wanted – they were going to be a couple, and there wasn't anything I could do about it.

Fun Night

It was midafternoon of the last full day of Transeminars – the next day, I was told, there would be a big picnic, followed by a gathering in the dining hall. We assembled, gradually, in the sheltered picnic area, Rafe assuming his usual place on top of one of the picnic tables, Diana on the seat below, and the rest of us settled in on the other tables. Morgana and Patrick sat in some proximity to one another, but she kept an apparently proscribed distance, as if she was observing a self-imposed restraining order. The Girls clumped together in the corner, working on their ever-present notebooks and drawing pads, seemingly removed but not out of earshot.

"Well, Seth," said Rafe, breezily, "about another 48 hours, and you'll be on your way back to – what the hell is the name of that place you're from, again?"

"Forget it," I said. "It's not important."

"Which, the name or the place?"

I shrugged. "Either one."

Grace looped her arm inside mine and latched onto my hand.

"So, you're now officially a veteran of Transformation," said Funk. "What do you think?"

I was at a loss for words. A big part of the reason was that, about an hour or so ago, Grace and I had made love behind the bathhouses. We couldn't use the Lone Cabin, because Rafe, Diana, Mishy and Funk had claimed it; Mishy had invited the two of us to join them, but we suspected this was just politeness on her part, and besides, we wanted to be alone. Our desire began to build, and we quickly sought a location as close by as possible – we had no patience to try to find a place in the Sitting Woods. Fortunately, there was a fairly secluded spot at the far end of the bathhouses, and we didn't take very long.

So, even as I sat with the others, my mind was still back behind the bathhouses with Grace. I half-wondered if Rafe or Diana could tell what we'd been up to.

Of course, asking me what I thought of my Transformation experience was a pretty useless question. Processing everything that had happened to me was going to take quite some time, I knew.

Nevertheless, I tried to answer Funk: "It's been, well, tremendous. I don't think I ever expected to find what I found here."

Grace squeezed my hand.

I happened to gaze at Morgana, and she had a fleeting look of anxiety on her face.

Then Funk, Diana, Rafe and Mishy started talking about their own first impressions of Transformation, which segued into a selection of anecdotes about this year: the best (and worst) meals Bill and Tess had served; the best (and worst) movies that had been shown; the stupidest thing they'd heard an adult say.

At some point, there was a pause in the conversation.

"It's different this year," said Morgana softly, her head bowed.

We all looked at her, surprised at how melancholy she sounded.

"What do you mean, Morg?" asked Diana.

Morgana raised her head, suddenly realizing she was the center of attention.

"I know you must all think I'm just a silly wee thing," she said, her voice sounding like a slowed-down version of itself, "and you're probably right."

She gave a very brief sidelong glance in Patrick's direction, but he was looking off in the distance and didn't notice. She pressed her lips together, and then continued.

"It's just that I see a lot more of the camp than you all do. You know, I play with the little ones, and sometimes with the not-quite-so-little ones, and when I'm with them and their families, I hear and see things. Or I just feel them."

Rafe and Funk looked at each other and simultaneously exchanged a light shake of their heads, but Diana focused on Morgana.

"What things, Morg?" she asked.

Morgana frowned slightly. "People just seem...unhappy."

"Unhappy? You mean unhappy with Transformation?"

"I guess so. I just sense that people aren't finding the pleasure – the satisfaction – here as they once did."

She fixed her eyes on all of us. "And I understand that the big meeting of all the adults on Skinny Day didn't go very well. There were a lot of complaints and disagreements. That's why it was so quiet in the dining hall at dinner that night."

I guess I hadn't been paying attention at the time – probably because I'd spent most of dinner thinking fondly about Skinny Day – but now that I looked back on it there did seem to be a pall over the room. Then I thought about what I'd observed during the past couple of weeks: the whole business with Therese (whom we'd barely seen in the past week; she appeared to be keeping a low profile around camp), the big blow-up at Ralph's seminar, Jerry's arguments with Howard and Marilyn.

"Morgana," I said. "Is it possible that this stuff has been going on all along, or maybe at least for a good while, and it's just now – because you're, you know, older – that you're catching on?"

Morgana considered this. "It could be, I suppose. However" – and here her voice and manner began to take on their more familiar character – "while I don't claim to be clairvoyant, I do believe I'm attuned in a certain way to minds and hearts." She held her gaze at me about two seconds longer than I found comfortable.

"Where once I could feel souls bounding and leaping," she said, "now they seem to be trudging along, merely going through the motions."

Rafe put his hand over his face and made a barely audible sound of distress. Still looking at Morgana, Diana gave Rafe's knee a quick slap with the back of her hand.

"You know, Jerry, Marcus, Howard, Marilyn – all of them – are 10 years older now than when Transformation began," I said. "I guess it's easy to think that adults – especially our parents – will stay like they are over time, but they can change, too. So maybe Transformation doesn't have the same meaning for them that it used to."

"But that's sad!" blurted Morgana, disconsolately. "I wish we could do something to make them feel about Transformation like when it was still new."

Rafe grunted. "Maybe we should bring back Fun Night."

I turned toward him. "Fun Night?"

"Yeah. It's what used to happen the last night of camp. People would do skits, or sing, or read poetry, stuff like that. Most of it was pretty lame, to be honest. But I dunno, I guess the adults liked it. Especially when the kids would get up and do something."

"So what happened to Fun Night?"

He shrugged. "Fewer and fewer people volunteered to perform. I guess everyone kind of lost interest. We haven't had Fun Night in, oh, must be four years now."

I thought about this. "So," I said cautiously, "would it kill us if we tried to think of something to do?"

Rafe made a face. "Are you kidding? Why would we want to do that?"

I looked around the room. "Well, if so many people seem to be feeling unhappy, like Morgana says, would it be such a terrible thing if we tried to cheer them up a little?"

Mishy giggled. "Sounds like something out of a corny old movie. 'Hey kids, let's put on a show!'"

I nodded at her. "Oh, believe me, I know. I can't believe I'm even suggesting it. But I think about Jerry, or Bill and Tess, some of the others my mom and I have gotten to know, and they've put a lot of themselves into this whole thing. Really, if not for them, would there be a Transformation? So maybe we can show them just a little appreciation."

Everyone was silent for a minute, but I could see Morgana had perked up at this turn in the discussion.

"What, just do a song or something?" said Diana.

"Yeah, why not?" I said. "Doesn't have to be anything complicated. Something we all know."

Funk began to sing, very badly, the beginning of "The Impossible Dream."

"Not gonna do show tunes," growled Rafe.

"No, it can be something that we know from the radio," I said. "Some song that maybe we just learned without even thinking about it. Something that doesn't take a lot of effort to remember."

Everyone was quiet again. Then Rafe began to laugh.

"Oh, man! I just had the wildest idea. It's probably stupid..."

For the next 20 minutes or so, we talked about Rafe's idea and mapped out a plan for putting it together – we had barely 24 hours, but that was still enough time.

The Girls broke into our discussion near the end.

"We want to be part of this!" said Min.

"Please?" said Dee.

Rafe looked at Lily, whose demeanor let it be known that they weren't taking "No" for an answer.

"Ah, what the hell," he said. "Just make sure you remember

when and where we're practicing. And speaking of which..."

Rafe slapped me on the shoulder.

"You and me got work to do."

Sometime after that, I caught up with Patrick. I saw him shuffling around on his own, and asked if he had a few minutes to talk. He nodded his head without alacrity, and we moved over to an isolated picnic table.

I'd been trying to sort out what exactly I was doing here. Yes, I was used to talking with people about their difficulties and dramas, but I wasn't in the habit of deliberately seeking someone out to get them to do so. In this case, however, it seemed necessary: I simply couldn't stand to see how downcast Morgana was, and felt vaguely that somehow it was my responsibility to try to put things right.

"Well, Patrick," I said, choosing my words with utmost care, "I don't know, exactly, what's been going on with you and Morgana. I mean, I do know you guys have been friends."

I paused to let Patrick give some kind of acknowledgement. He did not.

"Anyway," I continued, "maybe it's become, well, something else? It, um, seems lately that you two have been...closer."

I looked at Patrick again.

"Yes," he finally mumbled.

I think it was around then that something crystalized for me. Patrick was this vessel, this canvas Morgana used to express all her thoughts, ideas, songs, poems, recitations and whatever else came into her mind – including her fantasy of them as a romantic couple. Patrick's general lack of response she took for affirmation, so as far as she was concerned it meant she could read into him whatever she wanted. Until that day at the Lone Cabin.

It reminded me of how a little kid might play with a pet cat or dog: dress it in clothes, get it to wear a hat or a mask, carry or push it around to this place or that. But then comes that day when the kid crosses the line, and the cat hisses and scratches, or the dog growls and bares its teeth menacingly.

This situation, of course, was a lot more complex than that of a small child and a pet. Morgana hadn't been acting out some juvenile whim, but trying to deal with unfamiliar, very potent feelings in about the only way she could think of.

On the one hand, Patrick had done them both a favor: He'd asserted himself, at long last, and Morgana, maybe for the first time in her life, had to cope with outright rejection. Unfortunately, he had left too much unfinished. He needed to tell Morgana she had been out of line, but he also needed to reassure her – and himself – that she was still a good person.

That was all swirling around in my head as I gazed at Patrick, trying to figure out what to say next. I didn't want to betray Morgana's confidence, and I didn't want to make Patrick any more uncomfortable than he probably was.

Finally, I said: "I get the impression that, maybe, Morgana wanted something to happen that you weren't ready for, you didn't want. And maybe it kind of freaked you out. Would that be right?"

"Yes," he said.

I sighed. "OK. There's nothing wrong with that. You have a right to feel what you feel. If you told her that she crossed a line, that's perfectly all right. But don't punish Morgana more than you have to, OK? Let her know that she has a chance to make it up to you."

Patrick looked at me impassively.

I found myself getting a little irritated, but tried not to let it show.

I leaned my head forward in his direction. "OK?" I intoned, very deliberately.

"OK," said Patrick, imitating my tone.

- - - -

I also made a point of stopping in to see Bill and Tess, because I had officially finished my stint as kitchen/dining hall worker, and wanted to say a proper goodbye before things got too hectic. When I came in, they were getting food ready for the picnic, which would be buffet-style, with sandwiches, fruit and salads – about the easiest meal they'd had to prepare.

I thanked them for helping me feel welcome at Transformation, and complimented them on their cuisine – I'd never been particularly discerning about food, but I had genuinely enjoyed a lot of the meals they had served. They were both visibly touched. Bill started to shake my hand and instead gave me a bear hug. Tess hugged me even harder and planted a big wet kiss on my cheek. Then she told me to wait while she dashed over to a small table in the corner of the kitchen on which were stacked assorted cookbooks and papers. She picked up an index card and presented it to me.

"It's the recipe for ratatouille," she said.

Now it was my turn to be touched. On the days I had worked in the kitchen, Bill and Tess always let me sample what they were cooking – Tess would jokingly refer to me as their own personal food critic. For one dinner, they had made ratatouille, and I couldn't get enough of it; in addition to the portions they gave me beforehand, I must've eaten at least three servings. I'd given them compliment after compliment about it.

So now, here was the recipe, in my hands. I gave Tess another hug.

"Eat it in good health," she said.

"Or just eat it anyway," Bill chimed in.

We all laughed one more time.

And then, it was Fun Night.

I clustered with the other kids at the back of the dining hall. We gave each other hurried reminders and words of encouragement, until we heard Jerry call out for attention, and conversation in the dining hall died away.

"Well, gang," he boomed jovially, "we have a little treat to-night – an unexpected one, I must say. But some of our young-er folks have put together something they wanted to share with the rest of us. So, without any further ado..."

He motioned in our direction, to a smattering of applause.

It took a few minutes to get us all situated: Rafe and me in the middle; Grace, Diana, Funk and Mishy to our right; Mor-gana and Patrick to our immediate left, and just beyond them, The Girls.

Rafe and I arranged our chairs, sat down, picked up our guitars and settled them on our laps. After a few experimental strums to make sure we were in tune, we looked around at the others and exchanged nods.

I played the opening chord sequence while Rafe impro-vised. And then, sounding as if it were far away, I heard my voice start the first verse of "Peace Train."

I hadn't quite believed it when Rafe, after our group dis-cussion the previous afternoon, suggested we do "Peace Train."

"Why not?" he said. "I know it, more or less, you know it – I think most of us do. And probably most of the adults have at least heard it. Transformation is about the only place where I could ever imagine singing it."

(We knew we had to change some things about the song to make it work, especially the chorus, since all of us sang that. Slow down the tempo a little. Smooth out the rhythm. Pare those three rapid hand-claps – onetwothree – after the second line of the chorus to two moderate claps: one-two.)

Diana took the fourth verse. She had insisted on a solo: "I'm not going to have sung in my church choir all those years for nothing." Then we laughed as she recounted how several years ago, she'd been given a solo on "Oh Happy Day," and her voice had squeaked.

Our team of backing vocalists took to their task with varying degrees of expressiveness. While Grace seemed a bit self-con-scious – which might've been because she realized I was watching her – she moved easily with the music. Diana was clearly into it, swaying and rocking back and forth to the beat. Mishy was a little more reserved and somewhat clumsy, but as usual was enjoying herself. Funk and Patrick pretty much just stayed in place and sang what was required of them. Morgana seemed entranced, singing as if she were interpreting an Elizabethan ballad.

The Girls, as it turned out, weren't as familiar with the song as we were. At first, Rafe and I had suggested they simply clap along, but that idea didn't particularly appeal to them: "We're *not* going to just stand there like doofuses," declared Lily. Then Min remembered that there were some percussion instruments in the arts and crafts building, so I accompanied them there and looked on while they searched the various drawers, cubbies and closets.

"Found them!" yelled Min. Lily and Dee were right next to her, and the three of them excitedly held up their finds: a small hand drum, a maraca and a wood block with a small drumstick attached by a piece of string.

"Is that all there is?" asked Zoe forlornly. "Nothing else?"

It dawned on the other three that there was no instrument for Zoe. They each offered to let her have the one they'd claimed, but Zoe shook her head.

"No," she said, quietly. "You found them fair and square. I can just clap my hands or something."

Then I'd had an inspiration. I looked around, saw an old coffee can that was serving as a pen, pencil and paintbrush holder. I emptied it out, found a paintbrush with a good thick handle, and banged on the can a few times, then started to play a rhythm – OK, nothing that would ever get me into a band, but good enough. I held the brush and coffee can out to Zoe.

"You're all set," I said.

Zoe took them, studied them for a few seconds, then looked at me and beamed.

"Neat!" she said.

Rafe had arranged a section of the song where he and I would play chords while The Girls came in with their instruments. It had taken a while for them to get the hang of it, and not rush the tempo or play too hard (at one point I was afraid Lily would actually break the skin of the hand drum). They were keeping it together pretty well now, looking over at us for direction and encouragement; Zoe even gave me a little smile as she banged on the coffee can with the paintbrush handle.

Rafe, Diana and I sang the last verse together.

Although nobody recorded the event for posterity, in my memory – my emotional memory, if you will – the song sounds polished and cohesive, like something out of a movie musical. The actual performance, I know, was very different. Cues were missed. Transitions were ragged. Voices were in and out of synch with one another.

But I also know none of that really mattered because, at one juncture, I gazed out at the audience. I could see Mom smiling broadly, Morgana's mom lightly tapping her knee in time, even Rafe's parents exchanging contented glances. A few of the adults actually seemed to be choking back tears; Marilyn's face was crinkled with emotion, her hand over her mouth. Jerry looked delighted, practically elated.

In our last run-through, only a few hours ago, Rafe decided to end the song by having us all sing the last line of the chorus over and over, so that the audience could join in, too, which they did. Since all I had to do was repeat the same chords *ad infinitum*, I looked on either side of me. Grace was trying to dance with Diana, and she caught my eye and laughed as she sang, and Funk was cracking up at them. The Girls were pounding their instruments and essentially yelling the words. Patrick actually sported a small grin and shifted his weight from one foot to the other. And Morgana – she held her arms up above her head and swayed slowly in a small, tight circle, eyes closed and her face tight with concentration.

Finally, Rafe shouted, "Last time!" and gave his guitar an extended strum. Everybody sang the last line once more, drawing out the "train" at varying intervals, until Rafe played the final, resounding chord.

The dining hall reverberated with applause, cheers and whoops. I stood up and bowed with the rest, and then put my guitar back in its case.

The next several minutes were a mob scene.

My mother reached me first, giving me a huge hug and holding onto my shoulders while she shouted, "My wonderful, talented son!"

Then in quick succession there was Jerry, Todd and various other people – even Howard and Len (from the comic books seminar) – as well as complete strangers, all praising and congratulating me and the other kids. I could hardly make out what they were saying at times, since there was a continual stream of conversation all around.

Then I saw Grace, Rafe and the others heading outside and ran to join them. It was a relief to be in the cool, fresh night air.

Rafe abruptly leaned his head back and let out a loud "WOOOOOO!" The Girls all took hands in a circle and jumped up and down screaming. I hugged Grace and lifted her off the ground for a couple of seconds, and then Diana and Mishy embraced us, and then The Girls came up and chattered at me all at once, and then Funk and Patrick each shook my hand.

The hubbub died down a little, and Rafe looked at me and said, "That was freaking amazing, man. You did great."

He pulled me over to him and wrapped his arms around me, slapping my back. Everybody laughed. It was about then that I realized Morgana wasn't there.

We all kind of exhaled, just stood there or walked around in little circles, letting ourselves come down from the excitement. Inside the hall, we could hear Jerry calling for the audience to settle down again.

"That was sure a wonderful treat," he said. "Kinda reminds

us of why we're here, doesn't it? Well, this is the last night of Transformation for this year, so I wanted to share a few thoughts, and then open it up to anyone else who'd like to say something."

Out of the corner of my eye, I saw movement, and as I turned, Morgana came running up and embraced me tightly, resting her head against my chest. And would not let go.

I patted her back lightly, expecting her to relinquish her hold. But she held on even tighter. I felt her breathing seize up, start again, and continue unevenly; I realized she was crying.

"Hey, Morgana," I said, helplessly. "It's OK."

I looked up to see Grace several yards away, watching us with amusement, then bewilderment, then concern. I did my best to shrug at her, to show I was equally at a loss.

Grace walked over, put one hand on Morgana's shoulder, her other around mine. "Morgana, what's wrong?" she said.

Morgana didn't answer.

I saw Grace motion with her head to catch Diana's attention. Diana, who had been talking with Mishy, Rafe and Funk, headed over, with Mishy right behind.

"Morg," said Diana, running her fingers through Morgana's hair. "Talk to me. What's going on?"

Morgana still didn't answer. Diana and Mishy joined with Grace to further encircle her and me.

By this time, The Girls had noticed what was going on and hurried over, thinking that it was some fun group activity. But Diana made a silent *shush!* expression and they slowed down, gathering around us quietly.

Right behind them were Rafe and Funk, looking puzzled, but they too joined the growing circle. Rafe even put a large, hairy hand on Lily's tiny shoulder.

And last of all was Patrick. He advanced slowly, inserting himself next to Funk. The circle was complete, if irregular.

Morgana had stopped crying by then. She rose her head and surveyed us in quite some surprise.

"Oh my goodness," she said, sniffling, her voice ragged. "Look at all of you!"

She began to smile, with a little difficulty at first.

"Hello, everybody!" she said, sounding more like herself.

"Hello, everybody," we replied, not exactly in unison, but close enough.

"I'm *not* everybody," said Morgana, in that practiced haughty tone.

"Neither are we," we said.

"Yes, you are," said Morgana, her voice dropping to a whisper. "You're everybody I need."

The Girls dispatched themselves to find Morgana's parents, who slowly walked Morgana – spent and practically catatonic – back to their cabin. The rest of us talked for a little while, trying to figure out what had gone on. I offered speculation, but kept mum about what had happened at Lone Cabin, though I wasn't sure if there was any connection.

Finally, we scattered, and Grace and I walked out to the dock. The sun had set some time ago, but the lights from the dining hall and other cabins provided some illumination for us. We fumbled around with each other rather forlornly, until Grace finally wrapped her arms tightly around me.

"I'm sorry," she said. "I know you were probably thinking that we would, well, you know. I wanted to, too, but..."

I was grateful for that. As much as I wanted to make love, Morgana's episode had left me feeling disconcerted. I had a vague sense of complicity, what with the incident at the Lone Cabin the other day, yet at the same time I intuited that there was something far bigger going on.

Grace shifted her position so she could lean back against me and settle into my arms. We were uneasily silent for a few minutes, and then I spoke.

"Is this the part where you ask 'What's the first thing

you're going to do when you get home?'"

She laughed softly. "Sure," she said, with her familiar burr.

"Well, of course, the first thing I'm going to do is write you a long letter—"

She turned her head sideways so she could meet my eye with a mild smirk.

"Like hell."

"OK, what I mean is, the first thing *after* I unpack. And after I maybe stretch my legs for a bit. And have something to eat. Unless we stop for dinner on the way—"

"All right, all right, I get the idea."

We were quiet again.

"What will your letter say?" Grace finally said, quietly.

"What would you like it to say?"

"You mean I have to dictate it for you?"

"It would certainly save me time having to come up with all the words."

"What are you, an idiot?"

"Yes, I meant to tell you. You have fallen in love with an idiot."

Grace laughed a little, then was silent.

"Is that what this is? Love?" she almost whispered.

I leaned my head forward a little so I could catch her eye.

"Um, yeah? What do you call it?"

She was thoughtful for a few seconds.

"I hadn't actually thought about what to call it. I guess I've been too busy enjoying myself."

Then she sat up and turned around to face me.

"But you know," she said, "you said '*You*' – meaning me – have 'fallen in love.' What about you? Have you fallen in love?"

"My God! Of course I have! I mean, I know we haven't really known each other for very long, but with all that's happened these last couple of weeks – how could I not love you?"

In the darkness, I saw a smile spread across her face.

"I love you, too, shit pie."

I smiled back at her.

"Maybe for that first letter I write, I'll tell you the special name I come up with for you."

"It'll be tough to do better than 'shit pie.'"

"Oh, don't worry. I'll have lots of time to think of a really good one on the drive home."

She turned herself around again, lay back in my arms once more. Behind us, in the distance, we could hear a buzz of conversation and occasional laughter coming from what sounded like a sizeable group of people.

By this time tomorrow, we would all be gone.

Seth and Mom (Cont.)

The light was off in our cabin when I arrived, and I tried to be as quiet as possible coming in through the door.

Mom wasn't quite asleep yet, though.

"Hi, hon," she said drowsily.

"Oh, I'm sorry – I didn't mean to wake you."

"No, that's OK. You know, we haven't really kept up with our check-ins lately, have we? Sorry about that."

"No, Mom, it's not your fault. I guess we've both been" – I searched for the right word – "a little occupied."

She sat up, leaning on her left arm.

"Well, I don't want to embarrass you or anything, but I want to tell you, again, how proud I was of you for being in that concert. I wondered if you were ever going to play that guitar again, and you sounded wonderful. Maybe you'll give it more attention now?"

"Yeah, I guess."

"OK," she said, softly. "That's your decision to make, obviously."

She paused a few seconds. "Seth, I wanted you to know that I'm also proud of you for, well, giving Transformation a chance. I know you didn't want to come here, but it seems like you really got into the experience. That's really mature of you, you know?"

I thought for a few seconds as a whole kaleidoscope of scenes from the past two weeks flitted through my mind – all these various moments with Grace, Diana, Rafe, Morgana, others. It was almost overwhelming.

"Thanks, Mom," I managed to say. "I'm pretty tired. Gonna turn in now."

"Good night, sweetie."

Last Morning

I'd intended to get up early the next day anyway – Mom and I had to get a jump on packing so we could get on the road by at least midmorning – but Grace gave me another reason. She wanted us to spend a final bit of time together just by ourselves.

"That way, we can get the long goodbye out of the way," she had explained, "and you'll have time to say goodbye to everyone else before you leave."

It was overcast when we got to the Place of Grace. Although the hour was still pretty early, there was already a good amount of activity at the camp; breakfast had started, and we could see people trekking to the dining hall.

We didn't really talk. Instead, we just stood there, holding each other, sharing the occasional lengthy kiss. I felt sadness at the prospect of leaving Grace, and the camp, but my mind also was preoccupied with other details: what I was going to have for breakfast, how I was going to pack up my stuff, what Mom and I would do to get the cabin cleaned up.

Probably a half-hour or more had gone by when we broke our embrace and looked at each other. Grace gave a melancholy little smile and nodded her head. We kissed again, and started our way back to the camp.

We entered the dining hall and spotted Diana, Rafe, Mishy and Funk, so we got our food and went to join them. When we reached their table, we saw that Patrick was with them. And he was talking. A lot.

"...Hoover was famous for what he did to help Belgium in World War I, when they had a food crisis; Finland actually turned his last name into a verb, which meant 'to help.' But then a lot of people got angry at him during the Great Depression because they felt he wasn't doing the same kind of thing for America. That's why he lost to Franklin Roosevelt. Roosevelt didn't end the Depression, but he did a lot to help people, especially at the beginning of his administration, like with the Federal Emergency Relief Administration and the Civilian Conservation Corps, although he got criticized, especially by Republicans, for getting the federal government involved in so many things. Truman is interesting because even when he was vice president he hardly ever talked with Roosevelt, so when FDR died he didn't know about things like the Manhattan Project..."

The others were looking at him with varying degrees of amazement; Rafe's mouth was agape.

As I sat down next to Diana, I whispered, "What's going on?"

Diana whispered back, "Mishy just asked him if he was looking forward to going back to school, what's his favorite subject – you know. And he said he liked history, and in particular presidents of the 20th century. That was almost 10 minutes ago."

At last Patrick stopped somewhere around the Nixon Administration.

"Wow, Patrick, history is one of my favorite subjects, too," said Mishy. "I had no idea you liked it so much."

Patrick looked over at her placidly.

"Nobody ever asked."

The sun was starting to peek through the clouds by the time the car had been packed and the cabin swept and restored to its spartan appearance. Mom and I took a last look around to make sure we hadn't left anything behind. We walked to the parking lot, accompanied by Grace, who held my hand. At the fringe of the lot were the others.

Funk was the first to say goodbye, giving me the Vulcan "Live Long and Prosper" salute, which I returned with precision.

Patrick stepped forward and extended his hand. "It was nice to meet you, Seth. I hope you have a pleasant trip home." He shook my hand once, then stepped back.

Mishy engulfed me in her warm, fleshy embrace, and kissed me on the cheek. "Bye, sweetie! Please come back next year!"

I felt momentarily guilty, because somehow I'd never really connected with Mishy. I didn't know why: She was perfectly pleasant to me, always seemed to be in a good mood, hardly a discouraging word for anyone. So I conscientiously lingered in the embrace for a few extra seconds, reciprocating the squeeze that she gave me and patting her back a few times.

Diana's hug was more restrained, but she also kissed me on the cheek. "You take care of yourself, hon, OK?"

I went a little soft in my knees, then caught sight of Grace, her expression teasing, watching us.

Just then there was a high-pitched shriek, and The Girls came hurrying in from seemingly out of nowhere, almost knocking me off my feet as they collectively clung onto me.

"Bye, Seth!"

"I'll miss you!"

"Goodbye!"

Lily let go of me, crooked a finger, and narrowed her eyes. "You better come back next summer, or we'll come to your house and kidnap you!"

One thing about Lily: Even when she said something in jest, there was a perturbingly determined quality to her voice.

"Kidnap me?" I intoned dramatically. "Do you mean you'd steal me away and leave my poor mother in distress?"

195

On cue, my mother feigned advanced age and frailty, stooping crookedly with her hand on the small of her back. "My son!" she wailed in a feeble voice. "Where is my son?"

Lily couldn't restrain her smile, but she retained the stink-eye glare.

I leaned down and gave her a kiss on the forehead. Her face became a mere parody of a glower. I dispensed forehead kisses to Min, Dee and Zoe, and then all four scurried off, shouting farewells.

"Hey man!" said Rafe, giving me a bear hug and clapping me on the back. "Keep playin' that music, white boy."

Grace didn't say anything, just stepped up and held me for a few seconds.

"Oh! I almost forgot," said Rafe, and with that he went over to my mother and gave her a similarly bearish hug. "Goodbye, Joanne!"

My mother was surprised, but she patted Rafe lightly on the back. "Um, thanks and, uh, so long."

When they finished, all of us, my mother included, laughed.

As I got in the car, I realized there had been one person I hadn't seen at all. Morgana. I was a little surprised, but I figured she was still recovering from last night.

Mom started the car, everyone gave a final wave, and we slowly rolled across the parking lot to the road.

Just then, I saw Morgana. She was running in our direction, interspersing her gallop with bounds and leaps.

"Goodbye! Farewell!" she cried in her archetypal *dramatis personae* voice, her face radiant. "Adios! Safe travels! Bon voyage!"

I waved to her out the window.

We were on the road now, beginning to pick up speed.

And still Morgana followed us. I could see her shouting, but couldn't hear what she was saying.

At last, she vanished from our sight.

My mother shook her head and smiled slightly.

"Such a funny little girl."

Departing

I left believing with every fiber of my being that we'd be back at Transformation next summer. If not with Mom, maybe Dad – the experience might do him good. I suppose there was even a part of me that fantasized coming here with both Mom and Dad.

That certainty lasted about half an hour after we had pulled out onto the coast highway – Morgana by this time surely returning to the camp by now, perhaps still running. We were quiet at first, and I looked through my cassettes to find something we might both like for traveling music. At last I came across an album I wasn't as wild about as I'd once been, but I thought would be right. I slipped it in, and in a few seconds James Taylor's "Sweet Baby James" wafted out of the speakers.

Mom smiled and hummed along.

A few minutes later, she looked over at me.

"So," she began. "I guess you had a pretty good time?"

I smiled and kept looking straight ahead, nodding.

"Yeah, I'll admit it. You were right. I liked it." I paused a little before continuing. "It was a nice place, and there were some nice people there who were fun to be with."

My mother nodded. "Yes, there were. Well, I'm glad you made some friends and had fun." She cocked her head toward the back of the car. "Maybe you'll give the guitar another go?"

"Sure." I tried to keep my tone neutral and low-key, but in fact I was eager to get home and try some of the things Rafe had shown me.

When the first side of the cassette was finished, I started it on side two.

I could sense Mom was giving me an invitation to pose the question to her, and felt I really kind of owed it to her – for a number of reasons – to accept.

"What about you, Mom? Did you like it?"

Mom scowled a little.

"Oh, I don't know. I guess it was OK to just get away, be in a different place, be around new people for a bit. Some of the Transeminars were pretty good, but..."

She thought some more.

"But a lot of what I heard seemed to be things I already knew. Maybe I just needed to hear someone say them out loud to make them feel real. But I don't know how much I actually learned, you know?"

She sighed a little.

"And the people were – oh, I suppose they meant well and tried to make me feel at home and like part of the crowd. But I just – well, they seemed to act as if they were doing me some kind of favor? Does any of that make sense?"

I said I guessed I did.

The irony began to sink in: Mom's experience at Transformation was much what I feared I would have; mine ended up being far closer to what she had hoped for.

She continued. "Oh, and that big meeting last Sunday afternoon with all the adults? It seemed like hours of nothing but grumbling, moaning and complaining about how the Transeminars were boring or useless or irrelevant. And then other people would get up and criticize the ones who had complained."

She glanced over at me for a second. "By the way, I never did ask: What did you wind up doing that afternoon?"

A vision of soaking in the water with Grace at Far Pond stirred in my mind.

"Just hung out with the gang," I said.

Mom nodded and was quiet for a few seconds.

"Well, like I said, we went there, and I'm glad we did. But not a trip I'm planning to make again."

I didn't say anything. There was no point. Something in her voice let me know that, much as there was no talking her out of going to Transformation, it would be equally useless to convince her to return.

After a few minutes, though, I couldn't stop myself.

"So," I began cautiously, "you're not interested in spending any more time with Marcus?"

Mom furrowed her eyebrows, looked quickly toward me, then back to the road.

"Marcus? Why should I want to spend time with Marcus?"

"Well, I just thought that, you know, there was something going on with you two."

"Really?" she said, rather snappishly. "And what made you think that?"

No going back now. "Because," I said, evenly, "I saw you coming out of his cabin..."

Mom sagged a little.

"OK," she said, pointing to a very conveniently located rest stop up ahead. "I guess we need to talk."

Mom and Seth

Mom sat on top of the picnic table, much like Rafe had back at camp, and I sat next to her.

"OK, here's where it is with Marcus," she said, looking straight ahead. "You're a perceptive guy, you got a sense of what he's like: very attentive, welcoming, empathetic, kind of like a puppy wanting to cheer you up, right?"

I nodded.

"Yeah, well, I know all about his type. I ran into those kind of guys in high school, in college – the styles, the fashions, some of the words may have changed since then, but it's still the same. They want to try and attach themselves to a woman. And it seems like they have the best of intentions, but it's not so. Believe me, I know. So I had Marcus pegged pretty much from the start."

She looked over at me, then straight ahead again.

"Thing is," she said, a little wistfully, "I liked having that attention. I liked that a man seemed to find me attractive. It was nice to be able to flirt a little, just a little, and to be flirted with, just a little. Especially because I knew that nothing, and I mean nothing, would ever come of it. I mean, I had control of this situation, do you understand?"

I was amazed she was talking to me like this, like I wasn't some know-nothing 16 year-old kid. I nodded again.

"So, yes, we'd sit together at meals, or if we were at the

same seminars, or at the movies in the dining hall. And yes, we went on a couple of hikes, shared a few bottles of wine. But, from where I was, it was just a bit of fun, really low key."

She looked away from me and seemed as if she was debating what to say next. Then she turned back to me.

"In the end, though? I decided he wasn't worth any closer kind of...involvement," she paused, making sure I grasped what she meant, which I did. "And I tried to make that as clear as possible to him. After that, he stayed away."

She shrugged. "Didn't really raise his standing in my eyes, you know?"

I nodded. Then I took a deep breath and told her about my brief confrontation with Marcus.

Mom gawped at me for a few seconds. Then she began to laugh, deep and long, and after a few minutes tears ran from her eyes, and I realized she'd started to cry.

"Um," I said, trying to think of something to snap her out of this, "is this catharsis?"

Mom laughed again and hugged me.

"Oh, my sweet, wonderful son," she said, trying to catch her breath.

"What did I do?" I asked, warily.

"Oh," she said, sniffling a little as she released me, but with an arm around my shoulders. "I'm not laughing, or crying, at you. It's me. It's your dad. It's Marcus. It's all of us damn adults, and how we're supposed to be so mature and to do what's right. And you – you actually tried to defend my honor! Oh, my God."

And she laughed and cried again for a few minutes. Then she straightened up.

"God," she said, her voice quiet, staunch. "Marcus. What a fucking piece of shit."

I'd never heard Mom say things like that. It wasn't even the swear words, but the vehemence with which she said them.

"Can you imagine?" she said with pronounced disdain.

"He doesn't even have the balls to come to me and tell me that he's going to keep his distance because my 16-year-old son told him to. I mean, maybe – maybe – if he'd done that, I'd have been willing to let him have a cup of coffee with me. Son of a bitch."

"Mom," I said, rubbing her back. "He doesn't deserve you."

She laughed at that, from the heart, and it was glorious to see. I laughed with her. If there'd been anyone else at the rest stop, they probably would've thought we were crazy.

Yet at that moment, I felt she wasn't telling me everything. It took a while, but my instinct would prove correct.

We went back on the road, and were quiet for a while, listening to music. Then Mom began asking about the friends I'd made at camp. "Oh, and what was that girl's name – Greta? No – Grace, right?"

I knew she was fishing again. And I almost wanted to tell her everything, maybe even the part about sex with Grace. Certainly I could have talked about how it was just beginning to sink in how much I'd miss simply seeing her face, let alone touching her, let alone being within inches – less than inches – of her. And Mom had been so honest with me; maybe I owed her the same courtesy.

But I just couldn't do it. I guess keeping things secret was too ingrained in me by now. And besides, she had already told me I couldn't go back to Transformation, so I wasn't feeling especially grateful at the moment.

"Yeah," I said. "Grace. She's really nice."

Mom nodded, continued driving.

"Good," she said. "I'm glad you met nice people."

AFTER THE
SUMMER

Part One

A few days after we'd returned home, I went to stay with Dad for the weekend. So much had happened since I'd last seen him, but I wasn't sure how much of it I wanted to share. I certainly wasn't going to tell him about the whole business with Mom and Marcus, for one thing. I also thought about Grace's comments about whether my dad might have been pursuing new relationships, like I assumed Mom was with Marcus, and wondered if I should broach that subject.

I helped Dad move some furniture around in his apartment and lugged a few things down to the basement. He asked me what I was looking forward to about the school year, if I'd read any good books lately, whether I'd heard about this or that former neighbor. Finally, at dinner, I could tell he wanted to move on from small talk. We'd just started eating when he put down his fork.

"Seth," he said. "I just want to say I'm sorry. Sorry for the way things have gone the past several months. Your mom and I, we – I don't know how to explain it. We somehow wound up very far apart from one another, and we can't seem to close the distance."

He gave his perspective of how he and Mom had broken up. It was very similar to hers: There was nothing specific he could point to, no major dispute or transgression, just two people who had apparently grown tired of one another. The way he saw it, splitting up was the best way – the only way – to preserve the residue of affection and caring that remained between them, and to avoid something worse: that they might begin to resent or hate each other.

"I wish, really wish, it hadn't happened – your mom does, too – but I don't know what we can do to change things. It's not like we haven't talked about it. But we left you out in the cold, and you didn't deserve that. I can't predict what's going to happen, but I promise that both of us will do better to make sure you're OK."

It was obvious that Mom and Dad had spoken in the last few days, and she had clued him in on our discussions at Transformation. Part of me felt annoyed, somehow, by this – it was as if Mom had written a script for Dad to crib from. But I also knew Dad was being sincere and was seeking my forgiveness. I gave it to him.

"So," he said, looking relieved, "tell me about this Transformation place."

As I offered some basic details – the layout of the camp, how beautiful it was at Hilltop Lake, what our cabin was like – I speculated that Dad, however genuine his interest in Transformation, might also be compiling information to pass along to Mom so they could compare notes. Again, my reflexive teenage annoyance flared, but I knew, too, that Dad honestly wanted to hear about my experiences, because he cared about me.

Of course, there were many things I didn't tell him about those two weeks. Yet I wound up going into significantly more detail than I might have originally intended. I decided that, for example, The Sitting Woods and our cold-water immersion initiation made for colorful anecdotes, but – knowing my parents as I did – were not things they'd remember to any great degree, so it was safe to talk about them.

When he asked, specifically, if there had been any kids I'd spent time with at Transformation, I offered vague, generalized character descriptions: Rafe was "a hairy, hippie type of guy"; Diana "a really gorgeous chick"; Morgana "sort of art-sy-craftsy-spooksy-kooksy"; The Girls "these funny little kids who liked to pester us." On the one hand, it felt as if I was almost denigrating them with such minimalistic descriptions; at the same time, I considered this a way to preserve confidentiality, like I was protecting their secret identities.

Besides, even if I was more elaborate in my profiles of Rafe, Diana and the rest, how much would Dad – or Mom, for that matter – be able to relate to any of them? Better, I thought, to speak in terms my parents would understand.

Then Dad took a little sip of his wine, and – acting as if he'd suddenly remembered something – said, "Oh, your mom said there was one special friend you made. A girl?"

I closed my eyes and smiled. *Thanks, Mom,* I thought to myself.

"Yes," I said coolly. "Her name is Grace and she's just about my age. She's really nice, good to talk to, you know? So, yeah, sometimes we hung out when we weren't going to seminars or doing our chores."

I realized an opportunity might be at hand.

"Anyway," I continued, trying to sound casual, "I had a really good time there, and I'd kind of like to go back next summer. Hey, Dad – maybe you'd like to come with me to see what it's like."

I tried to come up with things about Transformation that might interest him: being out in nature (comfortably), meeting new people, going to Transeminars on business, or home improvement, or – I don't know – fishing?

Dad nodded his head and smiled absently. "Seth, I'm glad you enjoyed yourself. But it just doesn't sound like a place that I'd enjoy. I'm not sure I could get time off from work, either. Sorry, but..."

So much for that. Mom had probably warned him against agreeing to go. Well, there was a lot of time before the next Transformation, so maybe I could change his mind.

Things moved fast from there. Before I knew it, school began, and I found myself enjoying getting back into the routine and seeing my friends again. A lot of them asked me where in hell I'd been, and why hadn't I called, and was I going to stop being a fuckin' drag like I was for the last half of the year? I confided in a few of them – Chuck, Brent, Jen, all of whom I'd known for years – about what had happened with my parents, and to my surprise they expressed support and understanding.

My parents started behaving better, too, with each other and with me. Not to the point that they were ready to try again as a couple, but at least the tension level went down considerably.

At times, though, I felt strangely removed from events around me. All my life, my friendships had been tied to my immediate surroundings – my neighborhood, schools, recreational activities. Now, with Transformation, I had this new group of friends from a completely different setting, and who had little in common with my old friends. While I had shared anecdotes and observations about my hometown friends and classmates with Grace, Rafe, Diana and the rest, now I couldn't seem to do the reverse. I suppose I could've bragged about having sex, smoking pot and drinking booze, and skinny-dipping. I could've described what a strange yet poignant person Morgana was, or what a big asshole Marcus was, how wonderful Grace was. Doing so undoubtedly would've made me an interesting person among my peers: I would've been that guy who'd gone to some strange place, had taken the full measure of it, and come back in one piece. But, as was the case with my parents, giving my friends at home the whole story would have felt to me like a violation of the trust I had built with my Transformation friends.

I did try at first to integrate some aspects of Transformation into my regular life. I would try shouting "Laugh track!"

when something funny happened; other people either didn't notice or were simply baffled, so I stopped. I also wondered whether Chuck, Brent and Jen might like to commemorate the new school year with a water-immersion rite like that first day of camp; I quickly decided against it since, for one thing, the nearest body of water, Linwood Pond, was warm and muddy – nothing like Hilltop Lake.

Ultimately, I decided that there was no way Chuck, Brent or Jen, or any of my other friends at home, could appreciate what had happened to me at Transformation; hell, I was still trying to make sense of it myself. So I gave them a version little different from what I'd told Dad: It was really beautiful there, up in the mountains. Yeah, I'd met some kids there, who were pretty cool. We mostly hung out a lot, did this and that. The camp was kind of interesting, I guess: People would have these discussions about all kinds of different things – yeah, I went to a few, they were OK. On the whole, I liked it, wouldn't mind going back again.

It was as if I had traded one secret – my parents splitting up – for another.

Of course, through all this, Grace was constantly on my mind, and in my mailbox. We spoke on the phone occasionally, but it was hard to find much privacy, especially with our parents reminding us of the long distance charges. So we exchanged letters at least once every week, full of longing and quite vivid reminiscences of one another's bodies and shared sensations, as well as our various in-jokes ("You're still my little shit pie," she wrote in one letter). We signed them "Love, Always."

I made sure that I was the one who brought the mail in, so my mother wouldn't see how many letters I was receiving from Grace, which, of course, would prompt questions I didn't wish to answer.

Naturally, we tried to hatch conspiracies to get together.

But there were some considerable obstacles, starting with the fact that we were so many miles and hours away from one another. Our parents, we knew, were not interested in making such a long drive, not even to meet halfway, and going by bus would have been long and torturous since there were no direct lines between our towns.

I suppose Grace and I had ourselves to blame for not making it clear enough to our parents how we felt about each another. Both of us had been low key, even blasé in talking with them about our relationship, so why would they see any urgency in our wanting to reunite? Or maybe my parents – or at least Mom – knew more than they let on, and were consciously trying to prevent us from getting together.

Grace almost clued her parents in that fall. We'd spoken by phone one evening, and once again talked with despair about our exile from one another. This prompted Grace to go on a very uncharacteristic crying jag after hanging up, and when her mother asked what was wrong, Grace told her how much she missed me. Her mother – puzzled at such intense emotion over someone Grace had scarcely discussed – chalked it up to typical bizarre teenage behavior.

Winter, spring, into summer. Our correspondence and conversations continued, but not as regularly as before. The content of our letters became more mundane and less R-rated. And yet, we still signed them "Love, Always."

I thought about the others, too, even worried about them: Would Rafe find some direction in his life, and fix things up with his parents? Would Diana's folks reconcile with her sister? Was Morgana all right? At one point, I asked Grace for their addresses. I wrote a short note to Rafe, and was about to do so to Diana and Morgana, but then I balked. I convinced myself, somehow, that Diana would think I was coming onto her. As for Morgana, since I didn't know – neither did Grace, for that matter – about her emotional state, I wasn't sure if getting a note from me would be a good thing.

I did get a reply from Rafe a few weeks later that was perfunctory to say the least: "Hey man – nice to hear from you. I'm doing OK, still trying to get my shit together and not kill my parents (if they don't kill me first). Hope you're listening to good music and playing that guitar. Peace, Rafe."

Mom and Dad remained on civil terms, but were not in any hurry to try reconciling. My relationships with them continued to improve, slowly but steadily, over what they'd been months before, and I found solace in that.

I was busy with school, of course, especially because I decided to take part in the "Music Performance Club," a name the music teacher preferred over "rock band." This was a small group of kids – comprising bass, keyboards, drums, percussion, rhythm and lead guitars, vocals – that played popular songs mainly culled from Top 40, "It's a Heartache," "50 Ways to Leave Your Lover," "Dream On," "Tin Man," and so on. We'd be pressed into service for various school events as an alternative to the school orchestra. I wasn't wild about a lot of the repertoire, nor about some of the other members of the club, but it was generally fun – and certainly a good way for me to build on the inspiration and motivation with which Rafe had provided me.

Out of loyalty to Grace, I didn't pursue any relationships, and for probably just that reason I found myself attracting interest from a couple of girls I'd previously assumed had regarded me as some inferior form of life. No big deal or anything, mostly invitations to hang out at lunch with this or that group of friends, or to sit together at the basketball game. Early on, I thought long and hard about accepting these offers – was I betraying Grace simply by doing so? – but it became progressively easier to make the decision.

Once school was out, I wondered anew about whether I might be able to somehow get to Transformation. Mom hadn't budged from her position, so I tried to work more on Dad. He wasn't any more interested than when I'd first made the suggestion.

I had an idea: Perhaps I could attend Transformation in the care of another family. If not Grace's, maybe Mishy or Diana or Funk or...

"No," said Mom. "I'm not going to inconvenience someone else just so you can go to that place. Seth, I know you have friends there, but it's just not going to work out. Let's focus on other things – like you getting a job for the summer."

(Which I did: working at a local pet store for about 20 hours a week. I had to admit, it was kind of fun looking after the animals – even if I had to clean up their shit and piss – and I liked having a steady income.)

I reported my failure to Grace in a brief, disconsolate phone call about a week before Transformation started.

"It's OK," she said, her voice unsteady. "I know you tried. God, I'll miss you. We all will."

For the next few weeks, I tried not to think about what was going on down there at Hilltop. I visualized the cabins, the dining hall, the bathhouses, the lake, everything; I visualized the dining hall and kitchen, the Sitting Woods, Far Pond, the Lone Cabin, the Place of Grace; and I visualized everyone – most of all Grace.

I did have one modest achievement that helped lift my spirits somewhat. In the months after Transformation, I'd tried several times to make ratatouille using Bill and Tess' recipe, but the results had ranged from disastrous to unsatisfying. My mother had been surprised when I told her I wanted to try following the recipe all on my own – "I'd be happy to make it for you, sweetie," she said, but I was adamant about doing it, although I did consent to at least accept her consultation. This was a good thing, since my experience in cooking had been largely limited to boiling hot dogs and heating up canned spaghetti on the stove.

The first attempt wound up in the trash, overcooked and under-seasoned. I got progressively better at it, though, to the extent my mother hardly had to set foot in the kitchen. At last came the day when I followed every aspect of the directions perfectly, and it looked and smelled just like the ratatouille Bill and Tess had made. But the taste was...OK. That's it – just OK. Certainly nothing like what I'd eaten in the Transformation dining hall.

My parents, who'd gamely consumed each incarnation of the recipe, were supportive. They swore up and down each time that this was surely the best ratatouille they'd ever had. When Mom saw that I was disappointed even after I'd seemingly gotten everything right, she looked at me sympathetically.

"Do you know what I think is wrong?" she said.

"That I'm a crappy cook?" I mumbled.

"No, not at all. I think the problem is, you made it in the wrong place."

"Huh?"

"Well, the first time you ever had ratatouille was at Transformation. And more than that, you were present at the creation, so to speak: You got to see Bill and Tess make it. So, understandably, you associate everything about ratatouille with Transformation."

"I still don't get it."

She took a sip of her wine.

"OK, I'm hardly a gourmet chef or anything, but here's what I've come to believe. You have to make a recipe your own; you have to make it work for *you*, in your own kitchen. I had Bill and Tess' ratatouille, too, and yes, it was delicious.

But see, part of the reason was because of the meal being at Transformation, of the place that it was, the people we were around. You know?"

"I guess. But what does that mean? That I have to cook this in the camp kitchen to get it to taste right?"

"Not at all. I'm saying you have to go a little beyond what Bill and Tess wrote. Hey, even the ones who write recipes don't always follow them exactly to the letter. Experiment with it – maybe a little more garlic, a little less onions, or whatever. Just don't pretend you're at Transformation; realize that you're in your own kitchen."

As I thought about what Mom said, I remembered the "because you're here" discussion I'd had with Grace – about how Transformation had, directly or indirectly, contributed to the circumstances of our relationship. What Mom was suggesting seemed to me a paradox: To truly enjoy Bill and Tess' ratatouille at home as I had at Transformation, I had to separate the recipe from Transformation.

So several weeks after my last attempt, just a few days before Transformation would begin, I tried again. I honestly don't remember what it was I changed about the recipe: I scribbled the revisions on the index card Tess had given me, but sometime later I lost the card. It didn't matter, though. This time around, I was satisfied with the result – more than satisfied, in fact.

It also would be the last time I ever made ratatouille.

Later in the summer, I got a large envelope in the mail. I opened it to find a letter from Grace, and a folded sheet of paper that, when I opened it, turned out to be a drawing by Min of some people sitting in the middle of what was obviously a representation of the camp. I instantly recognized who the figures were supposed to be: Grace, Diana, Rafe, Funk, Mishy, Patrick, The Girls. All had sad faces; above them was "MISS

YOU!!!" in large letters.

There were signatures scrawled at the margins of the paper.

"PLAY THAT FUNKY MUSIC!!! Cosmically yours, Rafe"

"Hi Seth! Wish you were here! Hugs, Diana."

"Your presence is sorely missed. Stay cool, Funk."

"Hey there, sweetie! Hope you're having fun! Love, Mishy."

The other two signatures made me laugh.

"Best wishes. Sincerely yours, Patrick."

"Hi, Mr. Bathing Beauty!!!!!! Love, Dee, Zoe, Min and Lil (your Secret Sisters)"

Grace's letter was chock-full of news and gossip about the camp: Rafe's parents had finally kicked him out – or perhaps he left just ahead of their metaphorical boots – but he'd moved in with some friends a few miles away, was working odd jobs, so his parents agreed to pay half his way to camp this year; Patrick was still Patrick, but more sociable and talkative than he had been – the "How Many Words Did Patrick Say Today?" game had lost its significance; Joe and Denise had been so offended by the uproar over Therese that they decided not to come this year, maybe not ever again; Jerry had had another blow-up with Howard about his idea to bring in the financial advisor, and didn't speak for days; Bill and Tess got in a bit of hot water when about a dozen people came down with food poisoning.

It was then I realized that Morgana hadn't signed the picture, although she was included among the figures Min had drawn. *No Morgana this year*, Grace noted. *Nobody seems to know what's going on with her.*

At the very end, Grace wrote:

> *I took a walk to all the places we went, especially to the Lone Cabin. I think I must've spent two hours without realizing it, thinking about the afternoons we were there. Sometimes I wondered if it all had really happened, but of course it did. I was so, so sad you couldn't*

make it back, and yet, in a way, my memories were so strong it was as if you were actually here. I could see you, I could feel you. I even took off my clothes for a while, just sitting in the doorway of the cabin, feeling the air around me, and imagining you there with me.

It's horrible to think that we may not see each other for a very long time. But if I can conjure you up like this, where I can practically see you and touch you, then maybe that's some consolation.

Love, Always
Grace

I imagined Grace and the others, gathered near the bathhouses, or perhaps the sheltered picnic tables, Grace telling them about our frustration at being apart from each other.

Oh, you poor things! says Mishy, sympathetically.

Real drag, man, Rafe grumbles.

So unfair, Diana laments. *I wish we could think of something we could do, some way to get Seth here. He must be beside himself.*

Funk strokes his chin ostentatiously. *Yes, no doubt he's experiencing very strong emotions. If only there was some way he could harness all those feelings and convert them into a form of propulsive energy.*

Grace smirks at him, and Mishy giggles.

Yes! Yes! continues Funk, splendidly imitating every shlock sci-fi movie scientist. *Why, if he were able to do that, he could travel here in* – here he pauses melodramatically, fingers moving as if he were making calculations – *no more than five seconds; 5.8 seconds, to be exact.*

Hey, Rafe pipes up, *can you calculate this? The angle of the dangle-*

Shut up, Rafe! Diana interjects.

Laugh track! Funk proclaims.

And yet, the combined agony-ecstasy I felt from Grace's letter had largely dissolved by the start of school.

This was, after all, my senior year. I had started to contemplate college, and the prospect was actually quite exciting, if also a little scary. I thought about Rafe and all the anxiety he'd experienced about college, but mine was different – it felt positive, somehow.

My rate of correspondence with Grace had decreased to an exchange of letters – usually about a page, maybe a page-and-a-half long – once a month, or six weeks or even more. Our phone calls were even more infrequent, mainly because we both seemed to be so busy that it was increasingly rare for us to be at home at the same time. Or so we said.

In December, my parents formally, officially divorced. I was saddened, to be sure, but not as devastated as I thought I would be. It was all very cordial and businesslike, and the two of them seemed to get along better than they had in years.

That same month, I started dating someone in my class.

Her name was Isabelle, a transfer from New York City (technically, she would explain, she'd spent the first half of her life on Long Island, the rest in Manhattan) who'd arrived last year. Besotted with Grace as I was at the time, and in the midst of my post-Transformation hangover, I hadn't paid her much attention. And frankly, it didn't seem like she was looking for any: When I did encounter her, she appeared generally morose and averse to human contact – head downwardly inclined, eyes locked into a 20-yard stare, body hunched together as if she were encased in a sarcophagus. Nor had she been in any of my classes.

This year, however, we had homeroom together, plus two

classes, and our lunches coincided. Moreover, she now presented a very different image, and a striking one at that, especially for our provincial little school: stylishly askew shoulder-length black hair, lively brown eyes that seemed to take everything in, a mouth that constantly seemed on the verge of a roguish grin. There was an impatience to her movements, as if she always had to be somewhere else, that made most everyone else around her seem plodding and lethargic. And while rock-n-roll T-shirts weren't unknown in our school, hers had a certain gravitas – Ramones, CBGB's, Sex Pistols – enhanced by the strategic placement of a few safety pins.

She didn't exactly have a Noo Yawk accent, but when she got on a roll, she occasionally would mash together words in a way that sounded kind of like what you heard on TV: "Whatever you say" would become "whateva ya say"; "going over there" became "gowenovah theh." She also peppered her conversation with words like *yutz*, *shmuck*, *yuck-a-puck* and the like, which to us were positively exotic.

I don't remember our initial exchange, but before long we were sitting together at lunch, and we had reached a significant milestone. She told me she liked her friends to call her "Is."

"Is?" I said. "Hmm. I kind of like that. Isabelle, Is. It sounds as if you're, I dunno, the present tense come to life. Is – eating her lunch. Is – walking down the hall. Is – looking at the sky. Is—"

"Is – going to punch you in the face if you don't cut it out," she said, then slowly smiled.

"Sorry," I said. "Got a little carried away, I guess. I had this friend once who liked to play around with people's names." I thought momentarily of Morgana and wondered if she still did that.

"Aw, don't worry, I'm just the crazy kid from New York. Whadda I know?"

"So, have you been settling in all right? I get the feeling last year wasn't, well, that great."

"Oh, I was definitely a bitch," she said casually, sipping her juice. "No question about it. But it really didn't have to do with any of you guys. I was just so pissed at my parents for moving out here – especially my dad, because he was the one who changed jobs."

"Wait," I said. "Your dad moved you guys from New York for him to take a job in *this* place? Isn't that bass-ackwards?"

Is shrugged and popped a grape in her mouth. "You'd think. Dad just decided we had to get out of the rat-race, have a new start, yadda yadda. So he found a job at that electronics company. You know, the one in the industrial park?"

She waved her hand in what she imagined to be the approximate direction of the industrial park; I remembered having passed by there a few times, and had wondered if it was, perhaps, a minimum-security prison. I mentioned this to Is, and she laughed appreciatively.

"One's man prison is another man's freedom, I guess," she said. "He seems to love it."

Is took another sip.

"Anyway – yeah, I was pissed off, and I didn't feel like I should make any effort to, y'know, get used to the place."

She let go a little breath. "Thing is, it takes a lot of energy to stay mad like that."

"Parents have little appreciation of this," I said, nodding. "You really do have to work at keeping a good sulk going."

She held her palms up, feigning commiseration. "Tell me about it? Takes all kinds of self-discipline, and they give you absolutely no credit for it."

The moment of levity passed, and Is resumed. "But also, this is my senior year of high school, for God's sake. And it's going to be the only senior year I ever have, so I thought, might as well make the best of it.

"Besides, who knows: Maybe I'll get into Columbia or NYU, or somewhere back east, just to give my parents a hard time."

I crooked an approving finger at her. "This could be a very good learning experience for them: Don't piss off Is."

She smiled at me again. "Don't piss off Is. I like the sound of that. Maybe I should put that on a button and wear it."

"If it were possible, and if I had any kind of talent," I said, gallantly, "I'd make one in shop class, just for you."

She cocked her head and regarded me. "You're sort of a yutz," she said affectionately. "But you're OK."

I signed up again for Music Performance Club, whose unofficial name among its members and supporters was the Fucking Rock Band. I also started hanging out with one of the other members – Geoff, who played electric guitar and bass – and we worked on becoming a duo. Our repertoire went outside what most of our peers were listening to. We'd do stripped-down versions of, for instance, Peter Gabriel's "Solsbury Hill" or Tom Petty's "Refugee," or a couple of songs by Richard Thompson, who Geoff really liked. We'd trade off lead vocals, even try some harmonies; I'd play acoustic guitar, and Geoff either bass or electric, but sometimes he let me borrow his electric.

Just before Thanksgiving, our school – in what may have been its most progressive idea since the Lyndon Johnson administration – decided to hold an informal "coffeehouse night" for student musicians as an alternative to the usual assembly performance. It was a kids-only affair, very informal, set up in the cafeteria instead of the auditorium, with refreshments served (no coffee, however). Geoff and I decided this would be a good opportunity to make our public debut, and landed one of the 15-minute slots.

It went very well, probably better than I could've imagined – I was particularly gratified at the positive response to "Solsbury Hill," on which I took lead vocals and played that distinctive riff.

As I was putting my guitar back in its case, I felt a hand on my shoulder, and a female voice behind me said, in stereotypical showbiz huckster style, "Nice work, kid! Mark my words, you're gonna see yer name up in lights someday!"

I stood up and turned around to see Is grinning at me.

"No, seriously," she said. "I'm really impressed."

I told her I wanted to get a little fresh air, so she accompanied me outside to the adjacent courtyard.

"I didn't think you'd come out for something like this," I said, and when she seemed puzzled, I cited her collection of punk-rock/new-wave T-shirts.

"Oh, I like punk rock," she explained, "but it's not as if it's the only thing I listen to." She paused for a second. "I guess, for me, punk was more of a social thing – something my friends and I would listen to, because it was new and kind of outrageous, you know? But I like Peter Gabriel and – what was that song Geoff did, the one about the tightrope walker?"

"Oh, 'The Great Valerio.' It's by Richard Thompson, this English singer-songwriter."

"Well, I liked that, too. You guys have a nice sound together."

Is looked off to the side. "I'm kind of regretting all that time I spent sulking around last year. I guess I missed out on meeting some cool people."

She watched me for my reaction.

"Um," I began. "Thanks – I'm really glad you liked it. And I'm glad you seem to be feeling better about being in this place."

She shrugged. "I suppose it's not really the place," she said, still eyeing me, "but who else is in it."

My parents' divorce went through a few weeks later. At lunch the following day, Is remarked that I seemed down, so I told her what had happened. She was genuinely concerned, although I insisted I was OK.

"Look," she said, "I really think you should have some company. You want to do something tonight? Is there someplace where we could, I dunno, see a half-decent movie?"

As it turned out, there was: Words, Music and Pictures, a café and bookstore on the edge of town that also sold used LPs and cassettes (Geoff had gotten his Richard Thompson albums there), and a few evenings a week, showed movies – classics, obscurities, out-of-the-mainstream.

"How in hell could I not know about this already?" Is said, shaking her head. "So, you wanna go? My treat."

That night at Words, Music and Pictures, we perused books, browsed through record albums, and watched *The Producers*. At one point, late in the film, I felt as if I were back in the camp dining hall at Transformation again, and without thinking moved close to Is; by the time I realized it, I felt like I had to stay there for at least a few minutes – if I pulled back quickly, Is might wonder why I was behaving so strangely.

Is responded by moving closer to me, and the back of her hand rested very lightly against my knee. We remained so until the end of the movie.

Afterwards, we snacked on some doughnuts in the café portion. I talked some more about what had gone on with my parents.

Then I asked, "So how are you doing with your folks?"

She sighed. "Oh, OK, I suppose. Like I said, after a while, it gets really tiring to be angry all the time.

"But you know, I think about where I'll be this time next year: at a college, somewhere. So I'll really be done with this place – I mean, sure, I'll come home for holidays and maybe spend summers here, if I don't find something else to do. And then I graduate, and go out into the world. But Mom and Dad, they're the ones who have to make it here. And I worry: What if Dad comes to decide that this whole thing was a mistake? Or Mom does? Will they be able to deal with all that?"

"I understand," I said. "But, well, they're adults, and if they screw up, they're going to have to work it out for themselves. You have to live your life."

She leaned over the table, her chin resting on her hands.

"God, I thought I was supposed to be the one offering comfort. You sure you're OK?"

I nodded. "Yeah. You know, I'm in basically the same situation as you are. In a year, I expect I'll be at a college somewhere, too, and my mom and dad will be dealing with the consequences of their decision."

I picked up my glass of water and held it over the table.

"Here's to parents. You can't live with 'em," I said, grandly, "and you can't live with 'em."

Is grinned at that.

I drove us home (in Mom's car, with my recently acquired learner's permit), and parked by the curb outside her house. We said good night, how much fun this was, must do it again, good night again. And still she sat in the front seat, looking at me with an expression of anticipation and shyness. Finally, I reached over, cupped her cheek gently, and kissed her. We remained that way for several seconds, well beyond the quick-peck interval. And then she got out, looked back over her shoulder with a glint in her eye, waved, and walked toward her house.

There followed a succession of outings: Words, Music and Pictures, again; skating at the local rink; bowling ("Bowling!" she exclaimed when I'd suggested it. "Well, anything for culture."); even the school's first varsity basketball game of the season, to which we scarcely paid any attention, so involved in conversation were we. We began to express our affection regularly, in all the usual ways.

Somehow, through all this, I convinced myself that I wasn't

cheating on Grace. Ironically, I saw myself as simply fulfilling for Is the role that Grace had played for me: being a guide amidst new or uncertain surroundings and experiences, and in doing so, helping her get past her feelings of dislocation.

And if I was developing some feelings for Is, which I was, surely they didn't compare to the breadth and depth of what I felt for Grace.

About a week before Christmas, there was a card from Grace. Artsy representation of some festive outdoor scene on the outside, inside her inscription: *How did it get to be almost Christmas? I hope you are enjoying your senior year and everything else is going well. I miss you. Give me a call over the holidays, OK? Love, Always, Grace.*

It was then I realized: I hadn't told Grace about my parents' divorce.

One month, two months, three, four.

Is and I became a couple, with the blessing of various friends as well as our parents (hers looked upon me as proof that she had fully acclimated to the move; mine were relieved that I seemed to be pursuing normal social relationships). We were conscious of the fact that we'd be separated come the fall, but it was fine. This was something that, for whatever reasons, we both needed.

One Sunday afternoon at the tail end of winter, I went over to her house to study (no, really) while her parents were out on a shopping trip. We sat in her room, our textbooks and notebooks strewn every which way. About 45 minutes after I'd arrived, I looked over to see Is unbuttoning her shirt.

"It's time," she declared matter-of-factly, unbuttoning the last button and taking my hand.

We lay under the covers, our clothes lumped on top of the notebooks and textbooks we'd hurriedly dumped onto the floor.

"You certainly seemed to know what you were doing," Is said. "I'm guessing this wasn't a new thing for you."

I'd thought that, sooner or later, I would have to tell her about Transformation, and Grace. I hadn't imagined it would be in these circumstances, of course, but I felt like the time was right. So I told her – the first person, in fact, with whom I'd ever discussed Transformation in any full detail. I kept it brief, since her parents would be coming back at some point, and we really *did* have to get some schoolwork done.

Is stared at me as I spoke, and continued to do so when I was done.

"It sounds like it was a good experience," she finally said, very softly. "The camp, the whole trip, I mean."

She tensed a little. I knew what she was going to say next.

"So what happened with Grace? You're not, like, together anymore, right?"

Well, that was certainly the question, wasn't it? I thought of the best answer I could give.

"I'm here with you, aren't I?"

The question dogged me for weeks: *What happened with Grace?* I couldn't come up with the answer – or, rather, an answer more substantive than the one I'd given Is.

In early May, I got a letter from Grace, apologizing for not having written or called for so long. She offered belated best wishes on my turning 18, and congratulations on my upcoming graduation. Then:

> *I feel like I need to tell you something. You know how I mentioned going to the Junior Prom in my last letter?* [She'd said that one of the songs they'd played that night was "Wild World," which of course had made her think of me.]

Well, I didn't go alone. I went with this guy, Barry, who I've started going out with. It's nothing really serious, not really, but I do have feelings for him that I can't explain just yet.

This doesn't mean the feelings I have for you are gone, though. I know they're still there, deep down. It's just that, after so much time of not seeing you, not being together, I think these feelings are so deep inside now I can't get the same pleasure from them I did once before. It had gotten to the point where thinking about you became too bittersweet, because there haven't been any new experiences and memories to add to those before. I felt like I had to move forward somehow, or else I'd be in such despair that my feelings for you would actually become a burden. Does that make sense?

I hope you understand, and I want you to know that, whatever relationship I might develop with Barry – or anybody else, for that matter – I love you, and will continue to love you.

Love, Always
Grace

There it was.

I went up to my room, sat down, and immediately began writing a reply.

I'm glad you wrote me. You've put into words something I've also been feeling for a while. As I think about it, I realize how much of our relationship was shaped by being at Transformation. That's where we met, and that's also where everything that defined us as a couple took place.

I remember you said much the same thing during the conversation we had, up on that lookout point you like so much, when I asked you "Why me?" "Transformation made it possible," you said. And you also talked about how the fact I was someone new to the camp made me interesting – attractive – to you.

So when we went back to the "real world," we had no other points of reference for how we were with one another. Why didn't I make some incredibly bold, ridiculous romantic gesture, like running away from home and hitchhiking or whatever to come see you? Why didn't you?

The answer is, it wasn't within either of us to do so. We were both too anchored to our regular, non-Transformation lives to disrupt them.

That doesn't mean what we had was, or is, meaningless. I still feel something in my gut when I think about you, and Transformation. I'm sure I always will.

I know you didn't write me to get my "permission" about seeing Barry, and I wouldn't have wanted you to. If for some reason you do want my blessing, consider it given. You deserve happiness.

The fact is, I also have someone in my life now, too. I don't know how long or how far it can go, since we'll be headed off to college in about another four months – you may be facing the same situation with Barry at this time next year. I guess I feel I need this relationship at this particular phase of my life, much the same way I needed you, and Transformation, to help me get through what I was dealing with at the time.

Look, let's live our lives and all that, but let's promise to check in now and then, OK?

Love, Always
Seth

Part Two

One year since Transformation became two years, became three, four...

I graduated, had a fine summer with Is before we left for our respective colleges, hers in upstate New York ("Near enough, I guess," she said), mine a small liberal arts school in Washington state – it wasn't my first, or even second choice, but I was satisfied. We drifted apart, got back together the following summer, drifted apart again and finally acquiesced – amiably and gracefully – to the realities of time and distance.

During my sophomore year, Mom began dating a guy, Lonnie, she'd met at her exercise group ("Out-of-shape middle-age people jogging around a track" was how she described it). Lonnie didn't push things with me, didn't try to be my father or my friend, and from all indications treated my mother like royalty, so he was perfectly OK with me.

I kept up my music, but not to any great degree. I'd bring out the guitar for the odd dorm gathering or campus coffeehouse, and that was as much as I wanted to do.

There were a few relationships in college – one girl I even brought home for spring break – and these were nurturing and satisfying, but ultimately nothing anyone felt compelled to sustain any longer than we had to.

Grace wound up going to college in Arizona. We exchanged letters occasionally, usually at least one per academic year. She and Barry had gone through something similar to what Is and I – and untold millions of other college-age sweethearts – had experienced, but she was fine: "Between you and him, I figure I've had it pretty good in the boyfriend department," she wrote. She stopped going to Transformation after the summer of her freshman year, mainly because there were other things (jobs, internships, travel-study programs) that were of more immediate importance.

Her parents, however, still traded off going to camp, and through them she'd gotten news about Transformation. Things weren't going well, apparently. Attendance was down, and some of the long-timers weren't coming any more. There had been some continuing pronounced unhappiness with the Transeminars being offered, apparently – too liberal for some, too conservative for others, not practical enough for still others, not imaginative enough for yet others.

One item she thought I'd enjoy hearing about: Marcus had gotten in a whole heap of trouble at the most recent Transformation. He had set his sights on a new, unattached woman, eventually lured her to his cabin, then convinced her to let him give her a back rub that, apparently, became ever more intimate – and finally received a clout on the jaw for his trouble. The woman had gone straight to Jerry and raised hell. As word of this got out, a few other women came forward to tell how they, too, had received considerable, and discomfiting, attention from Marcus. Nobody suggested that he'd done anything illegal, but it made for an altogether damning portrait.

And since the longstanding rumors were now in the open, something had to happen. The solution was that he could continue as Transformation co-director/organizer, but was no longer welcome at the camp itself.

Grace had a little news about our gang. Rafe, after roaming around a little, had settled in Berkeley as a preschool aide, of all things. ("Seems to like it! And the kids like him even more"). Diana, Funk and Mishy were all finishing up college, and Mishy had actually gotten engaged. The Girls and Patrick ("Patrick!") had, for all intents and purposes, taken up the youth leadership mantle for Transformation.

But there was no word on Morgana, she lamented, except rumors – of her commitment to some health care facility or program, her family moving to the other side of the country.

Life is busy now, very busy, but my mind still does flash back sometimes to that summer, and it gives me a warm feeling.
Love, Always
Grace

I felt Mom might be interested in hearing about Marcus, so during my next visit home I told her.

I thought she might laugh, perhaps exult at the news, but she frowned and exhaled deeply.

"Well," she said, "couldn't have happened to a nicer guy."

She seemed lost in thought for a moment. I looked at her questioningly.

"OK," she said, finally. "I have to tell you something I didn't before, about what happened with Marcus. I'm sorry to have kept it from you, but when we had that talk the morning we left Transformation, well, I guess I didn't feel like I could share it with you. I mean, hell, you were just 16."

I nodded.

Mom frowned again. "You remember what I said about him and me, right? That we would sit together for meals, go for walks, that sort of thing? And I knew he was trying to worm his way into my good graces, but I tried to keep him at arm's length – just enjoy the company, but not the complications. So it was fine."

She paused again, took a deep breath, looking past me.

"And then he invited me to his cabin. I don't even remember the pretext. And I went. We're just sitting there, he on his bed, me on a chair, and he's asking me – for about the zillionth time – how I like Transformation, is it helping, do I feel any difference, blah blah blah. I told him that, yeah, I kind of felt a bit more relaxed than when I'd first arrived. So he zeroed in on that part about feeling relaxed and offered to give me a back rub."

I felt increasingly uncomfortable about this, but tried not to show it.

"He had me lie face down on the bed, raised my shirt and unclasped my bra – sorry, honey, don't mean to embarrass you – and I have to say, he did a very good job of massaging. But then, maybe 10 minutes after he started, I felt his lips on the small of my back. I looked around as best I could, and I saw that he'd taken his shirt off, so I knew where this was headed."

She raised her hand, as if to forestall any kind of horrified or critical remark from me.

"But – I was still in control. I could've yelled, made a scene, punched him through the wall of the cabin—"

I told her I actually liked the image of that.

"Except that, you know what would've happened? Guarantee you, a day or so later, he would've made his way back to me, all apologetic, and said something like, 'Emotions went beyond control, in ways we couldn't have imagined.'" She imitated that soft, simpering voice of his perfectly, and I couldn't help but laugh a bit.

"And he would've turned it around so that it was somehow *my* fault, that I had overreacted. Then he would've offered me a means of redemption – more moonlit walks, more bottles of wine, and so on."

I knew what she meant by "and so on," and she could see that.

"So what did I do? I just laughed a little lightly, and said very casually, 'Hey you know, Marcus, I think that's about all I need now. Really appreciate your kindness,' and I reattached my bra, pulled my shirt down and went out the door."

"And that's when I saw you," I said. "I guess you'd forgotten to take your jacket along with you, and he handed it to you."

"Yeah, I was a little surprised. I'd have thought he would have kept it, which would've required me to come back later on, and give him a chance to spin his little web again. And you know, somehow I think that's what he really wanted – not even sex, just the pursuit, the intrigue, or whatever you want to call it."

She looked at me again.

"It was stupid of me to have gone to his cabin, I guess, but again, I didn't lose control of the situation. And I thought I must've gotten through to him, because he hardly went near me again, except for once at lunch. We were getting coffee at the same time, and he gave me some line about how busy he'd been the last couple of days what with camp coming to an end, and sorry he hadn't been able to spend much time with me, etc., etc. I thought that was a riot."

She smiled at me. "That's why I had that outburst when you told me about telling Marcus to back off. It was such a sweet, caring thing for you to do, and I never would've expected it. I knew how angry you'd been with Dad and with me, and that you were feeling lost, just like he and I were. But you saw Marcus as a threat, not just to me but to our family – such as it was, anyway – and it was like, of the three of us, you were the only one who took any real action to try to keep things together."

Mom sniffled a little, and then was silent.

I didn't really want to say what I said next, but felt I had to: "Of course, in the end, it didn't 'keep things together.'"

She looked at me with a sad smile. "Yes, that's true. But maybe doing something made you feel better? At least a little?"

I thought about how Grace had questioned my actions and motivations in confronting Marcus. "I suppose," I said carefully. "At least for a few minutes."

"Well, anyway," she sighed, "now you know more of the story."

Then something occurred to me.

"That was why you didn't want to go back to Transformation, wasn't it?" I said, trying not to sound accusatory. "It would've just been too uncomfortable with Marcus."

"Oh, the business with Marcus was certainly part of that," she said. "But it's like I told you: I just didn't feel I belonged, that there was nothing of any sustained value I could take from being at Transformation."

I started to speak, but Mom anticipated my response.

"I know your experience was quite different from mine, and that you made friends there," she said. "I also guessed, pretty easily, that you got especially close to Gina—" She corrected herself, giving me a sly glance. "Grace."

She leaned back in her chair. "Obviously, you wanted to go back, and there was a part of me that wanted to give you that."

"So why didn't you?"

"You have to understand, Seth, that I had a lot on my mind those first couple of months after we got back from the camp. I was thinking about you, of course, and what your dad and I should do, but I also was going over in my mind all that had happened at Transformation, especially with Marcus. And the more I thought about it, I just didn't want you in the same place as him."

"Why? Did you think he would try to harm me or something?"

"Oh no, of course not. It's just that I didn't want you to be in the presence of such arrogance. Because that's what he was all about, this idea of doing as he pleased. It's not even so much how he acted toward women: If he hadn't done that, he might've embezzled camp funds, or taken people's stuff. Do you see what I mean?"

I nodded.

"But you know," I said, "and I can't believe I'm saying this, but Marcus did do a pretty good job of helping organize Transformation with Jerry. I mean, I'm not trying to defend him or anything, and maybe you didn't really think much of Transformation, but if you look at it objectively, that took a lot of work, making it happen all those years."

Mom looked at me a little sadly.

"Yes, that's true. But honey, if you really look at it objectively, well, there must've been people who knew what Marcus had been doing, or at least suspected. There must've been. And the fact that nobody did or said anything until there was no other choice? It doesn't reflect very well on Jerry or the others."

I didn't say anything, but Mom could see I was troubled by her remark. She leaned toward me.

"If it's not too much trouble," she said, smiling, "I'm curious to know whether I was right about you and Grace."

I let out a soft mock groan. "It's a long story." I returned her smile.

She pretended to glance at a watch she wasn't wearing.

"I don't have to be any place any time soon. What about you?"

I pretended to glare at her, as if I was 16-year-old Seth again. Then I shrugged, and started to tell her about Grace and me – not the whole truth, but some of it. I kind of figured I owed it to her.

Five years since that summer.

I was at home, contemplating the start of my senior year, and what might lie beyond. Graduate school? Travel? Work?

Mom and Lonnie were talking about getting married, maybe next summer, after I'd graduated. Dad, who had just started seeing a nice lady named Lori, and I kidded them: Whenever! Just get it done! (Mom never did marry Lonnie. They kept putting off the date – or, more accurately, Mom wouldn't commit to one – and finally, after three years, Lonnie felt he had to move on. When I asked her what had happened, she said she'd gotten used to being independent, to living on her own terms: "I've learned to like it so much, I'm just not ready to go back to being somebody's wife again.")

A few days earlier, I'd gotten together with Is for the first time in many months, at Words, Music and Pictures. She, too, was thinking of life after college. Sort of.

"Oh, for God's sake, don't ask!" she said with a pained laugh. "Everyone in my freaking family – even my goddamn 10-year-old cousin – has a plan for me."

She leaned back against her chair and gave out a controlled yell.

"I have no idea what I want to do!"

We were sitting outside by ourselves, so there were no other customers to be startled by such a display.

"I'm not sure I know what I want to do, either," I said. "How about we both yell?"

We counted to three, then burst out with a yell that lasted about 10 seconds, and laughed at ourselves. A dog down the street barked, and one of the Words, Music and Pictures employees stuck her head out the door to see what was going on. Is and I immediately pretended to be busy with our meals.

"God, I love you," I said.

"Me, too," she said. She reached for my hand. "Not a let's-get-married-and-buy-a-home kind of love, right?"

"Right," I said.

She'd spent the night at my house – or rather, the house that used to be all ours but was now Mom's. Dad had his own place with Lori. The next morning, Is and I had gone out for breakfast, talked each other's ears off some more, given each other a five-minute hug, and contentedly gone our separate ways.

And then a week or so later came a big manila envelope from Grace. Inside were several sheaves of paper, attached together with a paper clip.

Dear Seth,

How are you? If I remember correctly, you're about to start last year of college, right? That must be exciting. I've got one more year myself.

She spent the next couple of paragraphs bringing me up to speed on a few things, like her and Barry (still together, for now).

Then came the big news: Transformation was no more.

Early last fall, there'd been a fire at Hilltop – a bonfire, set by the crew hired to get the place ready for winter, that got out of control and spread to the dining hall, and a dozen or more cabins, and all had been completely consumed by the flames. Still, everyone expected that the camp would be restored, maybe even in time for the following summer.

But the trust decided it didn't want to rebuild Hilltop; apparently, the number of organizations and others using the camp had declined over the past few years, and the decision was made to put resources into other holdings and pursuits.

All through the winter, Jerry tried to get some of the Transformation long-timers – both those still involved as well as others who had left – to work with him on finding another site. But the attempt fizzled: There was so much disagreement on other matters regarding the camp that they hadn't even gotten around to searching for a new place. They'd finally thrown up their hands.

Then someone had an idea, Grace wrote: *If this was the end of Transformation, maybe there could at least be a farewell gathering.*

They found a large park about 10 miles or so from Hilltop and organized a big picnic; about 50 people, most of them from the first decade of Transformation, came and stayed all afternoon and into the evening. From what Grace and others saw, the overall mood was positive – no bitterness or divisiveness, just lots of good memories shared.

Aside from the initial, visceral reaction of sadness, I found that I didn't mourn the end of Transformation. I did feel bad for Jerry, and other people like Bill and Tess, or Ralph or Rick, who had obviously cared a lot about it. And I knew that Grace, Diana, Rafe and the others undoubtedly grieved the loss, since Transformation had been an important part of their childhoods, so I certainly felt sympathy for them.

But of course I didn't have the history with Transformation they'd had. What I'd seen was something coming apart at the seams, the shared vision and ideals falling away. It's not that people were lacking in commitment or purposefulness; these qualities simply had, over a decade, become invested in other things.

As I've thought about it, I wonder if this mirrored something larger taking place outside of Transformation. I remembered Jerry's little speech that first night in the dining hall, when he described the make-up of the camp's participants: "Democrats, Republicans, liberals, conservatives, Catholics, Protestants, Jews, atheists, business executives, teachers, contractors, writers, moms, dads." As that kind of consensus had deteriorated and finally broken down at Transformation, perhaps something similar had been happening in other communities – places where people lived, worked, raised families. Maybe ideas and beliefs taken for granted were no longer so strongly, widely held as before. I'm no political scientist, but that's about as good an explanation as I can come up with for what I saw happen on Election Day two years after that summer.

Mom's contention that Jerry and others might have been complicit, at least indirectly, in Marcus' misbehavior also weighed on my mind. I had a hard time fully accepting this, but I couldn't dismiss her point, either. If people had looked the other way, I wondered, was it because they regarded Marcus as a friend, and couldn't imagine him doing such things;

or did they close ranks because they believed it was necessary for Transformation's survival?

It also struck me that Zack was the only young adult I'd seen at Transformation, and he'd only come for Skinny Day. Grace, Rafe, Diana, Mishy and Funk had gradually stopped going. For whatever reason, the kids who'd grown up with Transformation did not return once they passed into adulthood. There was no fresh infusion of energy and ideas from a newly emerging generation that would guide Transformation forward.

The reunion included some quite unexpected revelations, Grace noted:

> I was talking with Jerry, and he said that many of the adults had known about Skinny Day, and had long suspected that Transformation kids were making use of the Lone Cabin. As you can imagine, I was shocked, and it showed. Jerry laughed and said, "Did you think we were that clueless?" And I laughed, too, and said that maybe we weren't as good at keeping secrets and covering our tracks as we thought. So I asked him why nobody had said anything or tried to stop us. Jerry said there'd been discussions about it, of course, but in the end the adults decided that perhaps letting the kids think they were getting away with something wasn't so bad – as long as they didn't progress to something even worse.

At the bottom of the page was this:

> There were all kinds of photos taken at the picnic, and others from "long ago" that were passed around. I thought I would pass some onto you (don't worry, I had copies made for myself).

I turned to the next page, on top of which she'd written:

Look at these two love-struck kids. Aren't we cute?

Pasted onto the page was a shot of Grace and me at Transformation. We weren't aware we were being photographed, so our attention was fully focused on one another. We were standing close together, each with an arm around the other, and smiling and chatting with obvious delight. I had to think about it for a minute, but after searching my memory I felt sure that the picture had been taken maybe an hour after our first time in the Lone Cabin.

Here's one of those kids, a little older.

And there was Grace, standing in front of a picnic table, with a few other people just barely visible on the left-hand side. She was definitely taller, had filled out a bit, and in the full flower of young adulthood. Her face was a little longer, a little thinner, though still with that same set jaw, and was lovelier than ever. Her eyes were welcoming, as I remembered them – once she had felt comfortable enough to put aside the teenage caginess and attitude.

I lingered on the photos, and the text, for what seemed like an hour. Then I went to the next page, on which were pasted more photos.

Here's someone you might remember.

At the top of the page was a photo of Morgana, almost certainly taken during that summer at Transformation – I could just make out the bathhouse in the background. She had undoubtedly been in the midst of one of her wild dances, just past the apogee of some great leap, wearing the tie-dye T-shirt dress. Her hair wildly fanned out above and around her, her eyes closed. She had an unrestrained, open-mouthed smile, seemingly lost in whatever flight of fancy had taken her at the moment.

And here's that someone as she is now.

Below the caption, another photo. It was Morgana, without question. Her childlike features were virtually the same, even after five years. But her smile seemed hard-won, and her eyes, although wide and expressive as I remembered, had a sadness to them that pained me to behold. Her hair was shorter, far less chaotic, and a little darker. I noticed she was wearing that same tie-dye T-shirt – as a T-shirt, not as a dress – and it now fit her very snugly, with a couple of inches cut from the collar down.

> *Morgana and I had a nice long talk at the picnic. She went through a lot that summer, and things got only worse after Transformation. The way she describes it, she felt like she was coming apart. When she looked in the mirror, she saw much the same face she'd seen for six, seven years. But there was all this turmoil inside her, about her changing self, these sensations that were definitely not those of a child – even though, in a lot of ways, she still felt like one. Basically, her parents had to pull her away from the outside world to save her, though not before she had some pretty bad experiences.*
>
> *When we talked, Morgana told me about what happened with the two of you that day in the Lone Cabin. I understand why you never mentioned it to me or to anyone else. But what's important is, you helped her more than you might have realized. She was in this incredibly vulnerable state, but you didn't take advantage of her, and in fact you showed her compassion. Believe me, there were plenty of guys – hell, some of them adults – who could have, and did, exploit that*

vulnerability. When she got into therapy, she was able to latch onto that episode with you as reassurance that there were good people – good men – in this world who genuinely cared about her. (She also told me about her attempted seduction, or whatever you call it, of Patrick, that poor lamb. Thank goodness he wasn't traumatized or anything, and the two of them were able to reconcile as friends.)

So that explains Morgana's breakdown after Fun Night, I guess. Maybe somehow she sensed that this would be the last Transformation for her, and it was all too much to bear. I do think she had feelings for you – hazy, unformed, but quite sincere – and she knew she could (literally) latch onto you for comfort. I gave her your home address, so she might write you about some or all of this one day, if/when she's ready. Just know that you are a special person to her.

I'd had a nagging sense of guilt about Morgana, and it had taken some time before I could identify what it was about: I couldn't help but wonder if, somehow, Grace and I had been a factor in her breakdown.

After all, Morgana seemed to take cues from Grace and me for her interactions with Patrick. And during our encounter in the Lone Cabin, she had waxed so enthusiastically about the fact that Grace and I had a physical relationship, and how much she desired the same thing – or thought she did – with Patrick.

So, had we – unwittingly, perhaps – set some sort of example for her to follow?

I discounted the notion, intellectually at least. I didn't know what other influences might have been at play, if there were other people whose actions were at least as meaningful to her as ours. Besides, where were her parents in all this? Didn't they see what was going on? Ultimately, wasn't Morgana their responsibility – not Grace's and mine?

Yes, I would tell myself that. But I would remember Tess lamenting about that couple, Cary and Brian: Transformation, she'd said, had failed them.

Maybe Transformation had failed Morgana. Maybe Grace and I had, too.

The last page contained a 5x7 showing a group of young people posing together in three rows, looking at the camera.

And here we all are, or most of us anyway. There were a few people you never met who showed up, and a few others from that summer who didn't – but of course they were in the much younger crowd, so you didn't know them that well. I think you'll recognize almost everyone here, maybe some easier than others.

Yes, there was Grace, and next to her Morgana, whose left hand rested in comradely fashion on the shoulder of Patrick – still looking soft and delicate. Diana, even more magnificent and self-assured, Rafe somehow even more hirsute and hearty. Mishy, earthy as always and glowing (good God, was she *pregnant?*). Funk had cut his hair dramatically, and was sporting wire-rim glasses. Those four girls on the left – no, it couldn't be. Yes, it was: Lily, Min, Dee, Zoe. They were so much bigger, and absolutely stunning, certainly not the skinny little things who seemed to find us older kids so fascinating. I practically laughed out loud looking at Lily, whose hair was now short and spiky. Although she'd grown a few inches all around, she was still the runt of the litter, and even with a smiling face she still sported that fiery look in her eyes.

I guess I never really knew what you thought about us – I mean as a group, a community, whatever. But I hope you know that whatever impression we made on you, you definitely made one on us, and in a wonderful way. As we talked at the dinner, we remembered your kindness (especially to The Girls, as well as Morgana), your graciousness, but also your willingness to question, even challenge what you saw – to Rafe, you'll always be "a bad-ass." And without you, there wouldn't have been "Peace Train." Zoe says she'll never ever EVER forget it.

In actual time, Transformation constituted a little more than a fortnight of my life. But in terms of its impact, there's no basis for measurement. And by that I mean it's simply difficult for me to gauge precisely where or how Transformation influenced me. There are only a few things I can point to, like the revival of my interest in guitar-playing or my attempts to make ratatouille (neither of them long-lasting), and say, definitively, "If it hadn't been for Transformation, this wouldn't have happened."

So why is Transformation still on my mind, all these years later, when I'm so much older than that Seth who I was then? Why, as I said before, do I find myself not just remembering, but inhabiting the memory of those two weeks?

Perhaps it has to do with an unexpected sense of gratitude.

I went in with such little expectations, but more importantly, I was arguably at my lowest ebb. I probably didn't realize it at the time, but I needed reassurance. I needed to know – especially being 16 years old – that I was OK, that I was somebody people would think was a good person, and that I could be out of my element yet not lose myself, whoever that was.

Being away from the familiar – as Mom had put it – helped me affirm who I was, not least because I felt the love (I know no other word for it) of a group of people who accepted me, and tried to help me, sometimes unknowingly, be a better version of myself. I knew I loved them back, even if there were things about them, and Transformation, I couldn't entirely understand. And I knew this uncertainty was OK; maybe in time I would resolve it, maybe I wouldn't.

That's why, after having traveled to Transformation wondering how I would make it through those two weeks, I left convinced I would be returning the next year, and the next, and the next. It didn't happen, but perhaps that was all right. Perhaps I'd gotten what I'd needed from Transformation. And for that, I was and still am grateful.

I hope you know, I really did love you, in each and every way. Yes, that was 15-going-on-16-year-old me – and I'm SO grown-up now, right? (Ha ha). Yes, I know it was so brief, and bright and brilliant, like the metaphorical shooting star. But I don't for a minute doubt what I felt for you was real and incredibly important. You were that guy, that First Love, my "little shit pie," and you were so good to me, and good for me. I do think sometimes of what might have been, if we'd lived closer to one another, or even if we had another couple of years together at Transformation.

I just hope you wind up with someone who treats you with tenderness and caring, which is what I would have given you.

Epilogue

The turn is coming soon. I don't even need a road map to find it now. After all, I've spent so many years tracing the route on all different kinds of maps – even geological survey maps – that I know it by heart.

I need to go back there, to Hilltop, to whatever remains of Transformation.

Ironically, I live far closer to there now, only a couple of hours away. So I rummaged through my cassette collection – my car has a tape player, too, though I'm thinking I might get one of those CD things – and picked out some traveling music: Cat Stevens, Jethro Tull, Cheap Trick, but also Talking Heads, Nirvana, Chumbawamba. I found myself wondering (and laughing) how many condoms I could get from Rafe now.

And just as David Byrne sings the last verse of "Heaven," I turn off from Route 1.

There is nothing.

No ruins, no rubble, no foundations outlined in the ground. Grass, weeds, trees, have overtaken everything. I guess the trust, assuming they still own the property, opted not to re-build; or if they did sell, whoever owns it now hasn't seen fit to develop the property in any way.

Theoretically, this should depress me, I guess. But I find myself moving easily and confidently through all the vegetation, as if the cabins and other buildings were still there. I spot where the dining hall was, and in my mind's eye I can see myself chopping vegetables in the kitchen to the comfortable chatter of Bill and Tess. I can visualize the picnic area, where I sit listening to Rafe and Diana argue about which one of them is right. Over there would be where I watch Morgana give one of her impromptu performances, in that damned tie-dye dress that was way too small for her – and yet, somehow, just the right size. I can see our cabin, where I'm jamming with Rafe, relishing the fact that I now know what a I-IV-V chord sequence is. I know I can find my way to the Sitting Woods, and even to the musty but cozy Lone Cabin, where I would have my arms wrapped around Grace, and hers around me.

This is a trip I could have, should have, taken years earlier, like right after I received Grace's letter about the end of Transformation. I had a car of my own by then – not anything great, but certainly capable of taking me to California and back. But I'd resisted the thought of going to Hilltop. Did I really want to wander around the burnt-out remains and other vestiges of the camp that were losing out to the advance of weeds and general neglect? What would be the point of it?

I know what the point is now. Over time, I've thoroughly wrapped myself in the memory of those two weeks, often experienced it as if I were still there, as if I were still that unhappy 16-year-old kid. But somewhere along the way, I've become content with just the memory. I've made no attempt to contact Grace, or Diana, or Rafe, Funk, Mishy, the Girls, Morgana – anyone. I don't know what their lives are like now, and God help me, I don't even know if they're all still alive.

I think about Mom and what she might say about this. How long has it even been since we talked about Transformation? A couple of times following her break-up with Lonnie, I'd

jokingly offered to see if Marcus might be available; sł
me to understand that she was not amused. After tha
than a passing reference – "It was a couple of years aɪtɛɪ ʍʋ
went to Transformation" – I don't believe we spoke about that
summer; my sense was that Mom regarded that as a troubled
time in her life, and not something she wanted to revisit.

Maybe, if I could find at least one of them – even Patrick,
if he could manage the words – they could tell me why I still
think about Transformation, if maybe it's because being there
changed me more than I had realized. I wasn't sure how important that was to me, but hearing it from their lips would
be wonderful.

It takes a while, but I find the path I want, and I climb the hill,
and I am in the Place of Grace, gazing out on the dining hall,
the cabins and all the other buildings of Hilltop, and the people who move among them, on their way, in some degree or
another – they hoped, even believed – toward transformation.

ABOUT ATMOSPHERE PRESS

Atmosphere Press is an independent, full-service publisher for excellent books in all genres and for all audiences. Learn more about what we do at atmospherepress.com.

We encourage you to check out some of Atmosphere's latest releases, which are available at Amazon.com and via order from your local bookstore:

Icarus Never Flew 'Round Here, by Matt Edwards

COMFREY, WYOMING: Maiden Voyage, by Daphne Birkmeyer

The Chimera Wolf, by P.A. Power

Umbilical, by Jane Kay

The Two-Blood Lion, by Nick Westfield

Shogun of the Heavens: The Fall of Immortals, by I.D.G. Curry

Hot Air Rising, by Matthew Taylor

30 Summers, by A.S. Randall

Delilah Recovered, by Amelia Estelle Dellos

A Prophecy in Ash, by Julie Zantopoulos

The Killer Half, by JB Blake

Ocean Lessons, by Karen Lethlean

Unrealized Fantasies, by Marilyn Whitehorse

The Mayari Chronicles: Initium, by Karen McClain

Squeeze Plays, by Jeffrey Marshall

JADA: Just Another Dead Animal, by James Morris

Hart Street and Main: Metamorphosis, by Tabitha Sprunger

Karma One, by Colleen Hollis

Ndalla's World, by Beth Franz

Adonai, by Arman Isayan

ABOUT
THE AUTHOR

SEAN SMITH has written for a living for almost four decades, as a journalist and an editor/writer in academia. While growing up in New York's Hudson Valley, he took his first stab at fiction: penning heroic short stories about football players and producing his own versions of Marvel Comics titles (for personal enjoyment, not profit). *Transformation Summer* is his debut novel. Sean lives in the Boston area, where he is known to haunt Celtic music events and jam sessions, and is trying to get the hang of tenor banjo.

Made in the USA
Middletown, DE
25 April 2023

29160671R00154